The Silent Bomb

The Silent Bomb

by
Charles Dodeman

translated, annotated and introduced by
Brian Stableford

A Black Coat Press Book

ISBN 978-1-61227-319-8. First Printing. August 2014. Published by Black Coat Press, an imprint of Hollywood Comics.com, LLC, P.O. Box 17270, Encino, CA 91416. All rights reserved. Except for review purposes, no part of this book may be reproduced or transmitted in any form or by any means, electronic or mechanical, including photocopying, recording, or by any information storage and retrieval system, without permission in writing from the publisher. The stories and characters depicted in this novel are entirely fictional. Printed in the United States of America.

Introduction

La Bombe silencieuse by Charles Dodeman, here translated as *The Silent Bomb*, was originally published in Tours by
Alfred Mame et fils in an undated edition that was widely re-
viewed in the last few months of 1916, which is indicated as
its year of publication in the catalogue of the Bibliothèque
Nationale. The timing is highly significant, partly because the
novel was one of the works that seemed to signal a change of
policy with regard to the use of works of popular fiction as a
means of building morale during the Great War of 1914-18,
and partly because of an unfortunate irony of fate, which determined that its particular morale-building theme was outdat-
ed by events in a matter of months, thus making it a particularly clear illustration of the perils of that kind of exercise.

Charles Dodeman was born in 1873—a date that is also
of some significance with respect to the Great War because it
meant that he was one year too old to be called up for active
service when the war began, and was thus able to continue his
normal employment, including his writing, during the war
years. His father was a colonel in the French Army—one of
several members of his family to attain that rank—and his
mother was an Englishwoman named Jenny Brown, the
daughter of a clergyman from Brighton who had met her future husband while on holiday in Paris. Her religious background appears to have had a powerful influence on his atti-
tudes; his novels are dutifully pious and sternly moralistic.

Both of Dodeman's parents died while he was still in his
teens. Both of his brothers followed their father's example and
enlisted in the army, but Charles did not, perhaps because his
health would not permit it. Instead, he devoted himself entirely
to reading and writing, while living on the money he had in-
herited, while it lasted. Most of his early works, including

poetry, short stories and plays, were published, if at all, in provincial periodicals, and brought in very little money. By 1898, he was effectively broke, and in need of a more reliable means of support. He stumbled into one while wandering along the banks of the Seine investigating the displays of the *bouquinistes*—the stallholders selling second-hand books—and found one of the pitches advertized for rent. He took it, and spent the next quarter of a century as a book-dealer on the Quai Voltaire, continuing to write in his spare time. He published a number of comic songs and scripts for one-act comedies in 1900-02, some written in collaboration with Raphaël de Noter, but that brief burst of publicity was followed by another fallow period

Dodeman's career as a writer must have come close to taking off when he sold a feuilleton serial to the *Echo de Paris*, "Le Cheveu et la Barbe," a rambling thriller in which a brother and sister are victimized by an evil hypnotist, but it was not reprinted in book form. When he did publish a similar thriller in book form, *Le Secret du livre d'heures* [The Secret of the Book of Hours] (1912), it had the advantage of illustrations supplied by one of the regular clients of his bookstall, Albert Robida, who also supplied illustrations to several of his other books, including *La Bombe silencieuse*, thus boosting their eventual second-hand value vastly, although it does not seem to have done much for their immediate promotion. Both those novels, as well as *Le Tailleur d'Images* [The Shaper of Images] (1913), also illustrated by Robida, were published in Tours by Alfred Mame.

When the war was over, Dodeman's literary career entered a new phase with the publication in 1919 of *Le long des quais, bouquinistes, bouquineurs, bouquins* [Along the Quays: Book-dealers, Book-buyers and Books], which was reprinted several times, becoming his most popular work by far. It is a charming and light-hearted patchwork of historical anecdotes about book-selling on the banks of the Seine, including his personal reminiscences and reflections on the locale. Its success prompted him to produce two further volumes of autobiographical reflections, alongside further novels, which continued to appear at intervals until his death. His demise is recorded in an obituary notice in the *Revue des Lectures* as having occurred on 29 December 1934, although the Bibliothèque Nationale catalogue and other sources derived from its annotation give the date as 1936.

La Bombe silencieuse is a hectic melodrama that shares many of the features of the popular feuilleton fiction of the period. In terms of its slapdash plotting it is not one of the most outstanding examples of the form—when an author is reduced to maintaining the threads of his plot by having his hero struck by a lightning bolt that evaporates his clothing and renders him cataleptic but otherwise uninjured, he is showing definite signs of desperation—but in that kind of fiction, rational plausibility is not really an issue. What makes the story remarkable, however, is its response to immediate circumstance; it is one of the earliest thrillers to be set during a war that was actually going on at the time of publication.

War had, of course, long been a major literary theme, but almost all novelistic accounts of warfare had been written with the benefit of considerable historical distance and hindsight. The Crimean War had introduced both London and Paris to war reportage relayed with great promptitude by correspondents close to the action, and had opened up scope for writers of fiction to react with similar alacrity, provided that they could work rapidly enough, but few could and few dared, only too well aware of the possibility that the interval between inspiration and publication might see their work drastically overtaken by events. In France, the Franco-Prussian War was over far too quickly, and its course and aftermath were far too surprising, to produce anything much in the way of immediate literary reaction, although the void was filled in retrospectively over the next forty years. The Great War was, however, a different matter. Not only did not drag on for four years, but the employment of the media as a vehicle for propaganda was raised to an entirely new level of sophistication.

Within the spectrum of wartime publication, entirely ruled by both formal and informal propagandistic intent, popular fiction initially played a subdued role, both quantitatively and qualitatively. It must have seemed to many publishers, writers and readers that there was something rather frivolous about the production and consumption of light popular fiction in dire circumstances; much of the fiction that continued the rich tradition of feuilleton fiction in the latter part of 1914 and throughout 1915 took on a new sobriety, tending toward deadly earnest. The fiction that dealt directly with the war—mostly short fiction in those years—was conspicuously naturalistic, attempting to deal realistically and artfully with the experiences of combatants and non-combatants alike, celebrating heroism in a determined fashion that was very different from the flamboyance of pre-war adventure fiction. By 1917, however, there was much more fiction produced that deliberately adopted the form and rhetoric of popular fiction with an evidently-calculated morale-building intent, heavily emphasizing a trend begun in 1916. That might well have happened spontaneously, but it was at least facilitated, if not actively stimulated, by the government, perhaps by Georges Clemenceau himself, given that he was an experienced journalist personally acquainted with many of the leading writers of popular fiction.

A significant lead in the adaptation of popular thrillers to wartime propaganda purposes was provided by Gaston Leroux, one of the *feuilletonistes* writing for the daily newspaper *Le Matin*, whose serial *La Colonne infernale* [The Infernal Column] appeared there between April and September 1916. Leroux went on to publish *Rouletabille chez Krupp* [1] in 1917, which overlapped with *Le Sous-marin "Le Vengeur"* [The Submarine *Le Vengeur*] (1917-18) in much the same rousing vein. The other players who joined in the game in 1917 included two well-established writers who were very obviously adding propagandistic material arbitrarily to works

---

[1] translated as *Rouletabille at Krupp's*, Black Coat Press, ISBN 978-1-61227-144-6.

that had been written with entirely different agendas, Félicien Champsaur, in *Les Ailes de l'homme*,[2] and J-H. Rosny, in *L'Énigme de Givreuse*,[3] but Dodeman and Leroux had obviously planned their works from the outset as morale-building exercises reacting with evident severity to the circumstances of the war.

The tactics of that kind of reaction are, of course, inherently problematic. Writers of such fiction have to beware of excess in making promises, having no idea how long the war might go on or how bad things might get. On the other hand, they cannot be too tentative, because the whole point of the exercise is to insist not only that victory is certain but that it will be brought about by the courage and resolution of the combatants and non-combatants alike. A further complication was introduced by the fact that it was abundantly clear by 1916 that courage and resolution, key determinants of war during centuries in which they were of secondary importance only to weight of numbers and strategic deployment, had been further reduced in significance by the technological advances that were transforming the nature of the war while it was in progress: the increasing importance of aircraft, the advent of tanks, the development and use of poison gases, and so on.

Given that context, it was natural—indeed, inevitable—that thriller fiction about the war produced during the war would deal primarily with covert struggles rather than formal battles, and that many of those covert struggles would revolve around the potential advent of new, game-changing technologies. In order words, the archetypal wartime thrillers were likely to be spy stories featuring embryonic superweapons. A few examples of that kind of story had been provided by war-anticipation stories published before 1914, and once the sub-genre was established it was maintained even in peacetime by

---

[2] translated as *The Human Arrow*, Black Coat Press, ISBN 978-1-61227-045.6.
[3] translated as *The Givreuse Enigma*, Black Coat Press, ISBN 978-1-935558-39-2.

its inherent melodramatic potential—it is still thriving today—but its difficult parturition took place in France in the year 1916, and *La Bombe silencieuse* was one of its pioneering endeavors. If the novel is inept—and it has to be admitted that it is—its ineptitude was due in part to the fact that it was feeling its way in plowing new literary ground, with precious few models on which to draw, and there is a sense in which its gaffes are as interesting as its virtues.

The most peculiar aspect of the story is perhaps the key motif that provides its title: the desideratum over whose possession and control the various parties contend—what Alfred Hitchcock was later to dub "the McGuffin" when summing up the formula of his cinematic thrillers. As potentially war-winning technologies go, it is not obvious that a silent bomb has any conspicuous advantage over the kind that go bang. After all, all bombs are silent until they explode, except for those equipped with what Dodeman calls an *horloge infernale* (a ticking timer), and the silence of the imagined bomb does not extend to its timer. Once the bomb has gone off, it hardly matters whether it makes a noise or not as it does its destructive work.

In fact, the invention featured in the novel has other virtues that a modern reader might deem far more important than its silence. One of its components is radioactive and is said to release particles with an unusual rapidity, thus increasing the power of its blast—in other words, it is a primitive atomic bomb—and in order to deliver it, the inventor is eventually persuaded to abandon the quest to build an unprecedentedly resilient cannon and employ miniature aircraft guided to their target by radio waves: what would nowadays be called a drone. Both of these features can be seen with the aid of hindsight to be far more important as advances in military technology than the bomb's silence, but in the author' eyes, they did not have anything like as much symbolic value, partly because the silence had the additional value of reflecting, in metaphorical terms, the occult work of the spy network trying to take possession of it: a kind of organization credited elsewhere with such titles as an "invisible column" or an "enemy within." It is in that light that the device needs to be considered.

In stories of this kind, it is compulsory for the author to refrain from showing his weapon in action on anything but a greatly restricted scale—because, after all, the real war cannot yet have given any evidence of the use of such a device—and Dodeman observes the rule conscientiously, so the actual use of the silent bomb in battle, although allegedly conclusive in the particular instance, is so peripheral as almost to be ludicrous. That factor too makes the presence of the invention within the text far more symbolic than literal, providing a striking illustration of the marginality of the work with respect to the genre of speculative fiction—but stories in which technological hypotheses are rationally extrapolated into untrodden narrative territory are vastly outnumbered by those in which they flatter only to deceive, and however frustrating it may be, it is the way the game is normally played.

It is also compulsory for authors of this kind of narrative to set the action in locations where the hypothetical events cannot clash with the experiences of their readers; when spies operated in Paris in wartime thrillers, they had to do so very quietly indeed, and had far more narrative scope for dastardly behavior in remote theaters of the war. Some such locations were attractive because they offered extra scope for melodramatic complication by virtue of their own historical contexts, and Warsaw, where *La Bombe silencieuse* is set, obviously seemed to Charles Dodeman to be rich in that kind of potential, given the long history of attempts to liberate Poland from Russian rule, and the intensive activity within the Russian empire of various revolutionary groups popularly lumped together as "nihilists."

Dealing with such materials, however, is not without risk, and the narrative obligation that Dodeman accepted to make Russian patriotism—even on the part of Poles—stand in figuratively for the French patriotism his novel was intended to shore up and stimulate, was risking far more than he guessed. He had no way to anticipate the Revolution of February 1917 (March for the rest of the world, which had abandoned the Julian calendar) and the forced abdication of Tsar Nicholas II—a leader very different from the character marginally portrayed in the novel, in terms of competence and benevolence. The Tsar's mobilization of Russian forces in July 1916, which plays a major role in determining the action of the novel, was almost certainly a terrible strategic error, which provoked a conflict that Germany did not want.

Politically as well as technologically, therefore, *La Bombe silencieuse* now seems more than a trifle silly—but it did not seem so to Dodeman, and it would be unfair to hold the benefits of modern hindsight against him too sternly. At the time of writing, France and Russia were allies, and confidence in Russian fighting spirit and prowess was a significant aspect to the morale that Dodeman was trying to maintain. In the hundred years that have passed between the time in which the novel is set and the time in which this translation was produced, everything relevant to the plot has altered dramatically, but that allows us a much clearer view of what the author was trying to achieve as well as its measured and problematic success. The novel's limitation and the awkwardness cannot take away from its merits as a pioneering endeavor, many of whose features became staples of the hybrid subgenre to which it belongs.

This translation was made from the version of the Mame edition reproduced on the Bibliothèque Nationale's *gallica* website. The BN's catalogue lists two versions of the novel published in 1916, which differ in their pagination, without indicating which was prior; the copy reproduced on *gallica* is the one with fewer pages.

Brian Stableford

THE SILENT BOMB[4]

PART ONE

Pierre Damidoff, an engineer at the Bargineff metallurgy and explosive factory in Warsaw, pressed the switch. The electric wire transmitting the fluid was connected to a kind of copper howitzer, to the mouth of which a nickel cylinder equipped with a helical propeller had been fitted. The propeller immediately began rotating at high speed, and the cylinder, describing a rather lazy trajectory, flew through the window into the garden, where it exploded. A young faun dancing on a pedestal was, so to speak, volatilized, but not the slightest sound was heard.

"A terrestrial comet!" murmured the inventor, with an indescribable pride. "A silent bomb! This is only a laboratory experiment, but if the State furnishes me with the capital and the necessary machinery, I'll be able to realize the sovereign engine of modern warfare within three months."

Damidoff left the physics laboratory, carefully closing the door. He picked up the scattered debris of the bomb and examined the fragment carefully. Then he headed for the villa situated on the far side of the arbor, still talking to himself.

"An inestimable result!" he murmured. "It's simple...everything is simple in nature. Anna was right: God em-

---

[4] *Author's note*: the idea of *The Silent Bomb* was born in Paris on the Quai Voltaire, from a conversation with Monsieur Merlet, an engineer of the State Railway Company. Thrown to the four winds by courtesy of the universally known and esteemed Maison Mame, may it pass from the realm of dream to reality and become, indeed, a redoubtable protectress of Justice and Right!

ploys the least complicated means to produce the most surprising effects; humans come closest to the divine method when they put simple methods to work. Poor Anna!"

While talking, the engineer had climbed the steps leading up to a door and gone into a study. He looked up at a portrait of a woman suspended between large photographs of two children, a boy and a girl.

"You're the one who put me on the right track," he said, nodding his head. "Bless you. What would have been used twenty years ago for futile and cowardly murder, for destruction without the possibility of rebuilding, will serve for the grandeur of the Fatherland, for its elevation to the head of the European powers—and that I swear on your memory, and on Nadia's head. Even if I'm offered a fortune, the invention will have no other aim. Thus, I'll be redeemed."

The engineer opened a drawer and slipped some papers into it that he had taken from his pocket.

"To think," he said, with profound sadness, "that the glory will go to the name of Damidoff, and that..."

The door opened.

"Papa, Papa, the mail!"

A little girl about five years old irrupted into the room and ran to her father, her arms laden with letters and newspapers. Bringing in the mail was her daily joy; no one in the house would have dreamed of depriving her of it.

The inventor closed the secret drawer in his desk and picked up the child, lifting her to his lips. He kissed her with a profound tenderness.

"Good day, little Nadia," he said. "Did you sleep well?" His face darkened as he added, to himself: "Still pale...she'll have her mother's nervous malady, poor child."

Nadia was, indeed, as frail as a flower, with a fine skin through which the meandering of the veins was visible. Her eyes had dark rings and her blonde hair seemed too heavy for her head, which she held at a slight angle.

Damidoff sat his daughter in a chair beside him and began opening his correspondence.

First he opened several envelopes bearing the stamp of the Office of Powders and Saltpeters; then he reached one that caused him to make a gesture of surprise; he thought he recognized one of those of which he habitually made use. As there was no reason for it to have come from his own desk, however, he dispelled the idea and unsealed the missive.

He went pale. He read:

Jude Iagow, the moment to strike a great blow and wrench Poland from the grip of the imperial power forever is near. Within a month, the whole of Europe will be in flames. It is necessary that that moment finds Russia in complete revolution.

You have in your hands what is necessary for that. You have discovered a silent bomb. We believe that you have not forgotten your ideas of justice and liberty, nor your oaths. You know what you have to do. You know where to find the brothers in grief and hatred. We are waiting for you. Act quickly, or you are doomed. You know that our threats are never vain.

The Committee.

"My choice is made," the inventor said. "My invention belongs to my fatherland. May my past be forgiven, and my name returned to me...but who told them, then? No one knows except Ivan. No, it's not my son. Georges Chantepie? The Frenchman? That loyal soul? Bah! What about Nitchef? Nitchef..."

Brows furrowed, suppressing the anger that was riding within him, Damidoff put a whistle to his lips. A shrill sound resounded.

Leaden and limping footsteps sounded in the corridor; the door opened; a man with a strange face appeared. He had long, flat black hair. His eyes were slightly almond-shaped, his cheekbones prominent, his face flat, coarse, bestial and expressionless.

At the sight of him, the inventor's anger died down as if by magic.

That brute? he thought. *Get away! Deaf, dumb and stu-pid—he's incapable of it. No, I mustn't...*

He indicated the window. "Open it. It's hot."

The temperature was, indeed stifling, although it was still early. The valet obeyed.

"Go!" ordered Damidoff, with a gesture.

Nitchef smiled at Nadia, who looked away, and left.

"Who, then?" the engineer said to himself. "The garden is enclosed and the walls are high; the laboratory is behind a clump of trees. Who can suspect? Who has been able to see?"

He slipped the letter into the secret drawer and resumed opening his correspondence. He pulled himself together, but he was more anxious than he wanted to appear.

His astonishments were not at an end. He had just re-moved the elastic band from the *Scientific Review*. His gaze had encountered a suggestive title, following an article by Dr. Mohr, a professor of neurology and head of a renowned sani-tarium situated a few versts from the villa: "A New Invention and a New Phenomenon."

He scanned the article, and was stupefied.

We cannot conceive of an explosion that is not accompa-nied by a noise. It is the molecules of the substance that sur-rounds us, the ether, colliding violently under the brutal pres-sure of foreign molecules, which produce the noise of the ex-plosion, the BANG. The contrary phenomenon would throw us into an inexpressible astonishment.

And yet, the phenomenon of the silent explosion, which is produced continually in interplanetary space, can also be produced on our planet and within its ethereal envelope.

Sound is nothing but vibration, like light. Luminous vi-brations are greater in intensity, that is all; but between the vibrations perceived by our hearing and the vibrations to which our retina is sensitive, there is a large unknown field. There are shrill sounds whose vibrations are too high in fre-quency for us to hear. Suppose that an explosion were violent enough to produce those unknown vibrations; that would re-solve the problem.

We are told that a scientist, a researcher of genius, is one the point of having found a scientific solution applicable to engines of war. The formidable result is in sight. Let us say right away that experiments have not yet crossed the bounds of the physics laboratory, but the indications are there. From Papin's pressure-cooker, our modern dreadnoughts emerged.

The article was signed: *V.O.*

"The wretch!" groaned the engineer, his teeth clenched. "The wretch! He'll be the death of me…!"

He got up abruptly and went to the window,

"How hot it is! It's overwhelming!"

Pierre Damidoff leaned on the windowsill, while, indifferent to the drama that was being played out around her, Nadia drew fantastic arabesques on a piece of paper, twittering like a warbler.

THE RAY IN THE DARK

Before the engineer's eyes extended a garden planted with trees and flowers, closed by rather high walls. At the back, there was an iron gate that opened on to the Moscow road. On the other side of the road stood a kind of manor house, built of brick and slate. A woman dressed in mourning was passing, at that moment, behind the hedge of the grounds; her eyes were obstinately fixed on the villa, with the attitude and expression of a cat lying in wait. She was striving to pierce the shadows behind the engineer; he did not see her, entirely occupied with his memories.

Twenty years before, in the course of a ball given by the governor of Warsaw, a bomb had exploded. The host had been mortally wounded. Around him lay officers, wives, and innocent young women. The bomb, a coward's weapon, had struck blindly, as usual.

Jude Iagowski, a pupil at the College of Higher Education, present at the parry and known for his subversive ideas, was dragged away from the body of his dying mother, whom he was embracing, and set before a military court. He vehemently denied being the author of the atrocity. Yes, he was affiliated to Free Russia, but he was not a nihilist. At least, his nihilism was purely theoretical. Furthermore, he was only affiliated with the secret society with the objective of achieving the emancipation of Poland, in accordance with the principle preached by certain philosophers that the end justifies the means.

That was already more than enough. He owed it to the absence of any proof that he was not put before a firing squad. He was condemned to the mines in perpetuity, while his close friend and brother in nihilism Pierre Damidoff was condemned for a fixed term.

The black hell opened for him.

Anyone who can read has surely encountered many descriptions of life in the Siberian mines. We shall not linger on that. Let it suffice to say that the gates of those prison camps might well bear the famous Dantean inscription: *Abandon all hope, ye who enter here.*

Jude Iagow suffered as much as a man can suffer. He suffered in his body, and he suffered in his heart, tortured by remorse. He could not rid himself of the memory of that scene of carnage. He could still see his mother's bloody body, dying while murmuring a supreme word of affection to him, and he thought: *Even if I did not do the deed, am I not nevertheless an accomplice to her death?*

And while he put his hands over his eyes, sobbing, uttering cries of despair and appeals for forgiveness directed at the dead woman, the specters of Schopenhauer, Hegel and Büchner,[5] the three apostles of German philosophy, sniggered behind his back, saying: "Ha ha ha! Naïve individual! That's how we undermine the social edifice of our neighbors, while waiting for our cannons to make the holes necessary for our big bellies. Ha ha ha! Are they poisoning you with that atrocious nourishment? Our dramatic authors will share it with the

---

[5] The addition of the eminent physiologist and Darwinist Ludwig Büchner (1824-1899) to this set of "apostles of German philosophy"—which will subsequently be further augmented with the name of Nietzsche—might seem a trifle odd to the modern eye, but his *Krafft und Stoff: Empirisch-naturphilosophische Studien* [Force and Matter: Empirical Studies] (1855) was so insistent in its scientific materialism that it got him sacked from his university post, and prompted him to write further works fervently attacking the ideas of God and the soul. The ill-fated playwright Georg Büchner (1813-1837), who spent much of his life in exile in France and Switzerland before achieving posthumous fame, was Ludwig's brother. There is no evidence in the present novel that the author knew anything at all about Hegel, Schopenhauer or Nietzsche, but he might have read Büchner.

French. For ourselves, we know the substance and we take advantage of it without using it, and we mock!"

And Hegel, the naturist philosopher, and Schopenhauer, the apostle of the incoherent will, and Büchner, the flag-bearer of gross materialism, appeared to the unfortunate convict as a cynically ironic trinity, surrounded by pestilential marshes in which an entire naïve humankind was bogged down. He bit his knuckles in anger, crushed by the certainty that the evil accomplished was irreparable.

But God had taken pity on his creature. He permits light to penetrate the deepest darkness, and permits beings born for sacrifice to bring hope to those in despair.

To those who spoke about destroying the idea of God, because matter alone is eternal; to those who affirmed the necessity of destroying society in order to reconstruct it thereafter—on what bases?—because the initial will had gone astray; to those who praised rational and pitiless murder, because only the goal was important and obstacles had to be removed; to all of them, the individuals of the elite spoke about God and his infinite bounty. They evoked the harmony of things for those who had gone astray; they showed them the fortunate life, the eternity of joy as the undeniable, logical, necessary goal of everything that exists, everything that thinks and believes.

Among those specters of hope was Anna Erloff.

Victims, for long years, of an erroneous conception of Roman Catholicism, the Erloffs had been expiating in the prison colony an excessive attachment to traditional religion. Anna had been born there, had grown up there and had drawn from scenes of the everyday life of the convicts and immense pity, and immense desire to soothe such great miseries. She had found the means in the very foundations of her faith.

Anna Erloff had a noble forehead, frank eyes, and an air of charming modesty; everything about her inspired confidence and commanded respect. She was about twenty years old.

She had soon achieved an ascendancy over the mind of the rebel. Her abnegation, her tireless activity, when it was a matter of helping and consoling, showed the disciple of the philosophers that resignation to the will of God might have grandeur. In the meantime, he had crises of terrible despair.

"If I was wrong to affiliate myself to a society whose objective is criminal," he said one day, "my inexperience is an excuse. To think that my life is over, that I shall never get out of this Gehenna, that my years will pass in this miserable village, while my intelligence, annihilated by coarse labor, will disappear like something useless! It's frightful! And yet, I was only wrong in the means; my goal was noble. Poland ought to be free."

"It will be, when God wishes it," the young woman replied, "but liberty should not be conquered by crime; injustice cannot be avenged by injustice. If you thought that, your sin is immense, but God's mercy is infinite. Be humble, repent, and merit human mercy by your conduct."

A year went by. One day, the young woman told the convict that she was obliged to return to Russia by family obligations. She would return in two years. She made him promise that he would behave well and would not try to escape.

He promised. Anna Erloff went away.

The Hell of the mine closed in again on the convict, more terrible than ever. There was a star missing from the ink-black sky. In vain, the condemned man exchanged a sustained correspondence with his protectress; in vain, he stiffened himself against chagrin, wanting to remain worthy of the woman who had transformed him morally, to struggle against the obsession with escape; all the time, a mysterious voice murmured to him: "Never! Never! You're a convict! You'll be here until you die! All your life, you'll be alone..."

He escaped.

THE INHERITANCE

The engineer was to remember throughout his life the slightest circumstances of his journey over the steppes, his struggle against the wilderness.

It snowed. He followed course of the highway, simply marked by a row of black stakes in the snow, at a distance. Fatigue and hunger sapped his energy. He was about to fall, vanquished and resigned to death, when a moving dot appeared on the horizon. The fugitive dragged himself as far as the road. He was about to play his final card.

The dot had grown. Jude had recognized a sleigh. It carried a single passenger.

When it came closer, the convict raised his hand.

"Pity, in the name of God!" he cried.

The man stopped his horse and looked at the man imploring his aid. "Who are you?" he asked. "Where do you come from?"

For his part, the fugitive studied the traveler, while an immense hope and an indescribable joy swelled his heart. In that emaciated face, in the eyes burning with fever, he had just recognized Pierre Damidoff, his childhood friend, a convict in another prison camp.

And Pierre Damidoff also recognized Jude Iagow.

"Pierre!" he exclaimed, advancing. "It's God who sent you. You've come from the mines?"

"Yes, I've finished my sentence, but death is at hand. I'm returning as quickly as possible, in order to repose in my last slumber beside my father, killed by my condemnation. That's why I didn't want to wait for the departure of the next convoy. And you? Have you escaped?"

"Pierre," said Jude, in a voice trembling with emotion, "Won't you have pity on me?"

The consumptive looked at his old comrade, into the depths of his soul.

"Jude," he said, after a long silence, "We've done wrong."

"Alas, yes! You see, Pierre Damidoff, we've been the victims of words and images. I've repented. Let me become an honest man again. Here"—he struck his beast—"I have what's necessary to redeem my sin, to render service to my fatherland and to humankind. To rot gradually in the mine…no, no! Not that! I don't want that. If you refuse, well, I'll lie down here and wait to die. You're the master of my life—but I beg you, permit me to become an honest man again."

"In the name of my father and mother, Jude, come. What will be, will be. God is the master."

"Bless you!" said the fugitive, fervently, raising his friend's hand to his lips.

He lay down among the luggage, under a pile of furs, and sank into a leaden sleep.

Pierre Damidoff left the highway. Versts followed versts, days followed days. Many a time, the convict was in danger of discovery. Fortunately, he avoided it. Nevertheless, the problem became increasingly difficult to solve, the danger becoming increasingly menacing. They were approaching the Urals, the Russian frontier. How could they get through? Afterwards, the difficulties would be ironed out, or very nearly, but it was necessary to get through. How? Jude Iagow had no papers, and the telegraph must have sent his description to all the posts. He could already feel the hand of a policeman on his collar.

Providence was watching over the prodigal son repentant of his errors.

The fatigues of the journey had exhausted Pierre Damidoff's strength.

His companion perceived his increasing weakness. "You're dying for me," he said to him, hugging him in his arms. "Brother, what can I do to thank you?"

"I'd have died anyway," the moribund man replied. "Yes, I would have liked to rest beside my family, but I've saved you, and that consoles me."

"Listen," he said, on day. "Heaven has sent me an idea. I can save you entirely. Yes, it's possible. I bequeath you my name and my petty fortune. You can collect it easily. This is how."

The dying man explained to his friend what he would have to do.

"I only ask one thing," he said, "which is that the new Pierre Damidoff should be and should remain an honest man, a good Russian, a good Christian. There alone is the truth."

"Do I need to swear?" exclaimed Jude Iagow, moved to the utmost depths of his being. "Your name will be the most esteemed of all."

"Thank you. And if you can...one day...eventually... have me transported...back there...next to my family."

The fugitive held out his hand, solemnly.

One starry night, the dying man rendered his last sigh. They were in a remote valley in the Urals. After having wept for his benefactor, Jude Iagow carried him into a little crypt naturally hollowed out in the bass of a crag. Stones covered the body, and the gravedigger prayed for a long time. The scene had no witness save for a large owl that had described broad concentric circles overhead.

Jude Iagow could only explain that unexpected aid he had found by superhuman, miraculous intervention.

When he reached the first frontier post his heart was beating strangely. He showed his papers—or rather, Pierre Damidoff's papers. The two men were the same age and height. The hard labor of the mines had, so to speak, rendered them identical. Moreover, they had both been educated at the same scientific college. The substitution was not discovered. Jude Iagow had abandoned his own identity thereafter to assume that of the dead man.

In Petrograd,[6] where he went, he wrote to the notary responsible for the affairs of the Damidoff family. Thanks to the information provided by his companion in that regard, he was able to take possession of the inheritance. He was not robbing anyone; the Damidoff line was extinct.

He set to work doggedly, passed the necessary examinations with honors, and went into the great Bargineff factory, where his intelligence, energy and hard work won him the esteem of his superiors. He had understood that order is necessary to society and that it is impossible for humans to remake the work of the Creator.

One day, Anna Erloff found herself in the presence of her former protégé. She did not seem surprised.

"I heard about your escape," she said, "but I thought I'd never see you again. How were you able to get here?"

"Providence protected me," he replied.

He told her the story of his extraordinary adventure. "Anna," he concluded, "you know who I am. Your decision will be mine, but since you've commenced a benevolent endeavor, why not finish it?"

Anna Erloff considered the young man. An immense pity sprang from her heart. She was the absolute mistress of the convict's destiny; she did not have the courage to send him back to Hell.

A year later, they were married.

The years passed. Ivan was born, then Nadia, and God recalled the young woman's pure and honest soul to His presence.

Jude Iagowski, to extract himself from his grief, devoted himself to studying the chemistry of explosives, which had always obsessed him. France had the inventor of the cold one; he wanted Russia to have the inventor of the silent one. Hidden in the little village of W***, a few versts from the factory

---

[6] At the time this scene is set, the city in question would still have been known as St. Petersburg; it did not become Petrograd until 1914 (it became Leningrad in 1924).

at X***, he pursued his research ardently. Finally, he had reached the desired goal.

Alas, as an inconsistent and futile mist is snatches away by a gust of wind, the twenty-year interval between his flight from the prison camp and the present moment, the twenty years of honest conduct and probity, entirely devoted to the service of the fatherland, had disappeared in the breath of the anonymous threat.

The past had just been welded to the present. Engineer Damidoff had become the convict Jude Iagow again, the condemned man in breach of his banishment, doubly guilty, since, having been sent to the mines for having thrown a bomb, he had hidden behind the appearance of an unsuspectable man in order to pursue a tenebrous project. God knew that his intentions were pure, but on putting the fact together, human deduction would infallibly conclude a criminal objective. His situation had become abruptly complicated at the very moment when Russia needed the collaboration of all her children, and the moment when he, Jude Iagow, was perhaps on the point of assuring her victory by procuring her an instrument of military might all the more formidable because it was silent.

Was not the sole means of avoiding a catastrophe so great in its consequences to seize the initiative?

THE DOLOROUS CONFESSION

"Good day, Father."

Jude Iagow shivered.

An adolescent about fifteen years old had come into the garden and was standing beneath the window, a smile on his lips. He was carrying books under his arm.

"Good day, Ivan," the engineer replied, trying to smile in his turn. "Is Monsieur Chantepie well?"

"Yes. He sends you his good wishes."

"Good day, Ivan! Good day, little brother!" On hearing the beloved voice of the young student, Nadia had abandoned her paper and pencil, and, leaping down from her chair, had run toward the newcomer, her arms wide and her pretty face lit up with joy.

The boy bent down to kiss her. He had noticed his father's pallor. "Is Papa ill?" he murmured.

Nadia looked up at the engineer. "Are you ill?" she asked.

Ivan straightened up, his brow furrowed with anxiety.

Jude did not answer. He seemed to want to pronounce words that hesitation was retaining on is lips.

He made an abrupt decision. "Come in," he said to his son. "I need to talk to you about serious matters."

He closed the window—not carefully enough, for it remained slightly ajar. And while the brother and sister, hand in hand, came into the study, the valet appeared, with a garden implement over his shoulder, and started hoeing a flower-bed immediately underneath the casement.

"Sit down there," said the inventor, indicating a chair near the desk, and handing him the *Scientific Review.* "Read this."

The adolescent obeyed. The little girl was already beside him, and had placed her blonde head on his shoulder, affectionately.

"So, Father," said Ivan, having scanned the article, "well-deserved glory will soon repay you for your lard labor. Our beautiful Russia will be the foremost nation, thanks to you." A sincere emotion veiled the voice of the young man, while a noble pride illuminated his visage.

"Alas," replied the engineer.

"What!" exclaimed Ivan, astonished. "Why this incomprehensible sadness? Isn't this a guarantee of imminent success?"

"If it's not an omen of misfortune."

"What do you mean?" the young Russian asked, anxiously.

"First of all, you know how severe and suspicious the Administration is—and quite rightly, especially where the manufacture of explosives is concerned."

"I know. Numerous political crimes have given them reason. But what are you worried about? Your past is there to plead in favor of your intentions. Who would ever accuse the engineer Pierre Damidoff of pursuing a criminal objective?"

"Now read this," said the inventor, handing his son the mysterious note signed by the nihilist committee.

Ivan's amazement reached its peak. "And this order was addressed...?"

"To me."

"I don't understand." The young man had put his hands to his head. "This comminatory letter, if I'm not mistaken, emanates from the secret society named Free Russia, whose aim is the destruction of imperialism and of society as presently established?"

"Yes," said Jude Iagow, nodding his head.

"But what has that got to do with you, loyal employee and patriot as you are?"

"I haven't always been that, Ivan," the ex-affiliate replied, in a grave voice, "and the time has come for me to reveal to you the secret of my life—a terrible secret. You need to know, because dolorous events might be imminent. You're a man now, you can listen to me and comprehend. Ivan, my name isn't Pierre Damidoff, but Jude Iagowski. I'm a convict in violation of banishment."

And the confession flowed from the unfortunate's lips.

"You see, my dear Ivan, I was born in the wake of the Polish insurrection of 1863—an insurrection that was harshly repressed.[7] I grew up under the rod of a suspicious administration, in the mist of dull rumbles of anger and hatred. Austria, by taking possession of the only part of Poland that remained free, and Germany, by persecuting our brethren in Danzig, taking their wealth in order to give it to its own people as the spoils of war, drove my sentiments of exalted patriotism to paroxysm, and I affiliated myself to nihilism, without giving any thought to the execrable projects pursued by that redoubtable association. One day, a terrible event occurred; innocent parties paid for the guilty, and my own mother was killed.

"That was a frightful revelation for me. Dragged before a military tribunal, I was condemned to the mines in perpetuity. The sentence was just, but I could not resolve myself to abandoning my intelligence, my activity and my life. I escaped."

Then the engineered related the story of his encounter with Pierre Damidoff, the singular inheritance from which he had benefited in the Ural Mountains, and his marriage to Ana Erloff.

---

[7] Following Russia's defeat in the Crimean War several of her dependencies made a bid for independence, beginning with the Polish-Lithuanian uprising of January 1863, with the Ukrainians and Belarusians soon joined in. It took two years for the Russians to crush the revolts, executing many of the insurgents and sending more than 18,000 to Siberia. The insurrectionists had hoped for support from other European countries, especially France, but did not get it—perhaps unfortunately, given the subsequent history of the Russian vassal states in question. Jules Verne originally made Captain Nemo a Polish insurgent, but his publisher thought the choice too sensitive and made him change the character's back-story.

"And that's it," he added, in a voice trembling with emotion. "Faithful to my promise to your mother, I brought you up with the sentiments of a good Russian and a good Christian. You know now what you have to do..."

"Oh, Father, Father!" cried the adolescent, hugging the unfortunate man. "What are you thinking? Can you believe that I'm cowardly enough to abdicate the respect and affection I owe you? You were bearing your secret alone; now there are two of us, that's all."

From the abode of the just, the dead woman saw them and blessed the child into whom she had breathed her pure and elevated principles. *Honor thy father and thy mother*: a divine precept, which no one ought to forget. A child must be blind and deaf when it is a matter of those whom Providence had given him for parents. For them, he must be all heart and all love.

The former convict's confession had not lessened Ivan's affection—far from it. The adolescent had divined the frightful distress of the soul that was unburdening itself, and had granted it, without any afterthought, freely and joyfully, the refuge of his filial piety.

The engineer felt consoled and stronger. He was ready to confront the obstacles that he foresaw being redoubtable. Furthermore, considering matters more closely, he was glad that circumstances had forced him to act. He wanted to be rehabilitated. It had become a need, especially now that he had confessed to his son. The latter had the right to demand it. He could no longer recoil; it was necessary not to fail in his new duty.

The embrace having relaxed, he had opened the door of the study, when guttural cries became audible, and vehement voice shouted: "Let me pass, I tell you! I need to see him!"

A PACIFIST

Jude Iagow returned swiftly to the window. An old man who had emerged from a plush limousine was at the garden gate, contending with Nitchef, who was stubbornly barring his way.

"I want to see him! I know he's at home!" shouted the visitor.

The valet obviously did not understand, for he did not budge an inch.

The engineer raised the whistle to his lips and drew a shrill, imperious blast from it.

Nitchef turned his head.

"Let him pass," he master orders, gesturing.

The valet obeyed, but with visible reluctance.

"Please excuse him, sir," said the inventor, advancing toward the old man. "He's a deaf-mute, and follows orders intractably."

"So I've observed," replied the visitor, with an enigmatic smile, as he came into the study, where he let himself fall into the chair offered to him. He was both furious and triumphant. He added, a trifle bitterly: "You're well-defended."

"It's sometimes necessary," Jude Iagow replied, coldly.

"Especially when one's employed in certain kinds of chemistry."

The unknown man reached into the pocket of his jacket and took out a section of the *Scientific Review*, which he brandished triumphantly.

It required all of the inventor's self-control not to let his astonishment and emotion show. How did the man know that he, Pierre Damidoff, was the scientist to whom the article referred?

"I don't know what you mean," he said.

The old man took a pair of gold-rimmed spectacles out of a case and set them astride his nose. The master of the house immediately had the sensation of having seen that face before somewhere. Where? He could not remember.

He looks like a German, he thought.

Nothing appeared to corroborate that opinion, however, except perhaps for an overly deliberate purity of accent.

"To whom do I have the honor of speaking?" he asked, gripped by an instinctive mistrust.

The old man's face expressed a sincere surprise. "You don't recognize me?" he said. "No? In any case, my identity is of no importance in the circumstances; I'm here as a representative of humankind." He darted an incisive glance at the inventor over the top of his spectacles. "I've read this," he continued, "and I don't approve. No, I don't understand anyone ambitious for such glory."

He spoke an overly grammatical, academic Russian. He directed a fiery stare at his interlocutor.

Ivan was watching the scene curiously.

"Personally, I understand it very well," the inventor replied, stung to the quick, and throwing prudence overboard. "I understand very well, especially when one's objective is the grandeur of the fatherland."

The visitor smiled ironically. At the first stroke, he had broken down the other's reticence. "The fatherland is a great and beautiful thing, I grant you. There are, nevertheless, other means of contriving to give it supremacy in the world. Above the fatherland, there is humankind, just as above humankind, there is God."

"Perhaps. However..."

"There is no perhaps, or however. Why seek new means of destruction? Does nature not have enough at her service? Come on, sir, think about it. You're intelligent, you must understand me. Why destroy?"

"But..."

"Why destroy?" repeated the old man, forcefully. "Here's a child, your son. You love him...yes, that's evident merely by the expression on your face. One day, he'll be a soldier. Why restrict his chances of escaping carnage?"

The stranger's vibrant speech, stirred the most secret fibers in the hearts of his listeners.

"Who are you?" the inventor interrogated, troubled in spite of himself, and increasingly in the grip of a mistrust that he could neither explain nor overcome.

"My name isn't important," the visitor replied, "and since you don't recognize me, let's pass on. Besides which, that anonymity of sorts is perfectly suited to my present role. I represent the hot of anguished fathers in the presence of the unremitting threat that your discovery is suspending over our young armies. So I've come, in their name, to buy your discovery. How much?"

Jude Iagow started violently. Suspicion passed from his heart into his eyes. The other did not seem to perceive it.

"How much do you want?" he asked. "How much? I'll pay." His hand reached into the inside pocket of his jacket. "State a figure, no matter what. I only put one condition on the bargain: you'll stop there, and promise not to do any further work on explosives. I have other fields just as interesting, and even more so, to which you can devote your need for knowledge and discovery. What do you want?"

As the words struck his eardrum, the inventor's face became increasingly cold and increasingly rigid.

I understand, Jude Iagow thought. *A jealous colleague. He wants to put a damper on my invention, and take my place. No chance!*

"I refuse," he said, in a low voice.

"Even for a million?"

"Even for two, five or ten. Goodbye..."

"After all..."

"I said goodbye," the engineer replied, in a dry one, bowing slightly.

"That's not your final word?"

"That's my final word."

"Impossible: think about it. Destroy? Why destroy? Aren't plague, cholera and cold steel enough? Yes, your invention is beautiful—no, not beautiful, curious..."

33

"Really?"

"Yes, curious...but you're trying to do the work of death."

"No, sir—not death but defense, defense and triumph, if masked enemies attack Russia some day."

"Enemies? What enemies?"

"Germany, for example."

"Germany! But Germany isn't anyone's enemy, sir, thank God! I have the honor of knowing many German scientists, and not the least. They all assure me—and I have no reason to contradict them—that their emperor wants world peace. He is, on principle and by divine destiny, a Mediator. Oh, now I think about it, you doubtless mean Japan, or even England?"

"I don't mean anyone, for nothing confirms, as yet, what is in sum merely a sentiment."

"I repeat to you, sir, that you're mistaken. If warlike intentions were on the rise the direction you imagine, neither Bebel nor Liebknecht would be left to expose their theories in broad daylight."[8]

The strange visitor definitely had an interest in cleansing Germany of perhaps-unjust suspicion, for he was putting real effort into it. He was probably one of those Don Quixotes obsessed with a mania for righting wrongs wherever he encountered them.

"But let's leave politics there," he concluded. "I don't understand it very well. Let's get back to your invention, the object of my visit. Sell it to me. I..."

---

[8] In fact, by the time this scene is set, the Marxist Auguste Bebel (1840-1913), who had long been the leader of Germany's Social Democratic Party, was dead. Karl Liebknecht (1871-1919)—one of the founders, along with Rosa Luxemburg, of the German Communist Party and a strident opponent of the Great War in the Reichstag—was imprisoned for High Treason in May 1916, and subsequently killed by the *Freikorps*—the remnants of the Imperial Army consolidated by the post-war government.

"That's enough," the inventor interrupted, his irritation having increased as his interlocutor exposed his humanitarian theories. "I don't have time to listen to your nonsense."

He opened the door, which collided abruptly with Nitchef, standing behind it. The valet made as if to flee. Jude Iagow stopped him with a gesture.

Good old Nitchef was on watch, he thought. *He need have no fear; I can look after myself.*

"Show this gentleman out," he said, in a loud voice, indicating the visitor.

"It's no, then?" said the latter. "Be careful—that might get you into trouble."

The engineer hesitated momentarily. His heart had just lurched under the influence of a muted presentiment. He was ashamed of the seeming weakness, and stiffened himself.

"Threats!" he mocked.

"May it please God that they're only platonic threats," replied the unknown man, shaking his head. "It will get you into trouble, I tell you. Unless…well, we'll meet again."

The old man bowed and went out, escorted by Nitchef, who was staring at him ferociously. Anyone seeing the two men, during their journey from the villa to the car, would have been astonished by the deaf-mute valet's gestures, and would have sworn that an animated dialogue was taking place between the latter and the old eccentric.

Meanwhile, a heavy silence had fallen in the study.

Jude Iagow was standing there, his head bowed, as if oppressed by the weight of a dolorous thought.

"This will get me into trouble," he murmured. "Yes, it would get me into trouble if my goal weren't so noble—nobler than might be convenient. But who is that man? How did he know that the article was about me?"

TOWARD DESTINY

"How could he have known?"

For three days, the engineer repeated the same question, without discovering an answer. The villa was surrounded by high walls. Moreover, the laboratory was, as we have seen, in a separate building, constructed in the middle of a grove of trees behind the dwelling. No one could intrude an indiscreet gaze, no one had ever come into it except him, Pierre Damidoff, and the stupid valet. How could the old man have known?

All of a sudden, Jude Iagow remembered having carried out an experiment with the silent powder some time before, in a gorge of the Vistula. That experiment might have had an invisible witness, who, if he was a true scientist, would have been keenly interested in it. An enquiry, rapid and quite easy, might have permitted him to discover the inventor's identity. From that, if he were jealous of any glory other than his own, to wanting to take possession of the discovery, was a short step.

Jude Iagow thought that he had deduced the truth. *I might have a powerful adversary in him*, he thought. *I'll have to hurry.*

He put his affairs in order, because, in view of his past, the game he was about to play was serious. He knew that.

The day fixed for his departure arrived.

It was 7 July 1914 (in the old style[9]). The weather was very hot, overwhelming. The air was supercharged with electricity. A violent storm was in preparation.

---

[9] i.e, in accordance with the Julian calendar; the difference between the two then being thirteen days, the Gregorian equivalent would by 20 July 1914—some three weeks after the assassination of Franz Ferdinand and eight days before the beginning of the Great War.

As night fell, he called Ivan.

The adolescent had thought a great deal. A week had matured him more than ten years.

The engineer opened the door of the room where they were slightly, and listened for some time. No sound broke the silence in the house and the surrounding area. Nadia was asleep upstairs. As for Nitchef, he ought to be in the kitchen, occupied in rocking back and forth, as was his habit, in a chair deprived of one of its legs. The idiot seemed to adore that kind of amusement. At any rate, it was his favorite pastime, as soon as he could get away from work.

Jude Iagow closed the door carefully.

"My child," he said, returning to Ivan, "I'm leaving in an hour. First, I'm going to the factory, to ask the director for leave on urgent business. From there I'll go to Petrograd and solicit an audience with the emperor. I'll put my invention in his hands, and make a full and detailed confession."

"He'll grant you mercy, I'm certain of it."

The engineer shook his head. "If I can get to him."

"Isn't it for Russia?" asked the adolescent, surprised.

"It won't be as easy as that, alas. To get to him, I'll need to get past many obstacles, which might prove insurmountable."

"What?"

"Jealousy, envy…and self-interest."

"So, Father, you've made an admirable discovery, but it might remain useless?"

"Many men are vile enough to prefer the servitude of their fatherland to the elevation, even merited, of someone else. I'll have to use cunning, solicit the most insignificant ministerial servants, beg them and plead with them to give my discovery some consideration. It will be a long process—very long. Anyhow, I've had the patience, and I'll have the courage. You'll need courage too."

The boy looked his father in the face. "I will," he replied.

"You understand what I expect of you. I might not come back."

"Oh! Why that dread?"

"It's necessary to be ready for anything. Think about foreigners—those who are always on the lookout for the slightest scientific progress in that field of ideas. Remember that Europe is going through a formidable crisis, and that if, in reality, war does break out soon, our enemies will do their utmost to destroy us. They won't neglect anything to rob us of whatever might promise or assure us of victory. Now, the visit of that stranger didn't tell me anything worthwhile. Who is he? Where does he come from? What does he want? His love of humanity! No, I don't believe it. Be on your guard. If he comes back, he'll try to soften you up with honeyed words. Be as hard as marble, and above all—above all!—watch out for Nadia."

"Would he have the audacity…?"

"He seems to me to be intent on getting hold of my invention. Be careful. Listen." The inventor moved his head closer to his son's. "You know where your sister's portrait is. Inside the frame, between the portrait and the cardboard backing, I've hidden the duplicate copy of the formula for my invention. It's necessary not to give it to anyone unless you're certain that I'm dead."

"Dead?" said Ivan, shivering.

"One never knows. In brief, is something bad happens to me and you've seen my dead body, or my death has been proven officially, only then should you leave for Petrograd and put my invention into the hands of the Minister of War. Is that understood?"

"It will be done as you wish, Father. I won't surrender anything until I'm sure."

"Even if you're in mortal danger—even if Nadia's in peril."

"Her!"

"It would be for the fatherland," said Damidoff, solemnly.

"That's true," replied the boy, gravely.

"Now, if I don't come back, I entrust your sister to you. Be her guide and her support in life."

"You can count on me, Father. I'll do what I can; God will help me."

"You're a brave lad. It's understood, then. Not a word, not a gesture! For the fatherland!"

"For the fatherland," Ivan repeated.

The engineer hugged the adolescent to his bosom. Then he went up to Nadia's room. The little girl was sleeping restlessly; she uttered a moan.

"The storm's troubling her," murmured the father, kissing her cautiously.

He contemplated her for a long time, stiffening himself against emotion. He went back downstairs. When he went past the kitchen door he saw Nitchef asleep, his elbows on the table.

Poor fellow! he thought. *What pure and elevated joys are forbidden to him! But also what troubles and miseries!*

He went through the garden slowly.

"Father!" called Ivan from the window where he was standing. "You ought not to go. The storm threatens to be frightful. Wait until tomorrow."

Jude Iagow was on the point of yielding to his son's reasoning, but he said to himself: "No, though. Minutes are precious; it's necessary to act. Anyway, I'll be at the tram station in ten minutes. I have time."

He put a finger to his lips to recommend absolute silence, made a gesture of farewell, and went out of the garden, as if forcing himself, and resisting a violent desire to go back.

Was that a presentiment?

THE VISION

Ivan Damidoff saw his father disappear with an easily-understandable anguish. The engineer would be obliged to travel a verst on foot through the, the tram connecting X*** to Warsaw having been stopped following an accident to the electricity generator.[10]

The sky was the color of ink. Lightning-flashes striped the sky, followed by frightful crashes of thunder.

Ivan was familiar with the kind of tornadoes that could knock down hundred-year-old trees, and he trembled for the traveler.

The night darkened rapidly. Ivan did not budge from his observatory. By virtue of a flash of lightning, he thought he saw Nitchef standing by the garden gate.

He's worried too, he thought. *My father should have taken him with him, especially as he'll have to go through the forest. If some evildoer...*

A blast of a whistle, modulated into three notes, interrupted his reflections. He shivered. "The nihilists," he murmured, leaning forward and pricking up his ears avidly.

A loud crash of thunder, followed by a scream from Nadia, tore him away from his post. He ran to the little girl's bed and found her awake, in a state of extraordinary nervous excitement.

"I'm scared," she said, hiding her head in her brother's arms.

"Don't be afraid, my darling," he said, striking her. "I'm here."

"I'm not scared of the thunder. I'm scared..."

---

[10] The author has forgotten that the villa was previously said to be in W*** rather than X***, which was previously given as the location of the Bargineff factories. W*** is never mentioned again

"Of what? he said, anxiously.

"I don't know. Why has Father gone?"

"For a reason you wouldn't understand. He's going to offer his invention to the Russian government."

"Oh? Where has he gone?"

"To Petrograd."

The little girl wrung her hands, weeping. "I'm scared that someone's going to hurt him."

"Who?"

"I don't know. There are men behind him."

Ivan shivered. The little girl's remark reminded him of his own secret fears, but he was afraid of being childish. He suppressed his anxiety.

"Calm down, darling," he said, kissing his sister. He added: "Anyway, Nitchef must have gone to join him. I saw him at the garden gate."

"Oh, I don't like Nitchef!" exclaimed Nadia, forcefully. "He's nasty."

"No, he's very devoted to Papa."

"No, he's nasty. He wants to hurt him."

That's prejudice, thought the adolescent, trying to dispel the bad feeling that was taking possession of him.

Was it the result of what the little girl said or an effect of the electricity in the air? He was becoming equally anxious. A kind of impatience, compounded out of unadmitted fear and a desire to see the storm end and daylight appear, robbed him of his ordinary self-composure.

But daylight was still a long way away. Hours separated him from it. As for the storm, it was just reaching the peak of its intensity.

The claps of thunder were succeeding one another rapidly, the fulgurant lightning-bolts changing the sky into a sheet of fire.

Ivan thought about his father, alone in the midst of the unleashed elements. As long as no harm came to him!

He was caught between two dangers: the lightning and his enemies. Was the bizarrely-modulated whistle blast the

41

signal for some maneuver by the latter? Had its significance been determined in advance? Might it not be: *Look out! He's leaving. There he is—get hold of him! Kill him!*

Come on, the adolescent said to himself. *In truth, I'm exaggerating. It's the storm. I wish Nitchef were here.*

But Nitchef did not appear. He had gone out. He must have gone to join his master. But if he had gone, was it to defend him?

What an idea! Had the deaf-mute ever show the slightest sign of rebellion or hatred? On the contrary, had he not given proof of an absolute devotion, at every moment of the day or night? What was he thinking?

"Oh, this storm—I wish it were over!"

Far from ending, however, the wind was increasing. The house was trembling on its foundations, as if it were about to collapse.

Nadia was getting more and more agitated. Her big blue eyes seemed to be looking through the walls at something that frightened her.

"Come on, calm down, calm down!" the boy never ceased repeating.

But she struggled, as if she wanted to escape his grip.

Ivan began to sense his reason slipping away.

The storm had become deafening. A thousand voices were howling at the same time, like an immense pack of furious wolves.

Suddenly, something frightful happened. A blinding flash of lightning split the sky, and an enormous thunderclap shook the ground.

"Papa! Papa!" shouted Nadia.

The adolescent stood up straight, his hair prickling, cocking an ear. He could no longer hear anything.

The last clap of thunder had doubtless exhausted the forces of nature, and the storm began to ease.

A few minutes later, the most profound silence reigned. Nadia, hand in hand with her brother, went back to sleep, finally calm.

Ivan waited a little longer; then, having put the little girl back to bed and tucked her in carefully, he went back to his own room, got undressed and went to bed in his turn.

He tried to think about his father; fatigue was stronger.

In the midst of his increasing torpor, he heard the door open and close and heavy footsteps resounding downstairs. *It's Nitchef coming back*, he thought.

He was soon profoundly asleep.

The next day, the radiant sun had chased away the phantasmagorias of the night. Nadia woke up smiling. Ivan felt hope reborn in his heart; his father must be on the train to Petrograd.

Only Nitchef was very pale, with something akin to a residue of terror behind his eyes—but the engineer's son did not even perceive that.

NITCHEF

While Nitchef was pushing rather than guiding the eccentric who had laid a fortune at the inventor's feet toward the garden gate, the old man had reached into his pocket and pulled out a handful of gold coins.

"Take this," he said to the deaf-mute. "I'll give you a thousand rubles if you can arrange a decisive interview with your master for me."

The lowest creature in the human scale understand the language of gold very well, and if Nitchef did not allow himself to be seduced, it was doubtless because only the sentiment of virtue lived in his obscure soul. He remained motionless for as long as the limousine was in sight, and after having carefully bolted the gate, he went back with strangely heavy tread for a man who had just expelled another with almost vertiginous rapidity.

Nitchef had been in Jude Iagow's employ for about a year.

One winter morning, Nadia, having wandered out on to the road, saw a man half dead of hunger and cold slumped against the garden wall. Moved by that distress, the child had taken the man by the hand. She had made him a sign to get up and follow her. Naively, she had led him to the kitchen.

The housekeeper who came in every morning to clean the villa's rooms and prepare lunch, raised her arms to the heavens.

"What's this you're bringing me?" she cried, contemplating the vagabond, who looked most unattractive in his rags. "Do you want to get us all murdered?"

"He's hungry," the child replied, simply.

It was necessary, no matter what the cost, to feed the stranger.

The inventory had reason to be wary of the appearance of suspicious individuals in the neighborhood, so the appearance of the wretch did not please him overmuch. When the latter was sufficiently fed, therefore, he slipped a ruble into his hand and showed him the door.

The man did not seem to understand. He maintained a stupid expression.

"I want you to go," Damidoff reiterated. "You can't stay here."

The stranger's throat emitted a few hoarse sounds.

"A mute!" exclaimed Ivan.

"And probably deaf," added the inventor.

He studied the man. Never had a more bleakly bestial expression, more sadly deprived of the divine spark, afflicted a human face. In the formation of that creature, nature must have stopped at the level of the fattened goose, the chameleon and the toad. One could shout an irrefutable truth at him, and he would not understand it. He was a living corpse, an amalgam of cells reduced to vegetal existence.

"What if we kept him?" Ivan proposed. "He won't be chattering to anyone."

Jude Iagow looked at his son. "And it would be a good deed," concluded the latter.

"We're keeping him!" said Nadia, clapping her hands.

The man's eyes turned toward her, and her joy vanished, like the fall of an overripe fruit. She was frightened. She ran to hide her face in her brother's jacket.

"He won't do you any harm," said the latter. "I don't think he's malevolent."

Jude Iagow having put a broom in the unknown's hands, the latter carried out his task rather awkwardly, but in a satisfactory manner, all things considered, for a scientist to whom domestic matters mattered little. Even so, the engineer hesitated.

A contest was engaged within him between pity, self-interest—he needed a discreet valet—and mistrust. All our actions are, however, written in advance in the book of the Eternal. For good or ill, the vagabond was adopted. His education demanded infinite patience. The whistle-blasts being the only sounds that could activate his eardrums, the master of the house devised a kind of acoustic alphabet consisting of long and short blasts.

Three months later, the deaf-mute was a passable valet.

They had hesitated for some time over what name to give him. As he could neither speak, nor hear, not think very well, Ivan suggested that they call him Nitchef, the root of which, *nitsch*, signifies "nothing." The name was apt, since the man did not even know where he had come from.

Over there, he responded, when asked, indicating a vague direction.

The name stuck. It did not seem to offend him, for good reason.

The engineer eventually congratulated himself on his find. He could invent anything at all—make gold, sunlight or create life—and the secret would be safe. The man did his work without manifesting any joy or pain. He was always obedient and impassive, not to say stupid.

Nadia experienced in his regard a terror that time had been unable to dismiss. The child was, it is true, extremely nervous, unhealthy and subject to crises that brought her bolt upright in bed by night, or caused her to stride back and forth in her room like a phantom. In brief, no sympathy, apart from the first glance they had exchanged, was possible between the man and the child.

That seemed indifferent to the man; his heart doubtless being as closed to sentimental life as his mind was to ideas.

Nevertheless, another person was to experience the same instinctive repulsion at the sight of the fanatic, this time cor- roborated by judicious annotations.

Georges Chantepie, a French teacher, lived some dis- tance away from the villa. Having come to visit his pupil he could not help demanding, on seeing the valet: "Where has he come from?"

"We don't know," Ivan Damidoff told him. "He doesn't know himself."

"Well, I'll tell you. He comes from Japan. I'd swear to it."

"Japanese, him?"

"He doesn't have a very emphatic semitic type, of course; some of his countrymen are much closer to the European, but that's where he's from."

"My father hasn't noticed that, though."

"Oh, that's not astonishing. The physiognomy of your compatriots has, more often than not, the characteristics of Asiatic peoples; the details don't leap to your eyes as they do to me, a Frenchman.

The tutor beckoned to the valet. "Isn't it the case that you're originally from the Far East?" he asked.

"He's deaf," put in the engineer's son. Deaf, dumb and notoriously idiotic. That's why his origin is, in sum, unimportant to my father."

"Ah!" said the tutor, simply. He feared being indiscreet by persisting further. Nevertheless, he turned round to dart a final glance at the domestic. He saw him occupied in attaching a branch of a pear-tree to an espalier, with a dexterity very considerable on the part of a quasi-imbecilic individual.

THE PIECES OF PAPER

The Frenchman kept his observation to himself.

Were his inductions accurate?

On studying the deaf-mute's characteristics one would not have failed, in fact, to recognize in his flat hair, his prominent Mongolian cheekbones, his almond-shaped eyes and in his skin, as if washed with rusty water—the distinctive signs of the races of the Far East—but nothing proved it in an irrefutable fashion. At any rate, the Frenchman had his established opinion, and on that point nothing could make him let go.

In the meantime, he learned, from the inventor's own mouth, that the "silent powder" had finally emerged from the limbo of theory and that steps were about to be undertaken with regard to the Government, in order to have it adopted by the army commissioners. A great and sincere esteem united the two men. They discussed the steps to be taken together.

"Monsieur Chantepie," said the engineer, "for reasons that I'll tell you one day, I might be absent for a long time. I might be brutally removed from my family, for long months. Can I ask you to watch over them?"

"My devotion is acquired, as you know," the Frenchman replied, simply.

He had understood, by his interlocutor's emotion, that some vital interest, some burdensome secret, was connected with his determination. Too discreet to interrogate him, he promised without unnecessary verbiage, and the handshake that concluded the conversation proved that his honest and loyal heart belonged entirely to his friends. At the time fixed by Damidoff for his departure, he was standing on his doorstep to wave to him as he went by.

The ink-dark sky and the repeated detonations of the storm that had accumulated above the region made an impression on him and added to the invincible anguish that he expe-

48

rienced in thinking that the mental tranquility his pupil's father seemed to enjoy was only apparent.

The traveler passed by, exchanging a salute of farewell, and hastened in the direction of the tram station, still a quarter of a verst distant.

As he was closing his door again, the tutor thought he saw suspicious shadows slipping from tree to tree in the direction taken by the engineer. In one of them, he thought he recognized, by virtue of a characteristic movement, the silhouette of Nitchef. He seized a revolver and ran out into the road.

At that moment, the storm burst in all its fury. He stopped. "I'm crazy to be afraid," he said.

He stood there for some time, indifferent to the hail that lashed him, peering into the deep darkness of the landscape. At one point, the agonized scream that had struck Ivan's ears made him shiver and snatched him out of his immobility. He walked for some distance without encountering anything abnormal. He spent a bad night, however, haunted by the idea that something bad had happened, and that it was his fault. The silhouette of Nitchef on the road never quit his eyes.

He was half-tranquilized the following morning, when Ivan appeared, holding Nadia by the hand.

"Did you hear the scream?" he asked, as if he could not help himself/

"Yes," the adolescent replied. "A child must have been frightened by a thunderclap."

"And where's Nitchef?"

"Oh yes," said Ivan. "Your *bête noire?* We left him to his morning occupations. He's sweeping."

The subject of the conversation changed. They talked about the inventor. The Frenchman sang his praises. "Such men honor their fatherland," he concluded. "I have no doubt that his efforts will have reached their goal within a year."

Then they evoked the difficulties that he would have to overcome, the ambushes that lay in wait for him, the enemies lurking in the shadows. Finally, they talked about Nitchef.

49

"Do you want to try a little experiment?" asked the Frenchman, with a tenacity that even astonished him. Go back home and try to take him by surprise."

"Oh! You want..."

"I need to know. A mania? So be it! Do me the pleasure. Hang on, let me ask you a question: yesterday evening, when your father left, where was he?"

"Nitchef? At the garden gate."

"Ah! And afterwards?"

"I don't know I had to leave the window, called by Nadia. You think..."

"I don't think anything. No, no...I'm trying to find out. I'm trying to form a conviction, now that you and your sister are alone in an isolated villa."

"My father has often slept at the factory for three days running. Nothing has ever happened to us. Then again, I'm no longer a child."

"That's why I'm talking to you man to man. I'd hide my suspicions from a child. Read between the lines of what I'm saying: above you there's your fatherland. I don't know any more than I ought to know, but it's permissible for me to guess a great deal. Would you care to grant my wish and go see what Nitchef is doing? I'll wait for you behind the garden wall."

"All right," said Ivan, vanquished.

He crossed the two hundred sagenes[11] that separated him from the villa, reflectively. The tutor was not a man to say anything lightly, and if he was advising him to be suspicious, it was because he had a reason that he was avoiding explaining, but which existed nevertheless.

His imagination immediately on the alert, he set about inventing the most improbable things, and when he set foot in the villa. He was no less reassured. He went into the vestibule

---

[11] There are five hundred sagenes to the verst, the latter being approximately equal to a kilometer in 1914, so the distance indicated is about 400 meters, or a quarter of a mile.

quietly and went through the house without finding any trace of Nitchef. Then he headed for the laboratory.

The valet had to be there. What was he doing there?

Arriving stealthily, Ivan darted a glance through the window and started to smile. Sitting on the parquet, the idiot was searching a waste paper basket, taking out the torn pieces of paper and composing a complicated design on the floor. It was a perfectly innocent occupation.

However, either because he sensed a foreign presence or the dread of having done something wrong surged forth in that puerile brain, he scattered the pieces of paper with a gesture and turned toward the window, his eyes imprinted with menace and anger. That expression soon disappeared, however, to be replaced by his habitual expression of stupidity.

Ivan signaled to him not to disturb himself, and turned away, murmuring: "I'd be very curious to hear him read me the algebraic or chemical formulas written on that page."

That irony was unfortunately lost to Nitchef—and that was a great pity.

"Well?" asked Georges Chantepie, who was waiting at the gate.

"In truth, Monsieur Chantepie," the adolescent said, with a sincere joy, "you were wrong and I was right. Do you know what he was doing? He was amusing himself with pieces of paper he'd taken from the laboratory waste-basket."

"In what fashion?" asked the Frenchman, with a gleam in his eye.

"He was putting them side by..." Ivan interrupted himself; his eyes had met the teacher's.

"Finish!" said the Frenchman, excitedly.

Ivan stared laughing, in a slightly forced manner. "Nitchef reading algebra! Him, who asked me by means of signs why I was looking at a book, what pleasure I experienced keeping my eyes fixed on blackened paper?" Before the severe gaze of his companion, however, his artificial gaiety suddenly faded away.

"If I were you," the Frenchman concluded, "not only would I immediately burn the pieces of paper left in the laboratory, but I'd strictly prohibit access to it to that lover of pieces of paper. Better still, I'd forbid him to set foot in the engineer's study. Do as you wish—it's no concern of mine. Nevertheless, I advise you to telephone your father and ask for his instructions."

"All right, but I can't do until tomorrow. He won't be in Petrograd until tomorrow night."

"That's true," replied George Chantepie. "In the meantime, leave Nadia with me, will you?"

A shadow passed over Ivan Damidoff's face. His father had considered him as a man in confiding his dark secret from him and putting the little girl in his care. He felt that he was capable of defending her against anyone who raised a hand to her. That paternity of sorts elevated him in his own eyes. In consequence, he expressed his gratitude for the tutor's offer, but declined it.

After all, even if Nitchef was an enemy, what could he ever have against that lovely creature?

But there was another cause of severe anxiety that surged forth: the day went by, and then the night and the following day, but the telegram promised by the engineer did not arrive.

Ivan was walking back and forth feverishly, with Nadia, in front of the post office, waiting for a dispatch, when Stapouloff, the burgomaster of X*** introduced his gross and imposing person into the office and demanded, in a shrill voice ill-suited to that enormous individual: "It is true that war has been declared?"

"War?" murmured Ivan. And he suddenly felt his mind dissolve in confusion, and his ideas become mixed up, as in the kaleidoscopes with which children amuse themselves.

THE PACIFIST AT WORK

At the same hour, in the sanitarium constructed on the summit of a nearby hill, the cupola of which Ivan Damidoff could see, looming over the part occupied by the director, Dr. Mohr was using his telephone.

"Hello! Is that you, Gorski?"

"Yes."

"How's Damidoff?"

"He hasn't given any sign of life."

"Have you tried electric massage? Warm air?"

"Nothing! The lethargy is complete."

"Well, I'll come and see for myself in a minute. Watch him, and don't let anyone near him."

"Understood."

Dr Mohr hung up the receiver with an abrupt gesture.

On a wooded hill, about two versts from the village of X , where the inventor of the silent bomb lived, stood the sanitarium constructed and directed by Dr. Mohr, an excellent man if ever there was one.

The hospice was a veritable museum of teratological monstrosities, in the midst of which an entire population of warders and medical orderlies agitated.

Inside the buildings, constructed in accordance with the latest principles of hygiene and modern comfort, was resplendent with whiteness. And Dr. Mohr reigned over that little kingdom like a lord, respected, if not loved, by everyone.

His reputation as a benevolent boor had long ago exceeded the boundaries of the Faculty of Medicine and penetrated into the world of the suffering and the disinherited, where we shall have occasion to see him at work. People talked about the miracles accomplished by that master of science, as well as his theories of emancipation and liberty, which took on an invincible persuasive power in his eloquent mouth.

53

Other stories also circulated, but covertly and quietly, accompanied by gestures of doubt. Among other things, it was said that he took the love of science so far as vivisecting human beings. It was said that his sanitarium contained a secret location known to him alone, where strange mysteries were accomplished. If the police had caught wind of these inconsistent rumors, they disdained them for two reasons. The first was that the scientist's situation rendered him unassailable—had he not saved the Emperor of Germany from an aposteme in the throat?—and in the second place, it was no longer the Middle Ages, an epoch of ignorance when sorcery was a crime against the State.

At any rate, that day, Dr. Mohr, sitting in the study from which he had just telephoned Gorski, a male nurse in his service, was in a very bad mood.

"Those imbeciles must have given him a knock on the head," he growled, "As if it's permissible to act brutally when it's a matter of a brain in which resides the predominance of an entire people over the world! Unless that wretched Nitchef administered him some drug of his own composition. Another famous chemist, that one! Idiot!"

He struck a gong. An office boy appeared.

"Who's waiting?"

"Count Krouptchine and a student, doubtless some wretched vagabond."

"Did he tell you his name?"

"A funny name: Thirteen."

"Send him in."

"What about the Count? He was here first."

"He can wait."

The usher knew his master. He knew that for him, there was no distinction between a poor man and a rich one. Suffering was, in his eyes, the great leveler. In the circumstances, however, the singularity bordered on impertinence. After all, the Count had arrived before the student. The usher thought it appropriate to apologize to the gentleman and address a haughty and scornful summons to the poorly-dressed young man who was waiting in the antechamber.

The latter had scarcely come into the study than the doctor stood up, carefully checked that the padded doors were closed, and advanced abruptly toward the person bearing the bizarre name of Thirteen.

"Well?" he said, in a low voice. "What does this mean? Why have you knocked him unconscious instead of grabbing hold of him and bringing him to me? Why have your stripped him? Where are the formulae?"

The individual made a gesture of impotence. "We didn't knock him out or strip him. As for the papers, it will be difficult to get them back..."

"Why?"

"Jude Iagow was struck by lightning. His clothes were volatilized, with all they contained. You must have noticed, chief, that he doesn't have a scratch on him."

"Indeed. I was rather perplexed, and wondered whether you might have given him some drug. Struck by lightning! He was struck by lightning? Very curious, yes, but inconvenient for us. Wilhelmstrasse is expecting the formulae. The lightning has done us a bad turn."

"Isn't there any means of bringing him out of this catalepsy?"

"It will be slow and difficult, if he doesn't die before recovering consciousness, and an active will—he might not recover intelligence and the power of speech at the same time. And time's pressing."

"Ah!" said Thirteen, shivering. "In...?"

Mohr raised three fingers. "Three days," he murmured.

The two men looked at one another; a ferocious joy irradiated their faces.

"Shh!" said the scientist. "Is it ready?"

"Everything's ready. Minds are at boiling point. Twenty-Four, at the Refuge, and Forty-Eight, at the Bargineff factories, will give the signal. The revolution will begin at Little Countess' Refuge and the general strike at the factories. Furthermore, the extension has been connected to the hospice circuit since yesterday."

The scientist pointed at a little bronze statuette on his desk, which was carrying a flower in its raised fingers whose pistil was formed by an emerald bulb. "So we can blow up the factory at the right moment by pressing that button. Perfect! The Emperor will be pleased."

The old man's face gradually resumed a cold expression. "Now it's a matter of getting the formulae. There must be a duplicate or rough drafts at the house. We have to find them."

"We'll do the necessary tomorrow night. The preparations have been made. The two children won't give us any trouble; they'll be given a narcotic. If they do get in the way..."

"No, no!" Mohr protested. "Don't take things to that extreme. Don't get the police mixed up in it. It wouldn't take much to ruin everything. We'll see later about getting the boy to talk—his father must have told him something. For the moment, be content with searching. Oh—one piece of advice: don't trust Nitchef. The mute seems to me to be playing a game that isn't clear. One might think that he's sniffed us out and knows too much."

"He knows that I can use a dagger..."

"Shh! Shh! Softly, softly! The time hasn't yet come to unleash the dogs. Let's go—goodbye, and good luck!"

The good Dr. Mohr accompanied Thirteen to the door, which he opened. The antechamber was full of patients, rich and poor.

"It's nothing," said the doctor, with a beaming smile. "We'll get your sister out of it."

With these words he rummaged in his pocket and drew out two gold coins, which, with feigned discretion, he slipped into the young man's hand. All those present had seen the gesture. As the student melted in gratitude he said: "Hush, my friend. That gold belongs to you, since I don't need it."

The scientist went back into his study and paced back and forth for some time, his brow furrowed.

"The silent bomb," he murmured, finally. "The dream!"

He opened a gold locket suspended on a chain of the same metal and contemplated a miniature representing Wilhelm II, Emperor of Germany, for some time.

"Sire," he said, "your time is nigh; you'll be content with me. *Deutschland über alles!* Germany above all, and everyone! Everything that humans invent of the beautiful and the great belongs by right to greater Germany. Sire, you shall have the silent bomb."

Dr. Mohr shut the locket and rang a bell.

THE FAKE

The next morning, a ray of joy penetrated into the villa darkened by anxiety. The deaf-mute received an envelope from the hands of the postman and handed it to his young master, who had hastened toward him.

"Nadia, Nadia, a letter from Papa!" shouted the adolescent, his eyes most with tears of joy.

The little girl dropped her doll and ran to her brother, who had just torn open the envelope feverishly. Ivan scanned the letter with a glance. His forehead darkened again immediately.

My dear Ivan,

To know where to find the formulas and the drawings. Give them to Nitchef and send him to me in Petrograd. I'll meet him at the station.

I've mislaid my portfolio. My attempts to find it have been in vain. You must understand my chagrin and my haste to begin the official steps. High hopes, all the same.

Your affectionate father.

Damidoff.

That was all. Not a word for Nadia.

Nitchef was waiting, with his most stupid expression. He seemed to be asking: "What is it?"

Ivan felt sick at heart. In spite of his love for science, his father was the most affectionate of parents. He adored Nadia. And not a word for her! Not one word!

Undoubtedly, in the anxiety provoked by the loss of his papers, forgetfulness was comprehensible. And yet...

Ivan had already taken a step toward the study when he stopped. He held the letter at arm's length, his eyes fixed on the signature. It was recognizable, but with one difference: the underlining flourish, usually energetic, enthusiastic and fiery, was marked at one point with an evident hesitation. One might have thought that the hand had made two attempts to depict it. He recalled his father's advice, and looked at the deaf-mute valet. The latter had not moved a muscle. Ivan immediately reflected. How had his father been able to imagine using that stupid being as a messenger in such an important circumstance?

There was definitely a doubt regarding the provenance of the letter. The best thing to do was make sure.

He ran to the telegraph office. The operator refused to take a dispatch. "Impossible! The wire's reserved for official orders. Go to Warsaw—you might have a chance of sending it there."

I'll go to Warsaw, then, Ivan said to himself.

He thought about taking his sister, but the little girl might slow him down, He confided her to Nitchef, and left.

He arrived at a city in turmoil. White posters issuing call-up instructions were covering the walls. Men were leaving workshops and warehouses to get ready. Others were heading for the railway stations. Trunks and suitcases cluttered the station forecourts, forming mountains along the walkways. Carriages, automobiles, charabancs and troikas were going in all directions at top speed.

War had not yet been officially declared, but the State was preparing for it.[12]

Ivan shivered as he went past groups of young men, calm but with a gleam in their eyes, haversacks over their shoulders, heading for barracks or the recruitment office.

If only I were two years older! he said to himself, angry at his weakness. *Anyway,* he added, *let's settle the matter of the letter—after that, we'll think about making ourselves useful.*

---

[12] The order for partial mobilization of Russian troops was issued by the Tsar on 15 July in the Julian calendar that the story's internal chronology is employing, although that internal chronology seems to slipped a few days since the 7th.

He went into the telegraph office. After waiting for an hour he was able to get to the operator, who could not guarantee that the dispatch would be sent for three days, and then...

He went out, feeling numb. He found the same animation and the same tumultuous sensations as an hour before. The vertigo of war and the love of the fatherland gripped his entrails again. Oh, if he had been free...! But he thought of Nadia, and resumed the road to the villa. Before leaving the city, he went into a church, in order to dispel the fit of moral weakness that he felt growing in his heart, and, after having prayed, felt new energy within himself. It was necessary to fight; he would fight.

His anxiety was for Nadia. Georges Chantepie had said so much to him against Nitchef that he was now so close to believing in the deaf-mute's malevolent intervention in the present events that he was afraid for his sister. He hastened his steps.

Night was closing in. The sky was cloudy and a light drizzle was falling. He went through the woods rapidly and on to the road bordered with white houses.

The Frenchman's house was still closed. He regretted that. He started running. He was in haste to see the little girl's sweet face again.

At that moment he was passing along the hedge that was mentioned at the beginning of this story. Through the trees, the gleam of a lighted window was visible.

The owner of the manor house was named Madame Wandowska. She was Polish, originally from Danzig. She had been very rich, but Germany, which had been preparing to absorb the world for many years, was intent on freeing its frontiers from possible and probable adversaries. The Poles were removed from their properties and transplanted into the plains of Hanover, while pure-blooded Germans shared out the spoils. All those who attempted the slightest resistance were shot. Madame Wandowska saw her husband perish in that way, under the gentle expansion of Kulturkampft.[13] She had taken refuge in the vicinity of Warsaw, with a little girl who had died one night of the croup. Those two great dolors had broken her. She had only escaped death by entering into a kind of meek and sad obsession, of which her dead daughter was the entire object. The manor was full of souvenirs of the cherished infant. She went so far as to take the child's favorite doll, dress it in mourning, and rock it in her arms, singing ballads to it.

When the weather was fine she went for walks along the road.

One day, she had met Nadia there. She had stopped, gripped by a sudden emotion, and had covered the little girl with kisses and tears. The child had returned her caresses with a politeness that had throw the poor woman into rapture.

Since then, they had seen her often. The widow's pockets were always full of treats. She was gripped by a powerful affection for the child. She had asked the engineer to let her take her home. He had refused, offering the excuse of a fear of being indiscreet; deep down, he feared that the grieving mother might be driven to a regrettable extreme in a fit of chagrin and jealous passion.

Since then, the widow had sulked. She had not ceased, moreover, to spy on the little girl's comings and goings. That is why we saw her, at the beginning of the story, lurking behind the hedge of the park, her eyes fixed on the Damidoff villa. Ivan did not spare a thought for her. He had other things on his mind—much more serious matters.

As he reached the garden gate, it seemed to him that he saw a shadow gliding from tree to tree in the direction of the villa. He ran forward. He was not mistaken. The woman—it was a woman—turned round as he approached, saying "Ivan!" and resumed her route even more rapidly.

---

[13] The anti-Catholic Kulturkampf program instituted in the 1870s by the Prussian Prime Minister, Otto von Bismarck, had been particularly ruthless in Poland.

The adolescent had heard his name. He thought he had seen a child in the intruder's arms. There was no doubt about it: Madame Wandowska—for it was her; he had recognized her, or guessed it—had just abducted Nadia.

His blood ran cold. He launched himself in pursuit. He tripped, fell, got up again, and arrived on the road just as the gate of the park closed.

He lost a great deal of time looking for a gap in the hedge.

He succeeded in getting through, not without difficulty, and increased the effort of his legs. He was visibly gaining on the shadow when he saw the latter stumble in her turn and fall face down on the first step of the perron, uttering a cry of pain. The door of the manor opened. A short stout man, whose spectacles were gleaming in the darkness, ran down precipitately, picked the woman up and went back inside. He disappeared just in time to close the door in Ivan's face.

The latter was getting ready to knock on the door when his eyes encountered a child-like form lying on the paving-stones. He bent down and straightened up again, with a doll in his hands.

The adolescent understood everything. Far from having malevolent intentions, the widow had wanted to bring Nadia a gift. His urgency in running after her had motivated her hectic flight.

The young man reproached himself for his stupidity and went back to the villa. He would come back the next day to offer his apologies.

It was a lesson; that would teach him to give events an importance they did not have.

He was already reassured as to the fate of his sister before he set foot in the house. He saw immediately, when he went in, how wrong he had been to be afraid, and especially to mistrust the deaf-mute.

The house was peaceful. A good meal was keeping warm on the stove. The samovar was purring softly. Sitting on his wobbly chair, Nitchef was rocking back and forth, as was his habit.

"Where's Nadia?" Ivan asked.

The deaf-mute understood, for he pointed to the upper floor and, resting his head on his hand, indicated that the little girl was asleep.

The engineer's son picked up a lantern and ran upstairs.

Nadia was, indeed, asleep in her little bed. Ivan leaned over and kissed her forehead. "Mama's protecting us," he murmured, gladly. "She'll protect us, and bring Papa back."

Nadia's arm was outside the covers. He took it gently and hid it underneath.

He ought to have been astonished by one thing. The child was usually a very light sleeper; the slightest presence in her vicinity woke her up. He had just taken her arm without her seeming to feel it. Her torpor was too profound to be natural.

Ivan did not notice the difference. Nadia was there, in her bed; he did not ask for anything more.

He went back downstairs on tiptoe.

The deaf-mute questioned him with a gesture.

The adolescent assumed that he was asking for news of the engineer. He responded with a gesture signifying that he did not know anything more.

"What a pity," he concluded, talking to himself, "that I can't explain it to him. He'd be a precious auxiliary. But what could I say? How could I analyze the incomprehensible and define for that inert creature what I can't define for myself?"

He made a gesture of discouragement.

He felt harassed. He let himself fall into a chair. "Serve the meal," he ordered. And he thought: *I have a headache. Tomorrow, I'll see Georges Chantepie. We'll confer.*

He ate absent-mindedly, without paying any heed to what he was eating and drinking. The tea tasted bitter. Perhaps it had been insufficiently sweetened.

Where's father? he said to himself. *Where can he be?* He stopped, his tongue thickening in his mouth. *Oh! What's wrong with me?*

Standing in front of him was Nitchef: a Nitchef he had never seen, a Nitchef whose face had taken on a normal expression. The heavy wrinkles in his forehead had been erased, and his eyes had a veritable gleam on intelligence.

There was a kind of pity in his eyes, and Ivan heard—or thought he heard—the deaf-mute mutter: "Poor child! Poor child! It's fortunate that I..."

Ivan widened his eyes in astonishment, but his eyelids were as heavy as lead. He stammered a few inconsequential syllables, and his head slumped on to the table.

He was asleep.

Nitchef picked him up, carried him away like a feather, undressed him and put him to bed.

After that, he went back downstairs, emptied the samovar into the stove, and washed the kettle and his young master's cup with abundant water. Then he went to the door and opened it. He put two fingers to his lips, and whistled.

VICTIM OR ACCOMPLICE?

When Ivan Damidoff opened his eyes, his tongue was thick, and his ideas were confused. He experienced a great weariness in all his limbs.

He recovered consciousness slowly, and not without difficulty.

He attributed his condition to the fatigues and emotions of the day before. He remembered running through the darkness after the shadow of Madame Wandowska.

"I was crazy," he murmured.

He darted a glance outside. The sun was shining softly. The foliage of the trees was swaying in the breeze.

He was pensive for a moment. *Perhaps Father's in the Urals*, he thought. *Before attempting anything, he's gone to pray at his benefactor's grave. There's no other reason for his silence. If the police had arrested him, they'd have searched the house.*

Mechanically, the adolescent looked around the room, and uttered a cry. Everything had been overturned, as if a hurricane had passed through it. The cupboard was open, the linen unfolded, mixed with his clothes, removed from the wardrobe. Boxes in which he had secreted small objects had been emptied on to the floor. Rubles and banknotes, money left by the engineer, were scattered around.

Ivan sat up on his elbow. He remained there for some time, open-mouthed and alarmed.

"Burglars!" he said, finally. But burglars would have taken the money.

Then he thought about a police search, and then about the invention.

He got up, got dressed in haste and ran to the study.

Nadia was smiling in her frame. The picture had not been touched. An indescribable disorder reigned throughout, however. What did it mean?

He went to the kitchen in the hope of encountering Nitchef. On the threshold of the pantry he recoiled. There was a large pool of blood there.

Anguish gripped him. He tried to call out to his sister; no sound emerged from his tight throat. He went back upstairs, trembling. Had any harm come to the little girl? Had she been taken away?

No! The child was in her bed, her eyes still swollen with sleep.

At the sight of her brother she put a hand to her forehead. "I have a headache," he said.

Nadia's face was, indeed, distraught.

"Didn't you hear anything?" he asked.

"No."

"That's curious—me neither. Where's Nitchef? That blood..."

"Oh! I'm scared!"

He shivered. He went to the window to call for help. He suppressed the impulse; he had just thought about his father.

"Impossible, impossible!" he murmured. "They'd discover the laboratory, and get hold of the thread...oh, not that, not that!"

He wanted to be the son of Jude Iagow rehabilitated, not Jude Iagow the escaped convict.

He put his head in his hands. Now was the time to show that he was a man. It was necessary to say nothing, not to breathe a word about the night's events. If only Nitchef had still been there. But Nitchef was gone. Was he the accomplice of the burglars? Had Georges Chantepie been right?

"Nadia, my darling," said Ivan, putting his arms around his sister, "stay in bed. I'll go make the tea. I'll be back in a minute."

The little girl had a sudden crisis of despair. "Papa! Papa" she said, sobbing. "I want Papa! I want to go with him."

"He'll come back—perhaps today."

"No, no! I want to go with him!"

Ivan had all the difficulty in the world consoling the poor girl. He only succeeded in part. Nadia was still calling for her father.

For a few days, those crises of despair had been frequent. The young man was anxious about it. The weight of responsibility was becoming heavier and heavier.

He went downstairs quickly.

"Nitchef!" he shouted.

The house resounded like an empty box. He remembered that the valet was a deaf mute—or at least might be. He took the whistle that was hanging from a nail in the corridor and blew it.

Then he thought he heard a groan coming from under the stairs. A cupboard was fitted under the flight. He went into it. His foot collided with two extended legs. He grabbed them and pulled them toward him.

Nitchef appeared, bound and gagged. A trickle of clotted blood was hanging down from his shoulder.

"Nitchef!" cried Ivan, taking off the gag. "In the name of Heaven, what happened?"

The wounded man moaned without making any reply.

"He can't hear me," said the bewildered adolescent. "What can I do? What Should I do?"

Then he thought that Providence had given his a friend in Georges Chantepie. He would provide good advice.

Forgetting, in his excitement, to free the deaf-mute from his bonds, he ran as fast as he could to the tutor's house.

The latter was getting ready to go out. At the sight of the young man's distress, he deduced that something bad had happened.

"Your father...?" he asked.

"No—come!" Ivan replied, his voice halting. "Thieves have pillaged the house, and I've just found Nitchef tied up, with a stab-wound."

"We need to alert the authorities, the police."

"No—not a word to anyone, I beg you."

"Why?" said the Frenchman, astonished.

"We mustn't. I don't even want anyone to see me running or to notice my pallor. It's true that I could say that Nadia's ill...and, in truth, she isn't very well at all. It's her nerves...oh, I'm very anxious. Come!"

The two of them went to the villa at a measured pace, in order not to excite suspicion. The gate was carefully closed. They went into the house.

"There's a revolver in the panoply in the study." said the Frenchman. "Is it loaded?"

"Yes. What are you going to do with it?"

"Render hearing to the deaf and speech to the mute," the tutor replied, unhooking the weapon and inspecting the mechanism. "Perfect! Where is the fellow?"

"This way...but he isn't as wicked as you suppose."

"You think so?" said Georges Chantepie, between clenched teeth.

He leaned over the valet, who had opened his eyes, and considered him in a hostile fashion.

"Those bonds were tied by a masterly hand," the young man said, finally. "Either this individual has an accomplice, or he's a veritable contortionist."

"You think he did it himself?" exclaimed Ivan. "What about the knife-wound?"

Georges Chantepie shrugged his shoulders "These people are capable of anything," he muttered. "Anyway, we'll see." He turned toward Ivan. "So you don't want to tell the police?"

"I repeat, Monsieur—we mustn't." Ivan's expression was grave.

"All this is very strange," murmured the Frenchman. "The boy is probably acting out of pity for this spy. So be it—but if my suspicions are correct, I'll act in spite of him, because such a comedy merits its punishment. And after all, what has engineer Damidoff to fear?"

He recalled his last conversation with his friend, however, and his brow furrowed under the influence of the anguish rising in his heart.

He shoved Nitchef back into the cupboard under the stairs. "Let's take a look around the house," he said.

"We can't leave the poor fellow like that!" protested the adolescent.

"A rabid dog is only harmless while it's tied up," the Frenchman replied brutally. And he dragged his pupil away.

THE MASK REMOVED

Ivan went to the samovar. He wanted to take some tea to Nadia. The samovar was empty and cleaned out. He had to make a new infusion, which he did as quickly as possible.

Georges Chantepie had already examined the various rooms.

"You accused vulgar burglars," he said, "but burglars would have taken that money."

"That's what I think," the engineer's son replied. "Perhaps Nitchef's arrival frightened them off."

"And they grabbed hold of him, beat him and tied him up, without waking you up?"

"It's true that I didn't hear anything."

"Nothing! What a torpor! And Nadia?"

"She didn't hear anything either."

"That's quite extraordinary. Look, she's fallen back into a heavy sleep." George Chantepie leaned over the sleeping child curiously.

"Reaction to the crisis," Ivan said, while busy putting things back in order.

"You ought to leave things as they are," the Frenchman advised, turning round. When his pupil said nothing, he added: "You're wrong. How did you feel this morning, when you woke up?"

"My head was heavy and there was a bitter taste in my mouth."

"What did you drink?"

"Tea, made by Nitchef."

"Where's the samovar?"

"Here. I found it empty and washed."

"Your tea must still be downstairs."

The tutor went down. The plate and dishes that Ivan had served were still on the table, but the cup had, of course, been removed, washed and replaced.

"I'm red hot!" said George Chantepie. "Decidedly, I'm on the track!"

Ivan had come back down in his turn and had started restoring order in his father's study. Traces of leverage were visible on the drawers; they had been searched.

"Leave all that," said the Frenchman, a trifle rudely.

"Since nothing of interest has been taken," the adolescent replied, in the same tone.

"Am I no longer your friend?" asked the young man, his vanity wounded.

"How can you think that?"

Ivan was hesitant. He knew that the Frenchman was offended by his visible constraint, by the reticence in his pupil's words. He ought to make him a full confession; then the situation would be perfectly clear. He opened his mouth, and then closed it again. Reveal that he was the son of an escaped convict? No! His pride revolted against such a confession, in spite of his veritable amity for the Frenchman. He had a profound need for his esteem, and feared coming down in his eyes.

Oh, how poorly he knew him, and of what support that pusillanimity deprived him!

The confession was on the tip of his tongue, but he swallowed it. "Certainly you're my friend," he said, "but you know as well as I do that my father was working on and manufacturing explosive substances. He might be exposed to a severe condemnation. It's better not to let the police in here."

"Undoubtedly," said Georges Chantepie, not at all convinced. "At any rate, I'm beginning to fear that your Nitchef might have something to do with engineer Damidoff's disappearance."

"Certainly not," the adolescent replied. "Otherwise, once again, he wouldn't be here, stabbed with a knife. In the second place, if the papers had been stolen from my father, the people looking for them wouldn't have come to search the house. They haven't found them, thank God!"

"On the contrary, my dear Ivan," the tutor put in, "that worries me a great deal. Your father—assuming that he's in the power of shady individuals—is a man who would die rather than give up his secret. He might have destroyed the papers he had on him. It's also possible that your Nitchef attempted a coup on his own behalf. It's possible that he refused to share with his friends, and when he had done so, they punished him as he deserved. Shh! Don't defend him. He gave you and your sister a narcotic, that's indubitable, and I'm certain that he knows where your father is. Come with me.

The two of them went back to the cupboard under the stairs. Georges Chantepie grabbed the wounded man by the legs and pulled him out.

"You," he said, "aiming his revolver at the man's temple. "You're going to tell us what you've done with Pierre Damidoff."

Ivan studied the valet. Now he was remembering a host of details that took on substance, in his mind, under the influence of the incident: Nitchef scarcely quitting the laboratory; Nitchef cleaning the scientific instruments with particular care—one might have thought that he understood how precious they were; Nitchef following the engineer like his shadow. A plausible explanation might have been found for that obstinacy in dogging his employer's footsteps, though: animal gratitude for the hand that fed him.

Then Ivan remembered Nitchef standing at the garden gate when his father left. He remembered the whistle-blast. He saw him once again stretched out in the laboratory, putting the pieces of paper together, doubtless to reconstitute a piece of work.

Finally, he thought about his singular disappearances, which had astonished the household and caused anxiety on many occasions.

Yes, definitely, the deaf-mute's behavior had been that of a spy.

And yet, he was there, his physiognomy more leaden than ever, appearing not to hear the Frenchman's pressing questions.

Angrily, the latter kicked him.

"I know full well who you are," he said, his teeth clenched.

The valet's small bedroom was above the kitchen. The tutor was there in two strides. Ivan heard him searching, moving objects around and muttering inconsequentially, and uttering triumphant cries. He soon saw him come down again abruptly, with a parcel of books under his arm and clutching pieces of paper covered in scribbling.

"Look, Ivan, this is what the idiot reads. Berthelot's *Chemistry of Explosives*. Büchner's *Force and Matter*, the works of Schopenhauer, Hegel, Spinoza, Max[14]... Here are lectures in physics from the École Polytechnique in France, and I found many others up there. Finally, here's the bouquet."

Having thrown the books on the table, the tutor unfolded the pieces of paper and read:

"We cannot conceive of an explosion that is not accompanied by a noise. It is the molecules of the substance that surrounds us, the ether, colliding violently under the brutal pressure of foreign molecules, that produce the noise of the explosion, the BANG. The contrary phenomenon would throw us into an inexpressible astonishment. And yet, who knows whether it occurs naturally on some other planet. At any rate, an engineer, an unknown scientist, is on the point of producing it scientifically.

"This article was signed *V.O.*, if I remember correctly."

"Indeed," Ivan replied.

"Well!" exclaimed the tutor, brandishing the rough draft of the article. "Have I found you out, rogue?" He continued, firmly: "My dear Ivan, I need to be more reasonable than you.

---

[14] I have reproduced this name as given in the original text because I cannot be absolutely certain that it is a misprint, and that the intended reference is to Karl Marx. There is no other mention of Marx (or Max) elsewhere in the text, although it is far more likely that a nihilist would be reading him than the other German writers routinely cited.

There's more at stake here than personal interest—there's a national interest."

"National?" asked the young Russian, with a start.

"National," the Frenchman went on, forcefully. "It's a matter of unmasking a possible traitor, because, to judge by the books that constitute this individual's favorite reading, he's something other and far better than an idiot and a valet. At a time like this, all disreputable beings, all masked or shady individuals, ought to be identified or handed over to the authorities. What do you think?"

Georges Chantepie looked his young friend directly in the eyes. He saw him go frightfully pale. Then he gripped him by the arm with a nervous gesture and drew him into the study. He put his hands on his shoulders.

"Ivan," he said, "Ivan, my friend—for a time when your fatherland and mine are standing up to resist a common enemy, we're brothers—there's a dolorous secret in your life. I've already understood that from my last conversation with your father. He promised to make me party to it. I'm not asking you, because it doesn't belong to you, but to him, and he alone will judge the opportune moment. I swear to you on my honor that he'll find my friendship ready to receive it, whatever the mystery might be, and grant him the refuge that men and Christians owe to one another. But Ivan, you can tell me: if we deliver this individual to the law, might there be any danger to you?"

"Great danger, Monsieur Chantepie," the adolescent replied, in a dull voice. "For if that man is the traitor that you say, he must have discovered our secret. If he talks, my father will die, and..."

"And?"

"And we'll be dishonored." The words stuck in the unfortunate boy's throat. "My father is innocent!" he proclaimed, immediately, terrified by the thought that the Frenchman might misunderstand.

"I don't doubt it, Ivan," replied the other, simply. "I'm certain of it. Well, Ivan, my brother, it's necessary to have this man arrested."

The son of the convict took a step backwards.

"It's necessary," repeated Georges Chantepie, with a sad gravity. He fell silent, and added, after a pause: "For the fatherland."

Ivan did not make any move to hold the tutor back. He remained motionless, entirely given to a vision that was advancing toward him menacingly: Colonel Archinef, the chief of the Warsaw police, coming into the garden and saying, rudely: "Jude Iagowski! Jude Iagowski, the escaped convict!"

The adolescent shivered, as if the vision were real.

A moan emerged from the cupboard under the stairs. "Ivan, Ivan, please let me loose! I'm thirsty! Oh, what a horrible thirst! How I'm suffering!"

Almost unconsciously, so astonished was he, the engineer's son opened the redoubt and pulled the wounded man toward him.

"A drink!" grated the latter. And as Ivan headed for the kitchen, the mysterious V.O. continued, gesturing toward his wrists, swollen by blackening blisters: "Free me from these bonds. I promise you that I won't run away."

Ivan picked up a knife and cut the cords binding the hands.

Then Nitchef leapt to his feet, shoved his young master away violently, leapt into the kitchen and locked the door.

"Ha ha!" he sniggered. "Destiny wills it, then! Well, its will shall be done."

And, having got rid of the cords that still bound him, he leapt into the garden, while Ivan, awakening from the kind of hypnosis into which he had been plunged, stood there, terrified by what he had just done.

HOW TO TRAIN A YOUNG WOLF-CUB

Meanwhile, the Russian mobilization was under way, like that in the west, in marvelous coordination. The sacred union had had tightened the bonds that old political quarrels and the brazen preaching of merchants of fraternity had failed to break.

The good Dr. Mohr was experiencing a profound rancor in consequence. His calculations had gone awry, and he was taking it out on his subordinate.

"Thirteen, this isn't what you promised me," he complained, the day after the staged burglary of which the Damidoff villa had been the theater.

Thirteen listened humbly and submissively, like an errant dog being scolded by its master.

"You were odiously deceived."

"I'm afraid so. These brutes are good, at best, for being our slaves, waxing our boots. At the first beat of the drum they got up as one man and went to put their necks under the yoke. I thought them more evolved, or closer to their Polish origins, and thus irremediable enemies of their conquerors. No, they're marching with the Russians, in a docile fashion, even though our people put revolvers in their hands."

"These people are Slavs, and you forgot that. But a game postponed isn't lost. When do you go before the Recruiting Board?"

"The day after tomorrow chief."

"Under the name of Michael Gregor?"

"Yes. Is it necessary for me to be admitted?"

"No, not yet. Something important is going to happen, it's said. The Tsar is coming to Warsaw to proclaim the autonomy of Poland.[15] Yes, the news hasn't yet reached the wider public, but I have it from an official source. It's a great

---

[15] There was no such visit; this element of the plot is fictitious.

blow against us—if not mortal, at least dangerous. Dormant sentiments are going to wake up and be revived, all the more so as the entire people think that the prophecy of St. Catherine's monk is coming true..."[16]

"Yes, the white eagle against the black eagle. Childishness!"

"Don't be so scornful, Thirteen, and let's look at everything, no matter how futile, as heaving considerable importance. It's necessary that the Tsar doesn't come to Warsaw, Thirteen. Do you understand me?"

Michael Gregor had been unable to help going pale.

"I have to…?"

"Are you hesitating?" asked the scientist, with a threat in his gaze. "You know that we don't admit hesitation in the execution of our orders. Take that as read. Good. I don't say you, but you have an instrument in your hands that will go straight to the goal without hesitation: Nitchef."

"Vladimir Obrenovitch is dead."

"Dead?"

"I suspected him of wanting to keep the invention for himself. If our expedition was a fiasco, the honor is due to him. In the second place, he showed more than mistrust in our regard—a muted hostility. He's been punished."

"Thirteen," growled Mohr, "you've committed a gross stupidity. I warned you: it's necessary not to alert the police."

"The police have too much to do at present. They won't worry about the death of a deaf-mute."

"Vladimir was an instrument to retain at all costs. Then again, killing the chicken isn't the way to get the eggs."

---

[16] This reference is probably to the fake late 16th century document supposedly written in the 11th century and known as the *Prophecies of St. Malachy*, which alleged that religion would be laid waste under a pope whose ranking in a list of 112 was identified by hindsight with Benedict XV, who became pope in 1914. There does not seem, however, to be any connection between Malachy and St. Catherine.

"The harm's done, if there was any harm. We have a better way. Ivan Iagow must know where the formulae are hidden. It'll be easy to make him talk. You have the father; take the sister—he won't hold out."

"Well, yes," said the doctor, visibly annoyed. "I've already thought of that, and but for the inconvenient arrival of the boy, Madame Wandowska would have succeeded in it. Anyway, let's move on. I'll see to the necessary arrangements. One more thing: the Bargineff factory is adding the manufacture of shells to that of powder. Forty-Eight is keeping me up to date by wireless of the daily production and the direction taken by the supply convoys. Make sure that a mobile crew is ready to move to any point that I designate. We'll strike the big blow"—he pointed at the statuette—"at the appropriate moment. Go!"

Mohr was visibly furious. Thirteen bowed and went out.

Then the master of the house rang a bell.

An office-boy in blue livery appeared.

"Go to X*** right away," he said. "Ask for news of engineer Damidoff and report back to me immediately."

The clerk went out to carry out the order.

"Whatever Thirteen, alias Michael Gregor, says," he murmured, "anger is a poor counselor. A secret agent must, above all, keep a cool head. I'll see about changing him, or else..." The sinister gesture of sweeping away a human existence completed the thought.

He picked up the telephone.

"Hello? Is that you, Gorski?"

"Yes."

"Is Constantinovitch any better?"

"His crises are diminishing in intensity and frequency, but he's far from being cured."

"Good—send him to me."

The doctor replaced the apparatus. "Semi-lucid," he muttered. "A marvelous subject, who will do exactly what I suggest to him."

Dr. Mohr saw a few patients, and then had Constantinovitch introduced.

The latter was a young man of seventeen. His very pronounced prognathism, and his eyes burning with excitement, full of cruelty and cunning, indicated a mental illness, an insanity.

There was a long conversation between the inmate and the physician, which the latter terminated by saying: "It's understood, isn't it? You'll take the automobile and offer a seat to the boy. When he's with you, you'll take off in fourth gear. If he protests, put a revolver to his throat. Finally, bring him to me. If you succeed, I'll send you back to your family; if not, I'll skin you alive—and you know that I never make idle threats."

On seeing the expression of terror that immediately spread over the patient's face, one could have guessed that the threat was calculated to obtain maximum effort from the will that it dominated and bent.

"I'll obey," stammered Constantinovitch. "When?"

"When I tell you. Go."

The scientist's eyes searched the dilated pupils that were trying to flee them, and were vacillating in bewilderment.

At that moment, the clerk came back. He told the physician that there was nothing new at the engineer's house, except for a false alarm caused by a French teacher's excess of imagination. He claimed that he had found Nitchef bound, gagged and stabbed, but there was no one there.

Good! thought Mohr. *Thirteen failed; I prefer that.* Aloud, he said: "Well, you'll be good enough to take your bicycle and install yourself in the vicinity of the Damidoff villa. Keep me up to date with anything that happens there, and if you see the engineer's son set off for Warsaw, come and tell me immediately. It goes without saying that you'll exercise the utmost discretion. The young man is subject to a nervous malady and must be brought here by surprise. His sister won't be long in joining him. I'm counting on you."

The employee made a gesture of complete compliance.

After his final consultation, Dr. Mohr sent the usher away, locked the doors of the antechamber, and carefully drew the double curtains over the windows. Going to a Gobelins tapestry, executed according to a design by Boucher, he carefully moved it aside. An absolutely bare wall in which no gap in the continuity was evident appeared to the gaze. The doctor applied a finger to a point that was familiar to him, and a panel rotated on hinges. A spiral stairway rose upwards. He climbed it, and, after opening a trap-door, found himself beneath a cupola. That retreat was fitted with a Marconi apparatus, connected to the lightning-conductor on top of the dome.

He activated the system and, listening carefully, sent out a call sign, soon followed by a response. Anyone familiar with the Morse alphabet who had witnessed the ensuing dialogue would swiftly have recognized that Dr. Mohr's distant correspondent was none other than His Majesty Wilhelm II, Emperor of Germany, by the will of Ahriman, the old god of the Hohenzollerns—of which he, Wilhelm, was a direct emanation, designated to be the master of the world for all eternity.[17]

---

[17] The connection between the Ahriman, the evil spirit of Zoroastrian mythology, and the House of Hohenzollern, whose ultimate sovereign Wilhelm II turned out to be, is not obvious, but Dodeman's citation probably owes something to the ideas of Édouard Schuré (1841-1929), one of the Parisian esotericists who numbered among his customers on the Quai Voltaire, and who was closely associated in 1912-13 with the Anthroposophical Society founded by the Austrian esotericist Rudolf Steiner (1861-1925). Schuré and Steiner both thought Ahriman a significant mythical figure, and distanced him considerably from his mythological origins.

THE TERRIBLE SUSPICION

Some distance away, in the vestibule of the villa, Ivan tore himself away from his dolorous meditation. Two young men with flags over their heads were going through the streets of the village, and their youthful voices rose up, as seriously as for a hymn:

> *God save the emperor,*
> *Sustain his glory*
> *And his memory*
> *And his grandeur.*

He listened, his hand clenched over his breast. He had set a wretch free, and betrayed his country and his sovereign!

Georges Chantepie came in, followed by the burgomaster, Stapouloff.

"Forgive me, Burgomaster, Monsieur Chantepie!" exclaimed the engineer's son. "He implored my pity. I untied him, and he's run away."

The burgomaster, it will be remembered, was a colossus with an enormous belly, little eyes and a ridiculously child-like voice. His small head contained just enough brain to satisfy the material exigencies of life; the rules and duties of his position were, in consequence, narrowly confined there. It took him an infinite time to discover the administrative decrees relating to any kind of circumstances, and to determine the attitude he ought to adopt. In his view, it was evident that the Frenchman had been wrong to set out on campaign and to imagine that a cripple might be a subtle criminal, but the child—Ivan was no more than that—was even more in the wrong for making a mockery of his tutor and, in consequence, the magistracy.

In his tormented voice, the mayor made a long speech—long in the sense that there were wide gaps between the words and the periods, necessary to the search for ideas and phrases. Then he went away, imposing and dignified.

"My dear boy," said the Frenchman then, in a dry tone. "You're definitely too much for me. I no longer understand you, and won't try to understand you. You've covered me in ridicule, and that's difficult for me to forgive. I didn't want to insist, out of pity for you and friendship for your father, although my loyalty to Russia, which has given me shelter, imposes an obligation on me. Let's pass on. If you've yielded to a charitable sentiment toward a doubly crooked and doubly vile individual, you were mistaken, but if you were obedient to some other motive unknown to me, you're extremely culpable. May you never have to repent of it! Nevertheless, I fear for your sister Nadia the inconsequence of your actions. I've asked for an engagement, but I won't have a formal response from the Recruitment Board for several weeks. My pupils have gone, or are ready to go. I'm free—would you care to confide your sister to me?"

"Thank you," replied the adolescent, with a hint of arrogance, "but I'll protect her if there's any need."

The two parted then, with a very chilly salute.

Ivan was, therefore, alone with Nadia, whose eyes were feverish. She talked and talked, and one phrase was repeated endlessly: "I want to go with Papa."

He did his best to console her; he tried to distract her. The child was obstinate in her grief.

The door opened silently and Madame Wandowska appeared, a bag of candy in her hand.

Ivan could not suppress a shiver, so sudden and silent had the mother's entrance been. One might have thought it the appearance of a black phantom with a large white face.

She leaned over Nadia, took her in her arms, rocking her and caressing her.

"What have I just heard?" said the madwoman. "Thieves got into your house? They didn't do you any harm?"

"No, Madame, no," said Ivan. "Nothing happened; they're just rumors."

"Yes, but it might happen. You're alone, the two of you. Two children..."

"I'm no longer a child, Madame!"

"Let me take Nadia. I'll look after her well. Would you like that, Nadia? Wouldn't you like to come with me?"

"No, Madame, no!" exclaimed the adolescent. "Thank you, but I can't let Nadia go. If my father came back, he'd be very angry. I'm grateful to you, believe me, but it's impossible, impossible."

Ivan had all the trouble in the world making her understand that her visit had lasted long enough and that he wanted to be left alone."

Finally, Madame Wandowska left, with tears in her eyes.

Ivan set to work—which is to say that he finished putting everything back in order and erasing all trace of the burglary.

While he went back and forth he analyzed the whole complicated adventure. He was beginning to understand. The demand from the nihilists, the article in the *Scientific Review*, the disappearance, the fake letter instructing him to give the drawings to the deaf-mute, the burglary, originated from the same source, from a very determined will to take possession of the invention.

In reality, were they not in the presence of a nihilist intrigue? Yes, why not?

Ivan paused in his work. He sat down and searched for the key to the enigma. And he found it—or thought he had.

The nihilists, the signatories of the threatening note, had carried out their threat; they had abducted the inventor, their former comrade; they were detaining him in some hiding-place. Nitchef knew where; he undoubtedly belonged to the redoubtable organization. Everything was explained now, and the deaf-mutes conduct became as clear a crystal.

At any rate, the revolutionaries did not possess the secret of the invention. Even the mysterious V.O. had not discovered the hiding-place of the documents, since he had nearly been executed by his companions as a traitor to their statutes. But why that determination to possess the silent bomb? With what immediate objective?

Ivan suddenly felt his hair bristling on his head. He thought he understood; he was afraid that he understood. Several times in succession he rejected the idea, which pricked him, obsessively and imperiously. A cry emerged from his lips. He leapt to his feet.

Was it possible?

A persistent rumor had been going round for some time. Was not the Tsar coming to Warsaw in order to make the gesture of liberation? He did not know the date of the projected journey, but the event would surely take place. Were the nihilists not pursuing the silent bomb for that purpose? To strike with so powerful a weapon, to be certain of impunity, thanks to the amazement produced by its strangeness—was not enough a tempt the scientific criminals that the nihilists were? And the frightful vision became more precise: the Tsar dead, governmental anarchy reigning, maintained by foreign plots, and Germany, taking advantage of the disorder, penetrating to the heart of Russia and imposing its law.

The principal author of the cataclysm was doomed to universal execration.

"But it's not him! It's not him!" protested Ivan. "You know full well that Jude Iagow has a pure hard. Jude Iagow..."

Jude Iagow! But Jude Iagow was an escaped convict. Jude Iagow had assumed the identity of an honest man in order to succeed more surely in his objective. Jude Iagow was a maker of silent bombs. The article in the *Scientific Review* said so. The secret laboratory, his chemistry apparatus and his technical library were proof of it. They would not look any further, and Jude Iagow would be hanged as a common criminal.

Oh, it was all well-planned! How well the nihilists would be avenged on their false brother, while chastising society, in the person of the Tsar, its representative, while precipitating Russia into the chaos of governmental and political intrigues, at the moment when order was most necessary to her salvation!

Ivan tottered like a drunken man. He felt his reason escaping him.

"Come in," he said, nevertheless. "Let's reason it out. There's no proof of any of it. For a start, the drawings of the silent bomb are in their place, in..."

He ran to the study. He took a chair, and reached up to the frame, unhooked it, and shivered. On the glass in front of the picture there was the imprint of a large spatulate thumb— obviously Nitchef's thumb, the phalanges of which did indeed have a splayed form.

Ivan removed the pins retaining the piece of cardboard fixed in the groove of the frame.

The papers were no longer there, and the photographic paper bore the same digital imprint as the glass.

The engineer's secret had been discovered, and stolen.

The adolescent put things back in their original place and sat down on the chair, overwhelmed.

What he feared had occurred.

All was lost.

What could he do?

When Ivan Iagow recovered his spirits, it was dark.

He went up to Nadia, who had fallen asleep from fatigue. He stayed with her, searching for a solution.

As his gaze strayed toward the window, a thin beam of light caught his eye. He got up and looked into the grounds, toward the laboratory. He could not see anything. Having returned to his place, however, he rediscovered the same beam of light, as tenuous as a thread. Someone was in the room where experimental work was done, and, in spite of his precautions, a crack in the shutter had revealed his presence.

Ivan suddenly felt calm and resolute.

Nitchef, the mysterious V.O., must be there, doubtless occupied in some chemical combination. He would go find the truth, and act in consequence.

He went downstairs, carefully closed and locked the door of the villa—Nadia was asleep, alone; he must not forget that—and slipped into the garden.

When he reached the laboratory, he slid inside through a subterranean ventilation-shaft. How many times, in his childhood, had he played that game?

Concentrating on what he was doing, he had not perceived a feminine shadow, hidden behind a tree, which he had almost brushed as he went past.

A few seconds later, he came out in the workroom.

A man with a glass mask over his face was bent over a receptacle from which vapor was emerging.

By his stature, the adolescent immediately recognized Nitchef.

THE FATAL CLOCK

"Thief!"

That single word escapes Ivan Iagow's lips.

Then a short and violent scene unfolds. The deaf-mute throws himself on the adolescent and place a brutal hand over his mouth. Is it to strangle him? No, for with a rapid gesture, the enigmatic V.O. has thrown a bell-jar over the flask and pushed it away from the heat.

"Fool!" he says, after taking off his glass mask. "Do you want to die?" That vapor is corrosive. Don't breathe in. Wait."

And Nitchef runs to the window, which he opens wide.

A gust of fresh air purifies the atmosphere in the room.

Ivan has remained standing, his arms folded, with a scornful smile on his lips.

"Thief!" he repeats.

V.O.'s face contracts, then resumes its phlegmatic expression.

"Words!" he said. "Besides which, Jude Iagow's invention belong to me, since it belongs to humankind. We're only cells in a vast whole. I have the absolute right to dispose of property that is everyone's, since intelligence is universal, since ideas have an independent existence and our brain is merely their temporary receptacle."

"My father's invention belongs to my fatherland," Ivan replied, coldly, "and you have robbed my fatherland, as you robbed my father, in his pity."

"My fatherland is humankind, and I know no other. Your Russian fatherland, like Georges Chantepie's French fatherland, I don't know, and I don't want to know. I only know human beings, who suffer under the rod of unscrupulous and heartless shepherds."

"They are great families who unite in times of danger, Nitchef. You've seen that."

"Families in which brothers devour one another, or rather, in which the strong devour the weak, without remorse, as the Carthaginian elephants crushed the humblest of mercenaries. But we're going to sound a terrible wake-up call."

"I'm not mistaken, Nitchef!" exclaimed the adolescent. "You're a nihilist!"

"Like your father, Ivan, At least, he was; at least, he had marched on the road of truth. Your father is a genius, and I admire that, in any case. Thanks to him, slaves will be liberated...soon."

"Slaves?" said Ivan, shivering. "What slaves are you talking about? There are only free men, defending their rights."

"Not their rights, but the rights of their owners. You're young, Ivan; I'll prove to you that I'm right. You claim to love your fatherland?"

"Above all else, Nitchef," said the young man, gravely.

"You'll deny it."

"I..."

"Oh—you fall silent. You dare not look into your heart. Haven't you already denied it once, this morning? And what if your sister were on one side, and your fatherland on the other?"

"Nitchef, you're a rogue, a tempter, a demon!"

"The problem will be put to you before long, and you won't resist, because people are cowards before pain." That was said with a kind of sinister and haughty scorn. How the man who pronounced such words must have suffered! "Listen," he went on. "I'll tell you some news. A German army is marching on Warsaw, and Warsaw will be taken, because your compatriots aren't ready. Courage is nothing against the inert and omnipotent machines that the others are bringing with them. The soul? Pooh! Force alone, with matter, is the mistress of the world—you'll soon see. They're coming, and Russia's final hour has sounded. It's your knell. Look, Belgium has been turned into a lake of blood, because it's weak.[18] What if I told you that that made me hesitate? But I was able, in time, to stifle those old sentimental whims, unworthy of a man. France is a heap of orators and demagogues, dead to action; it will follow Belgium. Your turn will come next."

"Russia won't die. We have numbers and we have courage. Everyone will rally to the appeal—everyone!"

"Except one."

"Who?"

"Me," replied the enigmatic V.O., with an indescribable pride. "And it's me, who is the sole conscience, the sole angel of punishment here, who will strike Russia in the heart and deliver her, quivering, to the enemy. He will strike her with the unforgiving weapon; he will strike her with the silent bomb, for the silent bomb belongs to humankind, avid for happiness and liberty, if not hungry for vengeance."

"I'll denounce you."

"It will make no difference. It's too late; you can't prevent the accomplishment of destiny. The proof is that I could imprison you, or kill you, but I won't do anything; I'll leave you free."

"Do you want Nadia to die, then?" said Ivan, softly, hoping to touch the wretch's heart at a sensitive point. "You're forgetting that Nadia saved you from starvation—or, at least, thought she was doing so, wretch!"

A cloud passed over Nitchef's face. "I was—oh, I was!" he said, in a muted voice, his teeth clench.

"You're forgetting that I saved you, this very morning."

---

[18] The German invasion of Belgium began on 22 July in the Julian calendar, so this is consistent with the date of 27 July subsequently given in the text (after some prevarication) for the assassination attempt, but it is unclear where all the time has gone within the story since Jude Iagow set out for Petrograd on 7 July.

"You saved me, that's true—but that was so that I could play my role to the end. I shall finish my work, and Russia will sink."

"To the profit of whom?"

At that direct question, the enigmatic V.O. started violently. Then he went on: "Truly?" he sniggered. "If I listened to you...a child...go on, shut up, and go find your sister."

"Not until you've sworn."

"It's too late; the infernal clock is in place.[19] The hand will arrive unstoppably at the detonator, at the appointed hour."

"Nitchef," Ivan begged, frightened to see what he dreaded so close to verification. "I beg you, in the name of your mother."

"My mother!" said the demon with the human face, with frightful sarcasm. "She sold me."

"In the name of your fatherland."

"I told you, I have none."

"Well then, I'm going to denounce you."

"It remains to see whether they'll find me. As for where the silent bomb has been placed, how will that be discovered? Who will know except me?" And Nitchef added, tranquilly: "The again, you won't say anything, because I have a hostage, and that hostage is your father."

Ivan went back to his room, crushed in body and soul. So his father was a prisoner of the nihilists! They had carried out a monstrous crime in the dark. He knew—he, Ivan—and his father's life was the ransom of his silence. Warn the authorities, after this morning's adventure? No one would believe him. What could he do?

---

[19] Nitchef refers to the timer attached to his bomb as an *horloge infernale* [infernal clock] because bombs were commonly known in France as *machines infernales* [infernal machines] after that title was given to one involved in an attempt to assassinate Napoléon. Bombs equipped with timers had been used (not with any great precision) since the 1870s.

The problem was suddenly staring him in the face, demanding an immediate solution: his father, or his fatherland!

Tomorrow, he thought. *I'm too tired to decide tonight. Besides, I have time; the Tsar isn't coming yet.*

For the second time, in a cowardly fashion, he made the sacrifice to filial love

He threw himself on to his bed and immediately fell into a leaden sleep.

When he woke up, it was broad daylight. The clock marked eight o'clock in the morning.

He got up, and his first thought was for Nadia. He went to her bedroom and leaned over the bed.

It was empty.

THE FOOTPRINT ON THE WALL

"Nadia!" Ivan shouted, in anguish.

There was no reply.

Naively, the young man looked under the bed. Nothing. Then he saw that the window was open. He put his leg over the sill and leaned out.

A ledge with a flat surface ran around the house a meter from the sill. A large wisteria extended its clinging branches even higher.

On returning from the laboratory he had locked the door to the corridor. It was still locked, as he was able to make sure. Having looked everywhere in the house, he went back to the window.

Nadia had gone out that way, but as it was impossible that the delicate child had accomplished that feat on her own, someone must have taken her.

Ivan immediately thought of the nihilists.

They've taken another guarantee, he said to himself. *Come on, stay calm*.

He went to the drinking-fountain and plunged his head into the water. Then he went out. On the perron, he found a woolen scarf. He immediately remembered having seen it on Madame Wandowska's shoulders. Her! That was a flash of enlightenment. He ran to the manor house and rang. The gardener's wife who fulfilled the duties of housemaid, came to open the door.

"Nadia!" cried the adolescent. "Give Nadia back to me!"

"But we don't have her," replied the maid, in a natural tone. She added, in the wake of her interlocutor's more or less incoherent explanations: "If she's been stolen, perhaps it was the deaf-mute. He hangs around with gypsies. He must have sold your child to them."

The woman might be right? How could the madwoman have scaled the wall and made off with a burden? No, only a man—not Nitchef, but someone else—could have carried off such an exploit.

Who, then? A nihilist?

It seemed plausible—even probable.

The man had climbed over the wall, climbed up the trellis supporting the wisteria, forced open the poorly-closed window, and gone back the way he had come. Wasn't there a ladder back there, leaning against the wall?"

Ivan returned precipitately to the villa. He ran to the ladder, climbed up and looked around. There was an apple tree beneath him whose branches hung down over a road that few people used, situated between two garden walls. At the end of it was the road running alongside the Polish woman's property.

A footprint! On the thin layer of earth deposited on top of the wall by the wind, next to a tuft of grass, the tiny bare foot of the little girl had rested on the damp soil and left an imprint.

The engineer's son went back down the ladder. He stood there motionless, prey to a profound disturbance.

He was agitated, though; and since Madame Wandowska had nothing to do with the matter, if the child really had been stolen, it was necessary to catch the kidnappers without delay. Once again, it was necessary to ask the police to intervene. All roads were definitely leading toward the same abyss.

Then he thought of Georges Chantepie.

I'll go to him...why not? He's good; he'll forgive me.

In a matter of minutes, the adolescent was at the Frenchman's house.

"Monsieur Chantepie!" he cried, frightened by his friend's coldness. "Forgive me! If you knew...and you shall know everything. Listen: Nadia has been stolen!"

"When?"

"Last night."

The engineer's son related how he had discovered the child's disappearance, and he added: "Are those who are holding my father prisoner the authors of the abduction?"

"With the intention of obtaining the desired ransom, it's possible," agreed the tutor. "It's also possible that the abduction has a different cause."

"What? Oh—the old gentleman who came to offer…?"

"No," said Georges Chantepie, shaking his head.

"Who, then? Who could have…? Wait, Monsieur Chantepie—come with me; perhaps you'll pick up a trail."

The young Russian dragged his companion away, and, having reached the ladder, made him climb up it. He showed him the imprint.

"Well, well!" said the tutor. "Where's her bedroom?"

"The first window over there, at the corner of the house."

"With that wisteria and the wooden trellis that reaches up to the ledge. Yes, yes, I understand—partly, at least. It happened last night…about what time?"

"When I went out to go to the laboratory it might have been nine o'clock, at the latest. I left Nadia asleep. A lamp was lit on the mantelpiece."

"Pardon me, but yesterday evening, between eight o'clock and midnight, no lamp was illuminating this window, or any other." At a gesture of protest from Ivan, the Frenchman continued: "For the good reason that, anxious not to have seen you all day, I came out to smoke a cigar on the road, and I didn't take my eyes off your house. Let's also say that Nitchef's escape worried me a great deal and I had a violent desire to put my hand on his collar. Besides which, the comings and goings of a certain cyclist dressed in the livery of Mohr's hospice intrigued me to the highest point."

"Yesterday?" said Ivan, nonplussed. "But it was yesterday that…"

"The day before yesterday, Ivan."

"Are you sure? Today is the twenty-sixth of July?"

"The twenty-seventh."

"But in that case," said the adolescent, passing his hand over his face, "I've slept for two nights and an entire day."

Georges Chantepie was no longer listening. He had bent down over the flower-bed at the bottom of the ladder.

"Did a woman come to see you, the day before yesterday?"

"Yes," the engineer's son replied. "Madame Wandowska."

"Ah! We're getting there!" exclaimed the Frenchman. "Everything is explained. During a fit of somnambulism, Nadia got up in order to go to join her father. She climbed out of the window and, with the agility appropriate to subjects in a hypnotic state, she climbed down the wisteria and scaled the ladder in order to get over the wall. Undoubtedly, the madwoman, haunted by the desire to possess the living image of her daughter, was on the lookout for her. She followed her. Look at this woman's footprint, deeply embedded in the loose earth, and that scarf, on the rosebush. She took possession of your sister at the moment that she reached the top of the wall, for the child's tracks disappear and the woman's subsist, even deeper. She's carrying a burden. I'm tranquilized...partly."

"We need to go and get her back!" exclaimed Ivan, forcefully.

"Hmm! Let's be prudent. If the unfortunate madwoman glimpses our intention, she might commit a regrettable and criminal action."

"Well then," said Ivan, decisively, "should we go to the police?"

"Today? Impossible—the police are on full alert; the Emperor's coming today. But Ivan. What's the matter?"

Ivan had raised his hand to his forehead, and then applied it to his breast, as if he had just experienced a sudden pain. A terrible conflict began within him. The struggle was only momentary, but in certain circumstances, a second is worth as much as an hour.

Finally, his resolution was made. He took a locket out of his bosom. On one side was a portrait of his mother, and the other a holy icon. "Isn't it you, Mother, who's instructing me?" he murmured. "And if my father has to die, your soul will welcome him joyfully, and forgive me."

He kissed the double image fervently.

"Monsieur Chantepie," he said, calmly. "What time is he arriving?"

"At eleven o'clock."

"It's quarter past ten. It will only take me twenty minutes to get to Warsaw. Goodbye!"

"In the name of Heaven!" exclaimed the Frenchman, amazed. "Where are you going? What's the matter? What about Nadia?"

"In fact, Monsieur Chantepie, if I don't come back, you'll look after her, won't you?"

"What! My poor Ivan, you're losing your reason! What does this mean?"

"It means that someone is going to blow up the Tsar."

And picking up his feet, the engineer's son runs at top speed toward the tram station, preceded by a cyclist posted near the wall of the villa, who is pedaling as hard as he can in the direction of Dr. Mohr's sanitarium.

They have already disappeared and Georges Chantepie is still standing motionless at the garden gate, muttering: "Blow up the Tsar? Blow up the Tsar? Get away! He's mad!"

Trumpets resound. A cavalry regiment rides past at a trot. The same martial energy animates the faces of the soldiers, the same flame of patriotism illuminates their eyes, and the Frenchman, impressed, adds: "A nihilist crime, at such a moment? Get away! The wind of war has passed over, and the infernal hollow idol has collapsed. There are only patriots now."

However, he is gripped by a grave anxiety. He has just thought about Nitchef.

PART TWO

THE MADMAN

While Ivan Damidoff heads for the station, a young man dressed in a khaki suit, leggings and a green helmet emerges from Dr. Mohr's sanitarium.

He has his fist on his hip and strikes a slightly grotesque attitude of self-importance. A luxurious automobile is stationed outside the door. There is no driver and no one inside; the owner is doubtless visiting the old scientist.

The young man abandons his martial pose. His smile blossoms and he laughs. He shows signs of the most intense admiration. He walks around the vehicle. He bends down over the starting handle and turns it over. The engine roars. The young man leaps into the driving seat, and away he goes! The automobile speeds along the road to the Polish capital.

The singular driver is delighted. He savors the pleasure of driving the auto—but enjoying a pleasure on one's own is nothing; it is necessary to share it with someone. Here is an adolescent, who is going in the same direction at a brisk pace. The unknown man's decision is immediately made. He stops. Then, with a slightly excessive politeness, he greets Ivan Damidoff.

The surprised adolescent replies to the greeting. He assumes that the other wants to ask him for directions—but no.

"You're doubtless going to Warsaw?" the driver asks. "Me too. Would you like a lift?"

The adolescent is on the point of refusing the invitation, but he thinks about the gravity of what he has to do. In such circumstances, speed is salvation. Perhaps the stranger is obedient to an inspiration from Beyond. Ivan jumps in beside him.

The automobile proceeds at a moderate pace. The two young mean strike up a conversation.

"You've certainly heard mention of Dr. Mohr?" the driver interrogates. There is something cruel about his face. His smile is sharp; his eyes, shadow by curly lashes, have a feline gaze. We have recognized him as Constantinovitch, Dr. Mohr's patient.

"A great deal," replied the inventor's son, for the sake of politeness.

"He has a mind full of utopias," the other replies. "The least of his follies is to want to abolish death, and for that he cuts open living dogs, mice and guinea-pigs. Human logic! Me, I've thought, I've seen, I've lived above wretches, above the rich and princes, and I say this: Dr. Mohr will never find the mechanism that makes human beings tick. And yet, he goes around day after day after day, and never gets a hint of it. I know where it is, but shh! Not so stupid! I'd gladly tell you, because I like you, but you'd tell him, and I don't want him to cut me open like a guinea-pig."

Ivan is embarrassed, and does not know what to say or think. He has the idea, however, that he is dealing with a humorist, a straight-faced joker duped by his exceedingly youthful appearance. He is disposed to accept it all without recrimination. The main thing is to reach the city as quickly as possible.

Suddenly, the young man bursts into strange, inextinguishable laughter.

"It's like the dead man," he says, finally. "There's a dead man there. He's been dead for two weeks, after having swallowed the thunder. What an idea!" The fantastic individual laughs even louder, and finally concludes: "The boss is keeping him to find out whether he'll surrender the mechanism, Ha ha ha! But he doesn't have it, the mechanism, he doesn't have it. The one who has it is the one who steers the world, the Tsar of Tsars."

The driver looks at his astonished and anxious companion from the corner of his eye. "You know the Tsar?" he asks.

"No, I've never seen him."

Constantinovitch has a mysterious smile. "What if he were shown to you?"

"I'd be very happy—but would you go more quickly, please?"

"Why?"

"Someone's going to assassinate him."

The driver jumps in his seat.

"Yes," Ivan goes on. "And that's why I'm going to Warsaw. It's necessary to warn the police before the train arrives. Faster, sir, I beg you. Take me to Colonel Archinef."

"To Colonel…?"

"The chief of police."

An abrupt change overtakes the madman's face; his features contract; his chin advances in a hideous prognathism; his eyes flash.

"Oh! Oh! Oh!" he wails. "Someone's going to assassinate me! Murder me! Someone's going to murder me! Who?"

"Not you!" protests the engineer's son, amazed. "The Tsar!"

"But I am the Tsar! Haven't you recognized me? I'm the Tsar, and it's me they want to assassinate. Oh! Oh! Oh!" Anger has given way to the craziest fear. "Yes, yes, I know," the strange driver continues, "it's Dr. Mohr who wants to murder me. He wants to cut me into pieces. Oh! Oh! Oh! He won't get me! No, he won't get me!"

Abruptly, he puts the automobile into fourth gear.

Ivan Damidoff does not understand his companion's incoherent speech, or his sudden terror. He tried to explain that it is not him that someone wants to kill, but the Emperor.

"Eh!" cries the other. "I am the Emperor! I am the Emperor!"

Is he mad? Ivan thinks.

The automobile races down the slopes of the hills that surround Warsaw at top speed. The city is visible in the depths of the valley watered by the sinuous course of the Vistula. A little closer, Ivan recognizes the tall chimneys of the Bargineff factories, and in the distance, toward the North, a cloud of smoke appears. Ivan's eyes have noticed it; he is gripped by anxiety.

"Faster!" he cries.

"Yes, yes," Constantinovitch repeats, his teeth clenched, his prognathism becoming so emphatic as to give him the face of a senile gorilla.

But he comes to a fork in the road, and he steers abruptly to the left instead of taking the correct direction.

"You've gone wrong!"

The driver doesn't want to hear it. He is fleeing his imaginary tormentor at a vertiginous speed. They are now going to meet the train. Abruptly, by courtesy of a beam of sunlight, Nadia's brother perceives the yellow flag with the badge of the imperial eagle carried by the locomotive.

He grasps the arm of the fanatic. He wants to force him to return to the right direction. "To Warsaw! To Warsaw!" he shouts.

The train has now passed behind a cape of hills. In ten minutes it will reach its goal; the inevitable will happen, unless he arrives in time. It is still possible; in spite of the wrong turning, they can reach the station in five minutes.

Ivan tries to grab the brake. The madman takes out a revolver and aims it at his companion.

"Make a move," he says, "and I'll kill you."

The ancient Polish city is beginning to dwindle behind them, and the train reappears. The shiny and sprightly locomotive is heading into the sun, toward catastrophe, toward death.

Now the road is going alongside a canal. On the other side is a towpath, a hedge and, not far away, a bridge leading to a footbridge over the railway line. At the moment when the vehicle goes on to it, with a desperate effect, Ivan succeeds in stamping his foot on the brake. The wheels stick, and jam between the parapet and a boundary-marker.

The train approaches. The engineer's son cries "Stop!" with all his might, in the hope—vain, alas!—that the engine-driver will near him and bring the machine to a halt. Perhaps he might succeed in attracting attention with his gestures, but he has to struggle against the madman, who has grabbed him by the collar and is trying to blow his brains out with the revolver. The train arrives at top speed.

The madman thinks he can kill his companion. He presses the trigger of his weapon. Fortunately, the adolescent has ducked, and the bullet breaks one of the windows of the locomotive.

The engineer stationed on the platform thinks that it is an attack, and speeds up the train, which will gain a few seconds on the anticipated timetable.

At that moment, the son of the convict slips out of his aggressor's grip, falls out on to the road, and runs away as far as his legs can carry him.

The brake released, the vehicle starts moving again. The boundary-marker gives way under the pressure, and, after accomplishing a terrible lurch, the auto surges forward again.

Ivan stops. Anxiously, he looks in the direction of the station.

The train is about to enter it. He closes his eyes in order not to see.

Must he open them? If he opens them, what frightful spectacle will be offered to his gaze? Heaped up on one another, the wagons in pieces, from which black smoke is emerging, while cries of agony emerge from the mass of debris.

He sees in his imagination the crushed body of the liberator Tsar, and, with a foot on the mutilated body, the emperor of Germany, enveloped in the huge cloak of the white guards, his head decked in a pointed helmet.

The silent bomb has killed Russia.

At the summit of the hill, in a belvedere on top of the sanitarium, the good Dr. Moher, his eye to the ocular lens of a telescope, is anxiously watching for the entrance of the imperial train to the station.

Finally, he utters an exclamation of wrath. "They're afraid! All of them, even Nitchef! Oh, the bunch of cowards!"

He goes back downstairs to his study, calmer nevertheless, and stays there for some time with his ears pricked. Impatient because he does not hear what he wants to hear, he sends for news. A few moments later he learns that the automobile has been found in pieces at the bottom of a ravine, with Constantinovitch dying in the midst of the debris.

"Was there no one with him?"

"No one."

Damn! he thinks. Aloud, he says: "Tell the steward to give the bill to the driver. That will teach him to leave my cars unsupervised."

THE ABDUCTION

Ivan Iagowski looked. He saw nothing but a crowd of employees around the rearmost carriage. He concluded that they were unloading the luggage, and his heart was inundated with joy.

Nitchef had been making fun of him.

With a light step, he headed for the nearest station. While he was waiting there for a tram, Georges Chantepie emerged from a vehicle heading in the opposite direction.

"I've been looking for you," the tutor told him. "Your last words intrigued me greatly."

"I've had a bad dream," Ivan replied, "and I mistook it for reality. In any case, I think I know where to find my father. He's in the hands of the nihilists."

The Frenchman started, while his pupil bit his lip. The great confidence he had in his friend had overtaken his prudence; he had just yielded part of his secret.

"Are you sure of that?" asked the tutor. "After all, it's possible, considering the kind of work to which the engineer devoted himself. We must go to warn Colonel Archinef. He'll discover..."

Ivan looked at him with supplicant eyes. "Please, Monsieur Chantepie," he said, in a low and tremulous voice, "don't bring the police into this business. No, no, I beg you."

The Frenchman studied his companion curiously. *Always that secret!* He thought, unable to help his heart contracting. *It must be very serious, very dangerous.*

"All right," he said to his pupil. "We won't go to the police. But the French consul in Warsaw is a close friend of mine. He might be very useful to us."

"What about Nadia?" asked Ivan, swiftly, desirous of breaking through the hint of embarrassment that had developed between them.

103

"Nadia?" replied George Chantepie, smiling. "I guessed correctly. She's in Madame Wandowska's house, being pampered like a little queen."

"You've seen her?"

"No, but from a certain pastry brought by the confectioner from X***, I've deduced that your neighbor has a guest."

"But the muzjik's wife..."

"Oh, the muzjik's wife loves her mistress too much to cause her the slightest trouble. She lied to you. Ah! Here comes our tram."

The two took their places in an empty compartment, and discussed at length the means of getting Nadia back without running any risks.

"The best thing to do," the tutor concluded, "is to leave her where she is—she's perfectly safe there, after all—and await a favorable opportunity. For the moment, we'll occupy ourselves with the engineer. I'm due to go to dinner at the consul's house this evening. Will you come to my house early tomorrow morning."

"Gladly," Ivan replied.

On returning to the villa, the adolescent experienced an indescribable sentiment of sadness and solitude. The lovely Nadia was not there.

A few hours later, he could no longer bear it; he needed Nadia. At least he wanted to see her, to be sure that she really was in the Polish woman's house, and that she was not in distress. If, by chance, he could succeed in getting her back without too much difficulty, he would make sure thereafter that no such misadventure could occur again. With the little girl entrusted to serious individuals, he could devote himself body and soul to the search for his father, as his duty commanded him to do.

The sky was clear. A searchlight on a nearby fort was sweeping the air with a broad beam of light.

An airplane passed overhead, droning. A zeppelin attack was expected, and it was mounting guard.

Ivan crossed the road. He got into the park through a gap in the hedge and made a circuit of the manor house.

The building was not huge: a ground floor and two upper stories. The residents must be plunged in darkness, because no ray of light filtered outside.

Ivan perceived a small window on the first floor that was open. A tree extended large branches toward it. He climbed up nimbly and slipped inside. He listened intently: complete silence.

To penetrate at night, by climbing, into an inhabited dwelling, was to risk the rigor of the law, aggravating a situation that was already complicated. Only one thing could excuse it: the presence of his sister—but if he raised the alarm, they would hide the child. What excuse could he offer then?

He was not about to retreat, though. He reacted against the advice of an untimely pusillanimity and moved along the corridor.

Step by step, his ears pricked, trying to make out, amid the confused background noises, the sound of breathing, or a cry emanating from the little girl, he chose a door at random. He put out his hand and gripped the latch. His heart was hammering. He was tempted to flee, to go back to the villa—but the door was already open.

Facing him was a widow, fully lit by the moon. He shivered. Behind the glass was a human face.

He stood still, holding his breath.

The man had to be on a ladder. A hand advanced, and with a slight scratching sound, a glass-cutter's diamond described a circle. Then, after disappearing again, the hand came back, armed with a mastic pad, which it applied to the glass. A hole was cut out against the sky. Then the hand reached in through the hole and released the window-catch.

Two seconds later, the man stepped down on to the carpet of the room.

A burglar, Ivan thought. *If I'm captured with him, all is lost.* He went back to the small window in haste. He was about to climb down the tree again when a voice said: "Above all, Gorski, don't do her any harm."

A second individual climbed the ladder while an old man whose spectacles were gleaming in the shadow, remained at the bottom.

Suddenly, Ivan remembered the old man that had been in Madame Wandrowska's house on the night that he had picked up the doll, and the spectacles that he had on, above a little beard as white and gleaming as frost. That same vision surged forth when the limousine of the famous professor of neurology at the University of Moscow, Dr. Mohr, went past him on the road.

He looked down at the watcher and thought: *How he resembles Dr. Mohr! I'd swear, though, that it's the same man who offered Papa...*

But it was very improbable that the director of the hospice would be in this place by night—and what connection was there between neurology and the soundless powder? The adolescent was surely the victim of a chance resemblance.

He was snatched from his reflections by a woman's voice.

"No, no! You can't. You don't have any right."

The woman was undoubtedly threatening to call the police, for someone replied: "Calm down, Madame; it will be better for you."

The man's voice became more menacing as the other raised her voice.

"Shut up, I tell you, and be careful! I'll lock you in a padded cell. Come on, enough! Anyway, no one will believe you. Hold her, Tcherniski—I'm going to administer the chloroform."

There was the sound of a struggle, then absolute silence.

It's curious that the muzjik hasn't heard anything, thought Ivan, astonished not to see the lady's servants appear.

Finally, a window on the ground floor opened. The man standing guard at the foot of the tree ran forward. A heavy package was passed to him. Then the other two jumped down from the window, and all three of them fled.

Ivan noticed that the man carrying the burden seemed to be taking infinite precautions. What was he carrying?

The adolescent felt an extraordinary emotion invade him, without knowing exactly why. What connection was there between those burglars and him, between the package and Nadia?

The three men having disappeared into the bushes of the park, the engineer's son let himself down from his post. He went toward the ground-floor window, which was still open.

A shiny object attracted his attention. He bent down and picked it up. At first there was a kind of disillusionment; it was a gold locket. The people he had perceived were vulgar thieves, then.

The boy was about to put it in his pocket in order to had it in to the authorities the next day when, having examined it more closely in the moonlight, he saw an N and a D engraved on the ornament's face. He uttered a cry of distress and anger; he had recognized Nadia's locket.

Then he ran after the abductors. They had already reached a limousine parked outside the gate, its motor running, ready to depart.

"Him!" said the old man, with an evident joy. "I didn't expect to be so lucky!"

In response to a sign, the other two leapt upon Ivan, and put a chloroform-soaked pad over his mouth. When they had got into the vehicle with him, it drew away at top speed.

HOW A CAT'S EAR WEARS AWAY
A SHEEPSKIN RUG

Ivan Damidoff raised himself up on his elbow.

Around him, the entirely white room seemed cheerful. The walls were white, the beds were white, the nurses were dressed in white caps and long white smocks. It was a white fairyland, into which the sun, shining through large bay windows put golden reflections.

At the far end of the room, surrounded by aides and interns, an old man similarly clad in a long smock, but with a black skullcap, was coming forward, stopping at each bed.

The adolescent looked at him. It seemed to him that the face was not unfamiliar. He got ready to speak to him and ask why him he was in a hospital bed, but the venerable old man went past without looking at him.

Ivan fell back into a profound sleep. How long he had been in that sort of lethargy, caused by the absorption on chloroform, he could not have said.

Finally, the recovered consciousness, and, still feeling very numb, he got dressed and demanded to be set free.

He was taken to the director's study, an order to do that presumably having been given.

"Come here and look at me," Mohr said to him, point-blank. "Do you recognize me?"

"It seems to me, in fact," said Ivan, passing his hand over his brow, "that…didn't you come to visit my father?"

"You don't know what became of him?" asked the scientist, by way of response.

"I don't know. He disappeared a fortnight ago, during a violent storm that burst over our region. There were enemies…"

"Are you sure of that?" Mohr cut in. "Do you think that only men can interfere with human affairs?"

"There's God."

108

"There's God! That's very true. Good. And on that basis, can't you admit the intervention of Providence in the disappearance of your father and your coming here? Yes…my question surprises you. Your father was an honest man…apparently." Seeing the adolescent go pale, the scientist went on: "Oh, I don't know anything—I'm assuming. We're all fallible." Those words had been pronounced with the secret intention of acting upon the adolescent's mind. He continued: "For in sum, is it very honest, on the part of an intelligent man, to invent killing machines?"

"When they're for the purpose of defending the fatherland, yes," Ivan replied, energetically.

"On condition that they don't fall into the hands of malefactors."

Ivan Iagow looked at his interlocutor and shivered. Oh, how well the other penetrated his thoughts!

"You see," the doctor added, "your father would have done better to sell me his formulae."

"Oh! I did recognize you."

"Your memory is accurate. Well, we're going to make a bargain. Would you like that? You know the whereabouts the formulae for the new explosive discovered by your father."

"If my father refused them to you, there's no reason why I, his son, should give them to you."

"That's a no, then?"

Ivan straightened up, and said coldly: "It's a no." He shook his head.

"You don't want to?"

"My father's invention belongs to Russia."

"Agreed, but by Saint Paul, invent marvels that might be useful to humankind, not horrors that might be harmful to it. For fifty years I've been struggling against nature without succeeding in vanquishing it."

"It's scarcely the moment to talk about such things," the adolescent remarked, ironically, "and I'm astonished that a scientist like you, a great patriot like you, is sustaining such a thesis at the precise moment when Russia needs the collaboration of everyone, as well as killing machines, to use your expression."

The strange old man let the remark pass. He stood up, put his hands on his interlocutor's shoulders, and looked him in the eyes.

"Even if I return your father to you?"

A violent emotion passed over Ivan's face.

"Even for that," he said, in a hoarse voice.

"And your sister, don't you think she's in danger?"

Ivan shivered. "Even for her," he murmured.

"Perfect!" said the old scientist, stepping back and beginning to pace back and forth, his hands inside the flaps of his smock.

There was a long silence.

Mohr came back to Ivan. "You have character," he said, in a singular tone. "I like that." He picked up a newspaper that lay open on a table "Listen. Look at this: your father has made bombs, and he, or other nihilists, his accomplices, have carried out an attempted regicide with his invention. That's why he didn't want to sell his secret. Shut up! Not a word! It's futile—I know everything now. I only have to raise a hand to doom your father, your sister and you. Are you ready to yield to my arguments?"

While he was speaking, the adolescent had pulled himself together. "Why are you asking me that?" he questioned. "Has something happened?"

"Yes, the attempt was made, but because the bomb made no sound, it was thought at first to be an incomprehensible accident, and the criminal was able to get away without being suspected. Now they're searching for him. You understand what I'm saying? They're looking for him."

"All right," said Ivan. "But since we're not guilty..."

"In any case, there's sufficient probability of your father's involvement, and yours. Listen to me: those imbeciles are spoiling a marvelous invention—marvelous, I admit that. They didn't even hit their target, since, instead of killing the Tsar, they stupidly murdered three railway workers. It can,

110

and ought to be, used for other projects. Listen: I won't ask you for the formulae; just give me one bomb. I'll study it."

"No," replied the engineer's son, firmly.

"You're making a mistake. It's probable that the guilty party will never be discovered—the man who threw the bomb, at any rate...but the man who made it..."

Dr. Mohr darted a glance sideways. Ivan shivered.

"Yes," the scientist went on, slowly. "Who knows what they'll find at his domicile? There's the article in the *Scientific Review*..."

The young man shuddered. The blow had struck home. He did not let his sentiments show, however.

"Do what you want with me," he said. "You won't get anything." And he thought: *I need to get out of here.*

"You're a brave boy," said the scientist. "You mustn't only think about yourself, though. There's your father. There's Nadia."

Ivan clenched his fists. "No," he said, again.

"Easy, now," concluded the head of the establishment, visibly irritated by that resistance. "Do you want to remain an inmate here?"

"What right do you have to detain me?"

"The right conferred upon me as a physician and neurologist, over a boy whose responsibility is attenuated."

The adolescent blushed with indignation. Him, a neurotic? Get away! He controlled himself. "All right, then," he replied. "It's not bad here, it seems to me. I'm the weaker, I admit."

The doctor pressed the button of an electric bell. A male nurse came in.

"This boy still has nervous disturbances," he said, "but there's no need to lock him up. Take him to a ward where there's a bed free. Watch him closely, though."

Ivan was taken through a long series of corridors to a ward where a bed was assigned to him.

Ivan Damidoff was a patient, or rather a prisoner, of Dr. Mohr, until he decided to speak.

In reality, he knew nothing about the invention, since the formulae had been stolen by Nitchef, but to confess that would be to give in, to fail his oath for a third time. In a firm tone, Ivan said: "The die is cast, and if it's necessary to die, I'll die. For in the final analysis, what interest does Dr. Mohr have in obtaining the formulae for himself and depriving Russia of them?"

THE MAN WHO SWALLOWED THE THUNDER

For about a week, Ivan was an object of curiosity for the hospitalized. He seemed normal; what extraordinary malady could he have? The adolescent had had time to think, and had arrived at the following conclusion:

Dr. Mohr has taken possession of my father, Nadia and me, in the hope of obtaining the formulae. Has he acted in a humanitarian spirit? No, no, because he had for an accomplice the confessed nihilist Nitchef, the author, or one of the authors, of the attempted regicide. Mustn't Mohr be a spy, if not a nihilist?

There was, in truth, a little madness in that notion of spies lying in ambush in every corner of Russian society, so Ivan could not be very certain about the matter. It might be better to think of his jailer and persecutor as an affiliate of terrorism. That seemed more probable; followers of Herzen[20] could be found, it was said, all the way to the steps of the throne.

I know where and how to strike, he thought. *Georges Chantepie and his friend the consul will help me, but for that, I need to be free.*

His escape plan was simple: to slip, by night, to the far end of the ward, go along a narrow corridor and go into a room that opened at the far end. After the door, a window, then a garden; a short run, a low wall to climb over, and that was liberty…salvation.

The following night, Ivan Iagow succeeded in reaching the intended door, and closing it behind him. The most difficult part was over. He took a deep breath.

---

[20] Alexander Herzen (1812-1870), popularly known as the father of Russian socialism, spent some time as an exile in Paris and exerted a considerable influence on the development of French socialism.

A moonbeam shone through the window.

A rigid human form was lying on a low bed. The man—a black beard cut across the whiteness of the sheets—had his eyes open, and was staring at the fugitive.

Ivan stood still, as if fascinated by that gaze.

He tried to shake off the charm that was nailing him to the spot. At the same time, he wanted to stay there.

Who was the man? A lunatic? A paralytic?

Patients, nurses and warders never tired of making witty quips about a mysterious individual found one night, deprived of his clothing, at the gate of the hospice, and cared for in a separate room.

Constantinovitch had not been unaware of his presence, since, Ivan recalled, he madman had burst out laughing when talking about the singular phenomenon. Everyone delighted in confirming, extravagant as it was, that the unknown man had "swallowed the thunder."

Day after day jokes on that subject were exchanged, in rather dubious taste, springing forth like fireworks. Many a time, Ivan had been on the point of questioning a warder, but in sum, what did it matter to him? What he had to accomplish, and the work of national cleansing that he had glimpsed, was much more important.

Now he found himself in the presence of the curious patient.

Yes, he said to himself, *it's the man who swallowed the thunder*. He said that in order to give himself courage, and he thought: *He's going to speak to me. I'm doomed.*

The window was two strides away. One bound, one gesture; he would open it; a quick jump, and he was outside. It was simple—and yet, the program now seemed to be bristling with difficulties, simply because of the presence of the invalid.

He had not thought of that. One squeak from the man, and someone would come, and he would be thrown into a padded cell.

Then he thought that lunatics, like children, are sensitive to amity. He made a friendly gesture.

"Have no fear," he murmured, as if the other could hear him. "I don't mean you any harm. Shh, friend!"

He put a finger to his lips and took a step forward.

The man was still looking at him. The moonlight put a luminous gleam into each of his pupils; one might have thought them silver dots in the darkness.

Ivan suppressed the atrocious anguish that was gripping him, and smiled.

He was close to the bed; he moved closer still.

He had to get away, at all costs; he could not abandon his plan. The entire house was sleep. Not a sound.

To make it clearer to the lunatic that he meant no harm, that he was not an enemy, he leaned over the hand that was resting on the sheets, diaphanous in its pallor, and kissed it.

An involuntary emotion gripped him. He peered at the man, but could see nothing but a bloodless face in a black beard and two eyes shining in the sidereal light.

He's dead, he said to himself, to explain his emotion.

The man who had swallowed the thunder had to be dead, in fact, because he was not stirring; his eyelids remained obstinately open, his pupils fixed.

Ivan made the sign of the cross.

I'm saved!

Having made that observation, and judging that Providence was favoring his plan, the moved to the window, opened the catch and pulled it toward him. The hinges emitted a creak that seemed very loud to him.

He listened, and shivered. Someone was coming; a sound of shoes on the parquet was audible, close at hand.

Ivan lay down on the floor and slid under the dead man's bed. Scarcely was he there than a watchman came in and leaned out of the window.

"Hmm!" he growled. "I could have sworn that the paralytic got up. Who could have opened the window?"

He looked out for a long time, scrutinizing the shadows in the garden. Then he closed the window firmly. Ivan Iagow was caught in a mousetrap.

THREE OLD COMRADES

The day after these events occurred, at eleven o'clock in the morning, an automobile furnished with the regulation papers emerged from Warsaw and headed for the sanitarium. Three men were inside.

"The boss says that they won't hold firm under our guns," said one of them. "Hmm! They don't seem to be as bothered as all that."

"Let it go, Forty-Eight. These savages have no depth. They won't hold firm against an army like ours, especially if we have the silent bomb."

"A famous invention, Thirteen! What do you think, Twenty-Four?"

"Famous," approved the man addressed.

"If the infernal device had exploded a second earlier, the police wouldn't have seen anything but smoke."

"The person who constructed and placed it is a poor clockmaker."

"Pardon me, Forty-eight; the intervention of some youth whose name the police don't know, but whose trail I picked up, was the sole cause of the failure."

"Who is he?"

Ivan Iagow, quite simply. Anyway, he'll lose nothing by waiting, for he's going to have a bad time."

"At any rate, his action proves that the plot has been partly uncovered."

"Nitchef must have said too much."

"No way to tell—he's an enigma, that Nitchef. Deep down, he hates and mistrusts us. He'd be a danger if he weren't blinded by hatred."

"In the meantime, he has the formulae and won't give them to us. In my opinion, we ought to leave the Iagows in peace and make that rogue cough it up."

"Impossible! The boss has plans for him. He's angry enough with me for having wanted to kill him."

"The boss is confident—so much the better for him. For myself, I wouldn't give ten pfennigs for any business that individual's mixed up in."

"That doesn't alter the fact that if we'd had more Nitchefs, we'd be further forward."

"You have your opinion, Twenty-Four; let me have my reservations. That man will do us a bad turn. It was probably his own fault that the blow failed; there should be no hesitation; he should be amputated."

"Al right! Nevertheless, we have to keep him. If we don't succeed this evening, we can still grab him and tear as many strips of flesh off him as it takes to get his secret out of him. When the emperor comes back to Warsaw, I want to greet him with the silent bomb."

"Behind Mohr, Twenty-Four, behind Mohr. Don't forget that."

"*Sic vos non vobis*,"[21] muttered Thirteen, aside. In a louder voice, he added: "That's not your concern. Do your duty, and you'll be paid in accordance with the services rendered. That's what I'm doing, and the Emperor is good to those who are collaborating in the great work. In the meantime, the purpose of tonight's expedition is to get hold of the silent bomb, or at least the formulae for it. We need to get the secret out of the boy or his father. The method employed by the boss doesn't lack originality; it's seductive. If it succeeds, I'll bow down before him as before a god, and proclaim German science as the foremost in the world. First of all, an idea as elevated and as…curious could only come from a German. Wasn't it Koch, a German, who found the secret of human longevity in the spinal fluid of a rabbit?"[22]

---

[21] A popular quotation from Virgil: "Thus we labor, but not for ourselves."

[22] The reference—somewhat exaggerated in its implication— is to the pioneering microbiologist Robert Koch (1843-1910)

That conversation had taken place in the purest Berlinese. Those who were engaged in it, and addressed one another by means of numbers, were spies of the lowest category, obscure colleagues of the great pre-war conspiracy.

We have had the opportunity to catch Thirteen twice in conference with Mohr. The other two were under the direct orders of the fake student, for the tenebrous service was as organized and as hierarchical as only an administrative body from beyond the Rhine can be.

While the members of the trio were conversing, the automobile was devouring distance. It stopped at the entrance to the forest whose dark foliage covered the hill. The headlights were extinguished and the vehicle was pushed into a side-path through the woods, behind a thicket. Having done that, the three men made their way silently toward the sanitarium.

Having reached a crossroads they stopped, and Thirteen whistled softly.

A human shadow moved away from a tree. The earrings and silver buttons on his rheingrave trousers, which gleamed softly in the darkness, were suggestive of a gypsy.

"Has the patrol gone by?" the spy asked.

"Yes, but you'll have to be very careful when you move into the open; the searchlights of the redoubt are sweeping the region."

"We'll be prudent. Anything new?"

"A big cannon arrived today."

"I'll inform the chief. Keep a close watch."

The gypsy returned to his post and the three men went forward. Having reached the edge of the wood they slid forward, keeping low and taking advantage of the slightest unevenness in the ground, toward a small door situated at the corner of the wall surrounding the hospice. They only had to push it, and they were in the garden.

Thirteen looked round.

"Anything suspicious?" he said, in a low voice.

"No," replied Forty-Eight, in the same tone. "But whenever I find myself on terrain beaten by that damned Mohr, I don't feel safe, although I don't know why."

"Shh!" the student commanded.

At that moment, a slender white silhouette stood out against the backcloth of the wall, and a shrill voice cried: "Ivan!"

"It's the little somnambulist," said Twenty-Four. "Mohr hasn't deceived us."

The child came forward rapidly. One might have thought her a light, pale apparition gliding over the ground.

Having reached one of the shuttered ground floor windows, she rapped on it with her tiny fit, and repeated: "Ivan! Ivan!"

Michael Gregor turned the Twenty-Four. "Prepare the bomb," he said.

He went after the little girl, to whom Ivan's voice now responded, and taking a two-part jemmy from a bag, he screwed the two parts together dexterously. Then, digging the tip in between the two panels of the shutter, he prized it open slowly but firmly.

THE HYPNOTIC VISION

This was what had happened.

The warder who had closed the window, intrigued, had made a round of inspection. He had found Ivan's bed empty and raised the alarm.

The fugitive had been discovered hiding under the bed of the man who had swallowed the thunder. Then he had been taken away, in spite of his protests, transported through a subterranean tunnel to an isolated pavilion, and locked in a padded cell with padlocked shutters.

The loudest noise could not get through those wool-lined walls, much less the empty space that doubtless surrounded the pavilion.

Lying on his bed, from which he has scarcely budged for several days, with his eyes wide opened, Ivan meditates in the dark.

Mohr is decidedly a redoubtable individual. What he wants, he is determined to have. He wants the formulae; he will get them.

"No, no," groans the young man, his teeth clenched. "Never, never!"

Anyway, he has a friend: Georges Chantepie. The tutor must be searching for him; he must have picked up his trail. He would save them, unless Mohr—the villain was capable of anything—declared all three of them, the engineer and his two children, to be neurotic, and dangerous to society. What could the Frenchman do? Nothing!

And the hope of rescue was extinguished, like a lamp running out of oil.

So, it's necessary to make a second escape attempt.

Why not? Full of that idea, Ivan gets up stealthily. He tries the shutters; they are solidly locked. At least he can see through a crack that he is on the ground floor.

He goes around the room, groping his way. His hand encounters the handle of a communicating door. Slowly, slowly, he turns it. The door yields, and he peeps through. The room is illuminated by a night-light.

He can see the foot of a bed…a human form under the covers; next to the bed there is a guard sleeping in an armchair. It's impossible to get through.

Ivan goes back to lie down on his bed. He is discouraged. The best thing to do is to wait. His heartbeats measure the passage of time.

"Ivan!"

He hasn't heard. Anyway, it was a dream.

"Ivan!"

What time is it? Seven o'clock? Midnight? Four o'clock in the morning? He feels chilled to the marrow. He slips under the covers and tries to go back to sleep.

"Ivan, it's me!"

What! One would think that was Nadia's voice!

He opens his eyes, widening the lids. He tries to pierce the darkness. He listens, holding his breath.

"Ivan, open up."

A small hand raps on the shutter.

With one bound, Ivan is at the window. Through the crack in the shutter, he perceives a small silhouette. He shudders.

"Nadia!"

It's her; it's Nadia, standing outside, rapping on the shutter with her closed fist.

How does she know that he is here?

He has to open the window. He must. How? He shakes the panel, in vain. It would need five times as much force as he has to obtain a result. He has no implement, no lever, and there is darkness, profound obscurity, hostility all around. If anyone some, Nadia will be taken away, and it will all be over, perhaps forever this time.

"Nadia!" he whispers, very quietly, in order not to wake the nurse sleeping next door, "I'm here. Can you see an open window a little further long?"

But the child does not seem to hear him.

"Ivan," she says. "Why won't you open up?"

The adolescent is on the brink of tears. He rakes the wood with his fingernails, bloodying his hands.

By what miracle is the little girl there? He doesn't ask himself that. She's there, that's all; she's separated from him by a panel a few centimeters thick, and he can't wait. It's enough to make him smash his head against the wall.

Now a grating sound becomes audible. Something hard is scraping the stone directly under the shutter; a shiny object slips through the groove. The panel creaks faintly; the wood splinters. The iron lock is beginning to come away, along with its screws.

Where is that help coming from? Ivan doesn't try to figure it out. He's about to recover his sister; that's the important thing. Afterwards, no human power will be able to take her away from him. Rather die than that.

Stiffening his muscles, he pushes the shutter; it opens. Nadia is in front of him, standing upright, very pale. He reaches out to her. Nimbly, the little girl clambers up on to the sill. The adolescent seizes her. He seems to be clutching a block of marble. He wraps her in a blanket.

"Poor Nadia," he says. "Where have you come from?"

The child doesn't reply. She struggles, trying to get up. Ivan needs all his strength to hold on to her. She gets away, and runs toward the communicating door. He catches her on the wing.

"Not that way," he murmurs. "Someone will hear you. Be good, Nadia, my little Nadia, I beg you."

"Papa! I want to see Papa! He's there! There!"

The adolescent shivers. The little girl has just shouted those words. Someone will come. But no, no one is stirring. The nurse next door, doubtless overtired, is sleeping profoundly.

If I only had a light, thinks the engineer's son.

If he had a light? But the night is pitch-black. Nadia is struggling with an uncanny strength. Ivan loses his balance, and in order to catch her he reaches out an arm and upsets a jug of water. The water splashes Nadia, who utters a loud squeal.

If he were able to see, Ivan would see the veritable terror expressed by his sister's face. It seems that she has woken up from a sort of lethargy. She shivers.

"I'm scared!" she exclaims in a changed voice—her natural voice.

Ivan notices the difference, and understands. Nadia has come to him in a crisis of somnambulism, guided by the mysterious sense that individuals in a hypnotic state possess—as on the night when she left the villa, when the madwoman, prowling in the vicinity, in the grip of her obsession to possess the child, had only to collect the little sleepwalker who had left her bed in search of him. Now she is calling for her father, affirming that he is there. Might that not be the man whose motionless form he had seen a few moments before? Might it not be the engineer that the sleeping nurse is guarding?

The adolescent murmurs: "The man who swallowed the thunder? The man I passed by while trying to escape? The man whose hand I kissed, and thought dead? His face? Yes…the beard had grown, and that's what deceived me. Suppose it's him. Suppose he's there!"

Moved to the utmost depths of his being, he says: "Tell me, Nadia, is that Papa in there, next door?"

But poor Nadia is hiding under her brother's arm.

She is weeping with fear. What could she say? When the crisis is over, somnambulists can no longer see, can no longer remember anything.

He places the little girl on the bed. Heart palpitating, he heads toward the next room. Already he has gone in. The guard has disappeared. He takes a step toward the bed. The pillow is hiding the paralytic's face.

He learns over; he wants to see.

A brutal hand grabs him by the collar, while another hand is planted over is mouth.

He tilts his head back. Two inches from his face is a masked visage, and a voice says, in German: "Not a sound, or I'll kill you."

In a trice, the two children are gagged, bound, and laid down to either side of the invalid. An infernal machine is placed on a table in front of them.

At the same moment, a deep and muffled noise, simultaneously sinister and singular, resounding in the depths of his chest cavity, provokes an unfamiliar sensation there. One of the steel monsters crouching in the vicinity of the fortress has just uttered a mortal howl.

Impassively, Michael Gregor explains to Ivan: "This dial is an infernal clock. It's constructed on the design of your friend Nitchef. It's the same system as the one he used to blow up the train carrying Little Father, whom your intervention saved from certain death...

"Do you see this glass ampoule? It contains an acid, which, when mixed with picrate placed in the inner sleeve, will set off the explosion instantaneously. All three of you will blow up, and the house with you, at the moment when the small hand, having reached this position—which is to say, at half past eleven—will put enough pressure on the glass to break it. Do you understand?"

He adjusts the gag over Ivan's mouth.

"When you've decided to give me the formulae for the powder, you only have to give me the signal," the German continues. "I'll stop the clock. If not, your death is inevitable. You hear me? Good." He turns to his companions, standing in the doorway. "You two get out, and wait for me down below."

Numbers Twenty-Four and Forty-Eight do not require the order to be repeated; they disappear like shadows.

Number Thirteen leans of the wall, near the door, dagger in hand.

And silence falls, absolute.

THE POISON

Half an hour before, Dr. Mohr had closed the door of the redoubt communicating with the wireless telegraph post.

When the panel had slotted into the wall with geometric precision, the old tapestry based on the Boucher drawings fell back into place.

The doctor sat down, lit a cigar and shouted: "Come in."

A valet appeared, presenting a visiting card on a tray. "This gentleman wants to see you right away."

At the sight of the name printed on the Bristol card, Dr. Mohr felt a strange surge of bile. His eyes became bloodshot, and his jaw advanced in a hideous prognathism. "That dirty Frenchman again!" he murmured; then he remembered that the valet was looking at him, and got a grip on himself. "Have him come in," he instructed.

Georges Chantepie appeared, manifesting a slightly aggressive attitude. He sketched a bow dryly. Forgive me, Monsieur," he said, "for presenting myself at such an undue hour, but circumstances demand it."

The old man indicated a seat with his finger.

A dull but imperious hostility seemed to have animated both men at first sight. To be honest, however, the tutor had told his pupil several times that Dr. Mohr was a worthy man, in spite of the immediate antipathy that he had felt.

Why that change of attitude?

Well, as the engineer's son had supposed, the Frenchman, surprised not to see the adolescent and the agreed time the next morning, had made enquiries. Madame Wandowska's gardener-valet had had no scruple about telling him that Dr. Mohr had come during the night, armed with a legal authorization—and in any case, was the master of the sanitarium not sufficient powerful to act without authorization?—to take Nadia away from the madwoman.

125

What! Why? By what right? Georges Chantepie had thought. *But Ivan...?*

He had demanded details.

"In truth," said the muzjik, "I was quite astonished to see the young man fall out of that tree over there after the physicians had gone. He ran after them. They must have taken him away."

So he's still out there, the tutor said to himself.

He went to the hospice, but was not let in. He was annoyed. His initial antipathy toward the scientist resurfaced.

Were the adversaries right? What kind of man was this Mohr?

He took the tram and went to the French consulate.

The consul informed him. Georges Chantepie was edified.

"A German!" he muttered. "A naturalized German, but a German all the same. And I could have shaken his hand and treated him as a worthy man?" He was furious with himself. "That fellow's playing a shady game. It's necessary to get the two children out of his clutches. We'll try an amicable approach, and if that doesn't work, we'll see about employing more forceful means."

And that is why our Frenchman, unable to hide his sentiments, allowed a hint of bitterness to show through in his first contact with the master of the house.

"To what do I owe the honor of your visit?" asked the scientist, drawing on his cigar and striking a pose devoid of all politeness.

"You have here," Georges Chantepie replied, irritated by that lack of etiquette, "three people who are dear to me: engineer Damidoff and his two children."

"Ah," said the doctor, phlegmatically, "You're interested in those people?"

"Very."

"Pooh!" said the old man, pulling a face. "To begin with, his name isn't Damidoff, but Iagow. Jude Iagow."

"Dami..."

"Iagow, Monsieur, Iagow. Damidoff is a false name, a name stolen from an honest man. A week ago—which is to say, on the day of the attempted assassination of the Tsar— Jude Iagow was what he was twenty years ago, by which I mean a nihilist. He blew up the palace of the Minister of Police during a ball. His own mother was killed by the blast. Condemned to a prison colony, he escaped. He doubtless murdered one of his companions, whose papers he stole. When he came back here he got a job in the Bargineff factory, a factory making munitions in case of war. Then, in the secret laboratory at his villa, he continued his studies of explosives."

"I knew that last detail," the Frenchman replied, hoarsely. An atrocious distress was gripping his throat, inhibiting his speech. Cold sweat was running down his temples. The revelation, made in a cold tone of voice, had fallen on his heart like drops of fire.

"He—I mean Jude Iagow—had made a marvelous discovery. Marvelous, I admit, and I say it loudly—but far from devoting it to the glory of his fatherland, as he claimed. He used it for the most cowardly of crimes, last week's attempted regicide."

"That's not true!"

"But he was punished," the satanic old man continued, "as he had not expected. At the moment of deflagration, the gas he employed provoked a kind of catalepsy, and the guilty party, punished by Providence, was brought to me by the other nihilist, a collaborator as anonymous as discreet as he was beyond suspicion, whom he had nicknamed Nitchef, and whose real name is Vladimir Obrenovitch."

"The V.O. of the article. But in that case, I don't understand that attempted denunciation."

"Attempted blackmail, you mean, either because he wanted to keep it all to himself, or a simple matter of personal animosity. It hardly matters which."

"It's impossible! Him, Damidoff? Ivan? Nadia?"

"Oh, let's not talk about Nadia. In truth, she's too young. But Ivan?"

"In fact, yes," murmured the tutor, despairingly. "Didn't he free the deaf-mute?"

"You see! As for the mother, you didn't know her. Where did Iagow meet her? In Siberia, where she was serving a limited sentence. Women are no less ardent in the doctrine of active nihilism. Her Catholicism, her piety, her charity? Masks! Oh, if you knew the Russian people as I know them…if…"

"Enough!" cried George Chantepie, violently. "Enough!" He was trembling with dolorous anger. What! The people he loved, the people he considered as his own family…!

Dr. Mohr was smiling internally; his eyes were sparkling behind his gold-rimmed spectacles. He understood that he had said enough. *You'll come back to throwing yourself at my feet!* he sniggered, privately.

"Fundamentally," he said, aloud, "That's not my concern—at least insofar as I'm a physician. I find myself at present, with regard to Jude Iagow, in the presence of a truly curious phenomenon; I'm only considering that, and nothing else. You want to know whether I have Ivan and Nadia Iagow in my possession; I reply: Yes, and I think I can soon set them free with the joy of having recovered a living father. In sum, a good wind brought you here this evening. Yes…you doubt that? In truth, your presence is precious to me, in the sense that you will be a trustworthy witness, the best witness that a miracle-worker could desire! A certain number of miracles illuminate my career. Let's understand one another: I'm not claiming to have exceeded the limits between which natural laws operate. No, I remain within the domain of terrestrial possibilities—which doesn't prevent some of my cures, with regard to the present state of medical science, being veritable miracles.

"In the case that concerns us, we find ourselves in the presence of a cataleptic, to whom neither massage, nor electric shocks, nor hot air treatments, nor any of the methods in customary use, can render movement or active life. Now, I'm reminded of a historical fact that is certainly known to you.

Croesus, the last king of Lydia, had a dumb son. Defeated at Sardes by Cyrus, an enemy soldier approached him in order to run him through with his sword when the mute, sensing the danger that his father was in, cried: 'Soldier, don't kill Croesus!' Filial love had given him the power of speech.[23]

"Well, I want to provoke the miracle of paternal love. That's why I took Nadia Iagow. Already, at this very moment, paternal love ought to have begun to provoke a salutary reaction, or at least to prepare the way for it. At this very moment, the girl—a somnambulist, as you're not unaware—has just knocked on the shutter of the lethargic's room. He hears her; he knows that it's his daughter. What he experiences must be intense. Can you imagine his state of mind?

"Of course I can imagine it!" growled Georges Chantepie. "Stirred to the marrow, he must be suffering terribly."

"Not enough, though," the scientist went on, with the coldness of a medical student dissecting a cadaver. "His daughter and his son will shortly, in twenty minutes, be in great danger."

The Frenchman leapt to his feet. He found the doctor's tranquility veritably atrocious.

"Calm down, Monsieur, calm down," the master of the house intervened. "these people can't interest you any more now; only an old seeker for the elixir of immortality like me can find anything attractive in that nest of vipers."

That was not the Frenchman's opinion. Atrocious as his disillusionment was in the matter of the family that he had once considered estimable to the highest degree, he could not still his heart. After all, even if the father and son were culpable, was Nadia not innocent? Well, he still loved, and ought to love Nadia, and—through her, still loved the other two.

"We must hurry!" he exclaimed.

"We have time," the old man replied, and mockingly offered a cigar, which was refused.

---

[23] This anecdote originates from Herodotus.

A few seconds later, a bell rang.

"Our men are here," said Dr. Mohr, getting up, his face suddenly grave. "Would you care to follow me?"

Georges Chantepie had risen to his feet. Suddenly, he shuddered. "What's that?" he said. "Did you hear it?"

"It's nothing," replied Mohr, placidly. "It's the cannon. Doubtless an alert." Between his teeth, he added: "An alert! No, but your knell, it's your knell that's tolling, O execrated Russia."[24]

Aloud, he added: "Come on, this way." His tone was dry, authoritarian, as if victorious Germany already dominated the world, and as if destiny and immanent justice gave him—a German, a member of a superior race—the upper hand over this Frenchman, this dullard, this serf, whose brain, still in the fog of ignorance, was unworthy to receive the light irradiated by his perfectly-evolved intelligence.

---

[24] It was the Russians who invaded Prussia to initiate armed conflict in 1914; they did so on 25 July by the Julian calendar. The Germans launched their first offensive in the Eastern front on 7 August; it was beaten back. The Germans eventually reached Warsaw the following year, as in the story.

THE MIRACLE OF PATERNAL LOVE

Ivan had his father's life in his power, along with Nadia's and his own. Lying beside the man he loved more than anything, he remained devoid of thought, still too stunned to understand, to feel, or to reason.

After a few seconds, he experienced something akin to an electric shock; he had just perceived a slight, regularly spaced series of sounds, with two distinct notes.

His hair bristled.

Have you ever, in hours of nocturnal insomnia, lent an ear to the singular voice of a pendulum clock?

Tick tock! Tick tock! Something mysterious is flowing and fleeting, in space and in time, something fluid, imponderable, ungraspable, which becomes part of you. You don't try to hold it back, because you know that's impossible, and you witness the inexplicable prodigy with an increasing anguish. It's your life that is dissipating, drop by drop; it's the spiral of your being that is unwinding, to lose itself in infinity; and you think that when the cup of life is empty, when the reel is entirely unwound, that will be death, eternity. And you're going toward that point in spite of yourself, possessed, carried away by an omnipotent, superhuman, divine force.

Tick tock! Tick tock! At each of those monosyllables, a little of ourselves escapes us, and we proceed toward death in little clicks.

Tick tock! Tick tock! In the same way that time seems long to us in insomnia, when our minds are occupied with material or terrestrial questions, it seems rapid, fantastically volatile, when that little sound evokes the ultimate end.

As for Ivan, his eyes fixed on the minute-hand of the clock, he thought that the nihilist was a thief, that he was stealing time from him, and that the metal finger was devouring the field of its course with a vertiginous rapidity.

He could feel the contact of the paternal shoulder on his own shoulder.

A curious thing: that shoulder, as icy as dead flesh a moment ago, was gradually warming up. The paralytic's imperceptible respiration was taking on a greater amplitude, and his chest, immobile until now, was beginning to rise.

The dead eyes, similarly fixed on the infernal clock, were now blazing.

The muscles of the face were taut. A formidable labor must be going on in that skull.

Entirely given over to his own thoughts, the adolescent did not perceive anything. He had found his father only to lose him again, and in what a manner! On the other side of his body, little Nadia was moaning softly. Oh, how she must be suffering in her bonds and beneath her gag!

Had he the right to allow her to suffer an atrocious martyrdom? Had he the right to let that tiny, innocent, charming creature perish frightfully in the flower of life? Did she understand the danger? Yes, perhaps a little. In any case, she was suffering. Poor little cherished being! To think that, with a sign, he could put an end to her torture, recover for himself and for her the joy of being surrounded by a beloved and tender father—so tender, so loving, so caring and loving!

Was he going to make that sign?

No, the voice of his conscience murmured in his ear. *No, you must not. Your sister's life, your own, your father's, are nothing. That of society, that of the fatherland, ought to be your only concern.*

I won't talk, Ivan thought.

A profound, immense silence enveloped the dwelling. Suddenly, another detonation rang out, followed by several others; then there was the whistling of rockets cleaving through the air, terminated by a dull explosion, like a full stop.

And dull rumbles, some distant, others closer, make the layers of the ether vibrate.

Zeppelins! Ivan thinks *Zeppelins over Warsaw!*

A horse sound emerges from the paralytic's mouth

He too has heard, has divined. The bandits are attacking civilians, women and children.

Leaning against the wall, Michael Gregor has not budged.

And the infernal clock repeats its little two-tone click. The minute-hand moves forward, and further forward. At least a quarter of an hour has elapsed—more than a quarter of an hour already!

Ivan starts. The paralytic has shifted. No, it's not an illusion.

A sudden revolt shakes the adolescent's limbs. The minute-hand is definitely moving too rapidly. He wants to bound toward it, to stop it in its speedy march. He writhes, his veins bulge, he croaks. His unusual effort is rapidly exhausted.

Michael Gregor looks at him, smiling frightfully. "Ten minutes more!" he says.

"No!" growls Ivan. And he looks toward the window. Isn't that someone walking? Yes, yes, someone's coming. Someone's in the garden. Who? Georges Chantepie?

There is another creak to the right. He turns his head. There is a window there, fitted externally with a curtain. That curtain has just moved, he would swear it. He wants to cry out. Impossible. Worse, he's choking...

And silence falls again, heavier, more sinister, only trouble by the tick tock of the clock. The zeppelins, their infamous work accomplished, are fleeing toward their lairs.

Is no one going to come?

Another five minutes...another four...

"Is it yes?" Gregor asks. Spy number Thirteen has taken a step toward the door.

Ivan makes an energetic sign of negation.

Bandit! he thinks, angrily. *You won't get anything. Too bad! Long live Russia!*

Three minutes...two...the German has almost disappeared into the next room.

"It's no?"

Ivan remains motionless.

Father, he thinks, *forgive me. You wanted it this way, and I obey. Adieu.*

He sends a mental kiss to Nadia, and closes his eyes.

The moment has come.

Another sixty seconds…thirty…twenty…ten!

Oh my God!

"Wretch!" howls a superhuman voice.

And the paralytic, the man who swallowed the thunder, leaps off the bed, and with a finger that doesn't tremble, pushed the minute-hand back.

The widow behind which Ivan saw the curtain move opens, and Dr. Mohr appears, transfigured by an indescribable pride, followed by Georges Chantepie.

"The miracle has occurred," he says. "Paternal love has rendered life to the living dead."

PART THREE

THE GOOD DOCTOR MOHR

Zemlya i Volya, "Land and Liberty"—such was the name of the society created by the disciples of Bakunin, the noble-man who became a revolutionary, the editor of *The Bell*, twice condemned to death, on whose head a price of ten thousand rubles had been put.[25]

Subsequently, the society had been subdivided into a multitude of cells, which covered Russia with a network to which a number of young men of the aristocracy belonged, carried away by their native generosity. And it is a remarkable fact that the augurs of those religions of murder and blood acted on the noblest sentiments of the soul to attract partisans and create disciples.

In that era, Hegel, Schopenhauer and Büchner had been relegated to the background. Nietzsche absorbed the intellectual space as the sun does material space. A monstrous appearance, his philosophy was enveloped in mystery. Behind cloudy verbiage, behind ostensibly profound sentiments, is the void, nothingness. Where his formula becomes material, it claims to save the world by sensuality, egotism and pride, as if humility and self-abnegation did not demand a much greater strength of soul to be affirmed and to act.

---

[25] *Zemyla i Volya* acquired its name, taken from that of a printing shop, in 1878, but the organization split shortly thereafter. It pursued a populist agenda only remotely connected to the Anarchist ideas of Mikhail Bakunin (1814-1876). The latter was in exile in London in the early 1860s when he and Alexander Herzen worked together on the journal *Kolokoi* [The Bell].

And as is well-known, in that doctrine the incendiarists of Louvain, and the destroyers of Notre-Dame de Reims found their energy-source.[26]

Unfortunately, those beings smitten with the ideal, naïve and too ignorant of life to mistrust it, took the asphyxiating cloud for the rampart behind which some celestial Jerusalem was sparkling. Among those victims of a shameless charlatanism, there are three people who merit immediate attention. One of those individuals is not unknown to us: it is the master of the sanitarium in which Ivan Iagow was to be interned, much against his will: Dr. Mohr, half-smiling and half-serious, his eyes shifty behind his gold-rimmed spectacles. The other two are Marie Sergines, known in revolutionary milieux as "the little Countess" and her brother Paul, a student of what is known as "human science."

The brother and sister, orphaned for three years, had allowed themselves to be seduced by the lures of a doctrine negligently emitted by the good Dr. Mohr: "Fortune is nothing if it is not employed for the benefit of humankind."

The two young people launched themselves wholeheartedly into that path, wide open to their aspirations. The millions of their inheritance would be a marvelous seed. The plan for a vast Refuge was drafted, discussed and put into execution, step by step. In the heart of the Vshi-Baja-Boiga[27] a construction rose up that enclosed refectories, dormitories, conference

---

[26] The Germans troops stationed in the Belgian village of Louvain looted and set fire to it on 12 August 1914 (Julian calendar), as a reprisal against reaction by resistance fighters—an incident widely reported in the Allied press as an atrocity. Notre-Dame de Reims was partly destroyed by German shellfire on 7 September as the Germans advanced through France. Nietzsche was actually far more influential in France than in Germany at this time.

[27] The text subsequently translates this phrase as "flea market." *Vshi* is Russian for lice; the remainder of the phrase remains enigmatic.

rooms and reading rooms. It was the ideal of modern creations for the use of the disinherited.

That was the façade. Behind it operated a kind of administrative council by which people more informed than the little Countess and her brother would have been astonished. It is insufficient, is it not, to create something practically? Its activity must be enveloped by a theory, as birdsong envelops the warmth of the Elysian fields. And young Russia—students, writers, thinkers—presided over the destiny of the refuge...and discussed the means of transforming the entire world into a terrestrial paradise.

They did not agree about the means, and it is a feature of many of these societies of universal fraternity that they never agree about the means. They divide into two entrenched camps: the partisans of slow, patient evolution, and the partisans of direct action.

The directive committee of the Refuge gradually became, without its noble founders having the courage or the power to oppose it, a nest of nihilists.

Marie Sergines was worried by that, and more than once she had confessed the fact to her old friend, who had assisted her parents in their dying days, the good Dr. Mohr.

The old scientist had tried to calm her fears.

"Children!" he said. "They talk, but that's all."

"Yes, but if the police get wind of it, the Refuge will be closed down—and what will become of the thousand poor people who find bread and patience there?"

What they find there, he replied, secretly, *is hatred, and I wouldn't want it any other way.*

The fears of the little Countess were mistaken, for at the first announcement of the declaration of war, there had been not one speech or protest. Simply and nobly, everyone went to the post assigned to him by the fatherland. Many were to fall on the field of honor for the ideas they had mocked and scorned. And while they drove bayonets into the sides of Austro-German, while the engineer Damidoff stimulated the production of the Bargineff factory, Marie Sergines transformed

137

the Refuge into a field-hospital under the direction of the professor, with the precious aid of Ivan, enlisted in the Russian scouts.

They only received the seriously wounded.

The honor of the fatherland, alas, demanded large hecatombs of the brave, and an incessant flood of the mutilated passed through the field-hospital.

But expiation was necessary, and people were ready to submit to the merited ordeal.

And the good Dr. Mohr, unaware of fatigue, half-serious and half-smiling, as if he were in his natural element, went from one injured man to another, examining wounds, diagnosing, prescribing, operating with an admirable reliability of intuition, clarity of mind, and manual skill and precision.

The military doctors allocated to the establishment, the ladies of the Red Cross, the aides and orderlies considered him with a respect that tended toward adoration. Even Ivan reached the point of reproaching himself for the low opinion he had had of the scientist and felt, at times, when he had saved a soldier considered as inoperable, that he was ready to throw himself at his feet and beg his pardon—all the more so as the doctor sometimes looked at him with a slight expression of reproach that went straight to the adolescent's heart.

THE ENEMY WITHIN

In spite of events, the miracle of paternal love provoked by Dr. Mohr had had an immense reverberation in Warsaw. It had further cemented the reputation of the venerable man whose science and purse were open to all suffering. Who, henceforth, would think of searching behind such a façade? Who would ever have imagined that the good Dr. Mohr held in his hand the threads of a vast system of espionage, which included, among other things, a monopoly on the silent bomb.

The engineer had vowed an eternal gratitude to his savior of genius. By a sentiment of delicacy of which he took account, the old man never raised the subject of the invention— or, if he did make allusion to it, it was while insinuating that he would gladly see the Government found a kind of ministry of inventions useful to the army, or while congratulating the little Countess—perhaps with a subtle intention of irony—on her passion for ballistics.

The engineer Damidoff was not unknown to the founder of the Refuge. In an environment of feverish cerebration like that of the hospitable house, Damidoff's research had often been a subject of discussion long before being known to the public, well before the conclusive experiment had taken place. We can guess by what channel they caught wind of it. Paul Sergines had discussed it with his sister. So, when she learned about the miracle of which the engineer had been the object, the young woman had asked her great friend Mohr to introduce her to him.

Nadia's gentility and grace had seduced the young aristocrat's heart. The intensive manufacture of shells required the almost continuous presence of the engineer at the Bargineff factory, and the local tram service in the vicinity of Warsaw having been suspended, for lack of staff, the young woman offered him accommodation in her house. The engineer accepted gratefully, and his installation there was accomplished immediately.

In the rare moments of liberty that their feverish activity left them, the conversation naturally revolved around the war and the chances of victory. It was then that Jude Iagow told his young hostess about his invention. The trials of the silent bomb had been successful; it was a matter of applying it to the war. The materials required were very costly, and the construction of furnaces and instruments was delicate work. The Ministry of War, entirely occupied with the mobilization, did not want to hear about it, besieged as it was in any case, by countess inventors with ludicrous projects.

"Well, then," exclaimed the young woman, one day, "I'll provide the necessary funding. My brother won't refuse it. Work on it, and may you succeed as soon as possible."

Emotionally, Jude Iagow leaned over the aristocrat's little hand and kissed it. "Thank you, on behalf of Russia," he said.

He set to work immediately. He recruited a dozen of the most active and intelligent workers at the Bargineff factory, and laid the foundations of a kind of secret society whose motto was: *For the Fatherland.* They would only work on the silent powder by night and in conditions of absolute security and solitude—which is to say, in the cellars of the factory, adapted for that purpose. Each worker had his own task, his material to manipulate. He did not know what his companions were doing. Each element was then handed on to a senior operative, who mixed them in his turn. The inventor was the last in the chain, and, alone and without witnesses, submitted the powder thus obtained to the requisite conditions of temperature and desiccation.

The invention was gradually finalized.

It was then a matter—apparently easier—of perfecting an electric cannon devised by the engineer, or, of the force of projection of the apparatus was insufficiently powerful, of discovering a kind of steel resistant enough to stand up to the deflagration of the silent powder without suffering any damage.

The popular imagination was working overtime. People had caught wind of the formation of the secret crew; mention had been heard of the marvelous invention that was in preparation. The advance of the Russian troops over the Carpathians striking the imagination, the belief spread that the famous Damidoff powder was in action. People were already envisioning the swarming Austro-German hordes reduced to the immobility of death.

As for Ivan, he could not bring himself to reveal to his father the scenes of which the villa had been the theater. As alert and sprightly in mind and body as before, the engineer had also acquired and extreme nervousness and irritability. He went so far to speak harshly Nadia, only to repent of it immediately and console her with tender words. The adolescent divined that the slightest shock might destroy a fragile equilibrium. If the inventor ever learned that the formulae had been stolen from him, that his discovery had served to carry out the most cowardly of crimes, it might have dealt him a mortal blow.

Thus, the young man had hastened to explain the disappearance of the valet by the rationale the drives an animal to flee of house whose master has disappeared, and when the conversation turned to the events of 28 July 1914, Ivan immediately changed the subject.

In any case, the war had brought forth a host of new ideas, new needs and new duties. It absorbed minds and hearts, extended toward the peril, the necessity of victory, drowning them in self-abnegation. The engineer had set aside his plans for rehabilitation in order to confine himself to his work, henceforth having only one aim: to render the silent powder applicable to engines of war, to take it out of the restricted domain of the laboratory on to the vast field of battle, which was gradually extending from the north and the south of Poland. Who would have dared, unnecessarily, to disturb the birth of such a prodigious and beautiful endeavor?

In consequence, retained by his filial love and his patriotic sentiment, Ivan had kept quiet. Along with Nadia, he was submissive to the mirage of the silent powder. They had begun to consider the inventor as a kind of enchanter, the possessor of a mysterious aura that made one dream of the knights of the Middle Ages, the possessor of the all-powerful secret that would ensure the victory of their fatherland.

They waited meekly for the triumphant hour. Dr. Mohr often surprised them in mid-conversation, and every time, when the old man came in, the adolescent experienced a shock to this heart. The other seemed oblivious to the constraint of his former inmate, no matter how visible it was.

"Did I scare you?" he said, playfully, tapping his interlocutor's leg with his foot. "What do you expect, my lad?—it was necessary. You don't hold it against me?"

"How can you think...?"

"And as you see, far from stealing your father's invention, I've advised Marie Sergines to supply him with the funds."

"Yes, that's true, Dr, Mohr, that's true."

And Ivan kept quiet, no longer knowing what to think or say. Oh, if he had been able to divine what the old man was thinking at that moment!

Mohr wanted to find out whether his father had talked to him about his work. "Tell me," he said, aloud. "Your father isn't suffering, is he?" And he tried, while entangling his interlocutor in false pity, to get detailed some explicit out of him. Fortunately, the inventor had not breathed a word about his work. The "chief," as Michael Gregor called the master of the sanitarium, had been reduced to relying on the rumors running around the factory, faithfully reported to him by number Forty-Eight.

One day, however, the latter told him that the engineer had introduced a new agent into the composition of the powder, which was definitely on the brink of readiness.

Now's the time to act, the old man said to himself.

And he had a long conference with Thirteen.

CONSCIENCE

You who fill with your presence
All of space and all of time:
Triple person, unique essence,
Being of existing beings;
Spirit, source, origin and cause
Of all spirit and all things.
Invisible, although everywhere,
Sustaining all by your empire,
Living through all that breathes.
O you whom we call God!

I cannot even trace the shadow
Of your features thrice holy God!
Glad however is my soul,
To sense those thoughts of flame
That your dive love pours forth...

Vladimir Obrenovitch put down Derzhavin's *Odes* beside him.[28] He was sitting at the foot of a tree in the midst of the silence of the forest. A few sagenes away was a gypsy encampment. The men were nonchalantly smoking long pipes; the women were weaving wicker baskets. An old horse was grazing on a bank.

Vladimir Obrenovitch put his head in his hands and drifted into a reverie.

Born in the horror of a Siberian prison camp, Vladimir had savored human misery all the way to the lees. He had been sold by his mother to gypsies in exchange for a few kopecks and had led an errant life for a long time. He had known hun-

---

[28] The ode "God" (1785) by the Russian poet Gavrila Derzhavin (1743-1816) was widely translated, and Dodeman is presumably quoting the French version.

ger, thirst and privations of every sort. He had lived on the margins of humanity, rejected, scorned or feared by city-dwellers and peasants alike. He had stolen; he had spent days and months in prison.

Finally, an epidemic of smallpox had ravaged his tribe and he had run aground in Moscow, at the Red Gates. His employment consisted of examining the boots of passersby. On perceiving a scratch or a disquieting gap between the upper and the soul, he quickly brought a stool a hammer, nails, an awl and cobbler's thread. The passer-by patched up his footwear himself, and rewarded that delicate attention with the gift of a few kopecks. Vladimir did not make a fortune in that trade, as one can imagine, and did not eat every day.

Splashed by the troikas of millionaire serfs or the automobiles of aristocrats, his hatred of humanity and the social hierarchy, already intense, was further increased. He joined the association of the nihilists.

The son of the Siberian woman had seen a great deal and remembered a great deal. He took advantage of the long leisure hours enforced by his trade to educate himself. He was intelligent; he became knowledgeable. Unfortunately, the baneful theories of the Schopenhauers, the Hegels, the Büchners and the Nietzsches came to the service of his rancor and enthused his mind for anything that might collaborate in the destruction of a society declared to be ill-made.

Avatars led him to Warsaw. There, when the nihilists, having discovered a former affiliate in the person of the engineer Damidoff and having got wind of the research he was pursuing, resolved to put him under surveillance, he offered to serve as the spy in question. He had quickly divined what he needed to do in order to introduce himself into the villa. He had no difficulty playing the role of a vagabond half-dead from hunger; he really was one.

The control he had over himself permitted him to assume the character of a deaf-mute without overmuch risk. In any case, entirely devoted to his invention, the engineer hardly saw what was going on around him. Ivan was still naïve, Nadia so young! Only the Frenchman was dangerous, by virtue of his penetration, but he only came rarely.

In brief, the fake cripple was able to track the progress of the discovery and take possession of the notes and formulae that revealed to him what no one but the inventor could know. And as he was an agent of justice, as his heart was too full of hatred to lend an ear to his conscience, awakened by Nadia's charming and tender action in bringing into the house a vagabond horrible in his appearance; as, in his view, Ivan Damidoff was only lending himself to the will of destiny in saving him; as the fate of Russia was nothing compared with the necessary vengeance, he had placed the infernal clock on the track.

According to his own theories and the laws of mechanics, the death of the Tsar was certain, and, in fact, the timer had triggered the bomb at exactly the right moment—but Providence had provoked a child, and the Tsar had been saved. His crime accomplished, the nihilist had fled the cadavers of the three employees torn apart by the bomb and gone into the forest, where a gypsy tribe was camped. He had been able to associate himself with them. Was he not one of their own? He found shelter there.

The police came and wanted to drive them all out, but, as if by chance, Dr. Mohr was there, and was the tribe as installed on sanitarium property, he asked that they be left in peace. The authorities yielded to the great man's desire, and the gypsies were able to devote themselves to their occupations in peace. Nevertheless, as a favor cannot go to waste, every evening, their leader went to see the doctor every evening to give him a report on what the women had overheard, or what they had observed, regarding troop movements or the establishment of artillery batteries in the vicinity.

One day, the approach of the Austro-Germans was announced, to within seventy versts of Warsaw. At that news, Nitchef had felt a frisson stir the depths of his entrails. He had raised his head, his lips taut and his nostrils palpitating. He had immediately repressed the involuntary reaction and expe-

145

rienced a violent anger against what he felt vaguely within himself.

"What does it matter!" he exclaimed. "Let them come— we'll see afterwards what to do about it."

And he had plunged back into the covert struggle that was taking place the old man—the one he called the atavistic slave—and the truly emancipated man that he had become, thanks to the philosophers.

Days and weeks went by. The most various and contradictory news circulated. One day it was announced that the enemy was in full retreat, the next that they had advanced ten versts. Then the nihilist shuddered. He began to interrogate the women when they returned from the city, with an insistence that surprised everyone, because he hardly ever spoke.

Finally, the definitive retreat of the Austro-Germans became known, and the progress of the Russians over the Carpathians. Calm was restored. Nitchef plunged more deeply than ever into his thoughts. He asked one of the women to bring him back a book. She handed him a volume of Derzhavin's *Odes*, bought at random.

Dusk was falling. The forest filled up with shadows; mysterious voices were whispering in the branches. Nitchef resume reading.

The gilded chains of verse gradually enveloped his heart. He tried to resist their persuasion but went back to them in spite of himself.

I am nothing, but in my soul,
I sense a divine fire burning.
Your spirit warms and inflames me.
I feel you living in my bosom.
I am nothing, but I have life;
And toward you, infinite grandeur,
I aspire; and your finger leads me...

The nihilist lowered his head. He suddenly stood up, with an energy he wanted to render superb.

"Lies!" he cried. "Childishness and lies! There is no God, and I'm free! I'm a man, and therefore master of nature, and I have the right to reform what seems to me to be bad. Too bad for those who fall! Only the goal is important."

He had not said "what is bad." He had said "what seems to me to be bad." He was, therefore, no longer completely sure of the goodness of his cause.

A guttural cry called him toward the camp.

A woman dressed in multicolored garments, with baskets on her back and a child in a bag suspended around her neck, had just arrived from Warsaw. She was telling an extraordinary story, like those that run round in cataclysmic periods, with an unusual luxury of detail. It could be summarized in brief as: "The Russians are advancing victoriously, thanks to an engine of marvelous power." Lord Kitchener, the English minister, had announced a few months previously the entrance on stage of a formidable factor whose possession would assure the allies of victory. That formidable factor had been found by a Russian, the engineer Damidoff of the Bargineff Factories. The little Countess had furnished the capital. Experiments had been carried out on a flock of sheep; eight hundred animals had been pulverized by a single blast.

"And the most curious thing about the whole business," Nitchef added, "is that no one can hear anything at all."

"So it's said," replied the woman. "How do you know?"

Nitchef wanted to ignore the fluctuations of the titanic conflict that had thrown humankind, divided into two camps, into collision. Why, then, did he experience an indefinable joy on hearing that the Russians were victorious? What did it matter to him? Did he not hate those authors of his misery?"

He shrugged his shoulders and went away.

No, he said to himself, raking his chest with his fingernails, *no, the Russians are not evolved; the Russians are savage brutes. They're unworthy of victory; they shan't have it. Oh, why didn't I let Jude Iagow die?*

147

As if a genie were replying to his thought, the woman who had brought the news called him back. "Someone gave me a letter for you," she said.

"Who?" he asked, astonished that anyone should remember him.

He opened the letter:

Come right away. M.G.

"Michael Gregor? Him!" A violent sentiment contracted his features, creasing his Mongolian eyes.

I won't go. But if I don't, he'll think I'm afraid. I'll go. What does he want with me?

As night fell he headed for the caravan and went in. Five minutes later he came out again, unrecognizable. A white wig covered his head beneath a woolen hood. A growth of fake flesh half-obscured his left eye, and his right foot was supported by a wooden pin.

In that get-up, he headed for the city.

A BARGAIN CONCLUDED

Vladimir Obrenovitch went into the ancient Polish city without anyone bothering him. He went into the Vshi-Baja-Boiga, or flea-market.

That place is the most extraordinary in the world. Everything that rag-pickers have been able to extract from dustbins, everything that wear and tear, caprice, changes in fashion has caused to be discarded—shoes, garments, cracked crockery, broken trinkets, pictures with holes in, coverless books—winds up there…and finds buyers.

A muzjik will gladly put on a pair of boots that an aristocrat has given to his butler and has passed from his feet to those of a student with luxurious tastes but a meager purse, finally to be collected by a street-sweeper who, having eventually found them unworthy of his high status, has thrown them out. And it is the same with hats as with boots, and all the garments in between.

The strange destiny of things!

The heaps of worn and dirty rags in that market-place offer a safe retreat for the horde of parasitic insects that give the location its name.

If the contents are bad, the surroundings are even worse. The shops are oozing damp, the houses black and leprous. They are the refuge of a wretched population living on the alms they receive, or the meager wages of sordid employments. And this is not a paradox: the poor are legion, but credit is unknown to them.

Among the crowded hovels, Vladimir Obrenovitch searched for the Stork Hotel. He found it at the end of a nauseating back alley. He slipped into a bar-room that one reached by going down three sticky steps. A gas-jet gave poor illumination to two rows of tables furnished with benches. Beggars were eating from metal bowls.

The proprietor approached, his expression roguish.

"Michael Gregor?" asked the cobbler, soberly.

"Upstairs," was the reply.

He went past and through a low door, reaching an atrocious spiral staircase. He went up several flights and stopped at a worm-eaten door. Beams of light shone through the cracks. He opened it without knocking.

A bearded man, still young and almost as wretched as Nitchef had been, was sitting at a rickety table and reading, pen in hand. It was Michael Gregor, graduate student of political sciences.

He remained impassive when Vladimir Obrenovitch came in.

"How did you know where to find me?" Nitchef asked.

"Don't we know everything that might interest Free Russia?" Michael Gregor asked. "We discovered Jude Iagow beneath Pierre Damidoff."

"I thought you'd gone off to war with the others."

"The others," said the student, disdainfully, "are children and cowards. At the first call they went to the barracks, in spite of their oath to start the revolution. Oh, people haven't yet got rid of their servile habits."

"And you?"

"Me, I've been turned down."

Nitchef could not hide his astonishment. Michael Gregor was solidly built and seemed exempt from physical flaws.

"In fact," said the ex-shoe-repairer, "I was forgetting your relatives. They're said to be influential."

"It scarcely seems so," said the student, indicating his wretched lodgings with a glance.

In reality, Mohr had furnished his acolyte with a drug that, taken before the recruitment board, had given him serious palpitations of the heart at the opportune moment.

"At any rate," that individual added, "I'm glad. I'm reluctant, in fact, to shed blood for any other cause than the one to which I've devoted my life. The Germans are our brothers. There are slaves and the oppressed among them, as there are here. You share my ideas, I know, and have given proof of it.

Damn! You work well, and but for that child…in brief, I regret stabbing you and I offer my apologies. You alone dared, out of all those who had sworn."

"Let's not mention it again. What do you want with me?"

"This. The sole means, it seems to me, of achieving a practical result, is to put Russia in a state of inferiority. It has an inexhaustible reservoir of men. What would it be if it possessed a superiority in munitions? You hate Russia."

At that direct thrust, the nihilist was momentarily confused; it only lasted a second, but the hesitation was nevertheless manifest. "Yes," he said, "with all my heart; they've made me suffer too much."

Thirteen, alias Michael Gregor, having noticed his interlocutor's slight—exceedingly slight—hesitation, relaxed. He even deigned to smile with satisfaction. "Perfect. Well, the Damidoff powder, that marvelous invention, is known to you—at least, you know the fundamentals. Oh, what you know no longer interests me as much as it did. If I can believe a comrade from whom I get my information, Damidoff—Iagow, I mean—has completely changed his formula. He has introduced into his explosive, or will, an agent that will be a radium whose particles are liberated with prodigious rapidity. The results, obtained on a small scale thus far, will be frightful. Nevertheless, the powder isn't ready yet. Whatever public rumor says, a realization of that sort—as you know—isn't brought about solely by an effort of will. *Fiat!* For the crowd, the man who doesn't succeed at the first attempt is a fool or a traitor. Imbeciles! At any rate, the invention is gradually being perfected, thanks to the capital of a renegade."

"Marie Sergines?"

"The little Countess, yes. She's infatuated with the idea of the silent bomb, as she's infatuated with our theories of emancipation and liberty."

"Who knows?" said Nitchef, questioning himself aloud.

"Eh? What do you mean?" asked the student, frowning.

"I simply mean that those who accept things as they are, are saner and happier than us, who want to destroy in order to reconstruct. Reconstruct what? The temple will never be large enough to contain humankind entire. Some will lie down on the threshold, others in the courtyard, others still on the carpets of the nave. I've killed—what benefit have people obtained from that? But let's leave vain words aside. If I've understood you, it's a matter of strangling the bird before it lays the egg?"

Michael Gregor had listened to Nitchef's speech with increasing anxiety.

Damn! he thought. *He's gone off the rails.* After a moment's reflection, he added: *After all, he won't betray me. The comrades are watching him, and his involvement is clear.* Aloud, he said: "No, no, it's not necessary to choke anything, at least for the moment. On the contrary, it's necessary to stimulate the laying of the egg. Now, you can do that."

"Yes, perhaps," said Nitchef, with a flesh of pride in the eyes. "Oh, if I weren't obliged to hide! If I were rich! I have an idea—an idea that would greatly simplify the research of that unknown genius Jude Iagow."

"He's some scientist, isn't he?"

"He has the spark. Yes, I admit it; I'd be proud to collaborate in his work."

"Be careful—he's working for Russia, your mortal enemy."

The nihilist shivered. Oh, how that man was stirring his heart, and how skillful his needling was!

"What does it matter," he said, finally, "what his goal is. The science is so beautiful! Oh, to create force…to create! There are moments when I admit that I'm only a man, and take pride in my intelligence. If I knew that the Russians were to be victorious, thanks to me, well, I'd be proud of it."

"Damn! You've changed, my dear fellow!"

"Yes," Nitchef agreed, in a dull voice, shaking his head, "I've changed."

"However," the student went on, tight-lipped, "it's a matter of understanding one another. If you become Iagow's collaborator, it's not for your own pleasure, but in the common interest. You're bound to Free Russia by oaths from which nothing can release you. You have a choice: to die, as surely as you're in my presence right now, or to surrender the secret of the silent bomb to me. No one will know anything about it, because it will only be utilized in a distant future—very distant. It's good, in sum, to anticipate and make provision for the unexpected. We won't prevent the Russians from making use of it. As for you, you'll be paid, and generously, for your troubles, from the secret funds of the *Zemlya i Volya*. You'll be rich, and therefore free forever. We're generous, when it's appropriate to be. Are you ready? Yes?" Michel Gregor continued: "So, you're going to be taken on at the Bagineff factories. Don't worry about it—Mohr will support you; you'll be accepted right away. Is that understood?"

Nitchef experienced a disturbance that he had never known before. Objections came to mind. He was both ashamed and angry in feeling a quibbling and pusillanimous double awakening within him, gradually undermining his savage determination to be an avenger.

After all, he said to himself, repressing that double into the depths of his consciousness, *what do this man's intentions matter to me? Why should I oppose them? Whatever Derzhavin says, if there were a God, he wouldn't have permitted a mother to sell her child. My own religion is hatred; my duty is what the people who possess and enjoy the wealth of the earth egotistically call evil. I shall therefore hate until the end, and I shall do evil. Too bad for those who fall!*

"Of course," said number Thirteen, having divined the subject of the soliloquy. "Oh, there's one delicate point: a special crew, regulated by statues more rigorous than ours, is working on the fabrication of the Damidoff explosive. You'll have to be admitted to it."

"What about Iagow? Ivan must have told him what he knows about me."

"We've thought of everything. No one will recognize you. Do you accept?"

Nitchef replied: "I accept."

153

Was he accepting in order to render to the cause the redoubtable service that was demanded of him? Was he accepting for the joy of collaborating in a scientific endeavor for which he had a sincere admiration? Or was he accepting for some other reason—a secret and confused reason to which he did not want to admit?

Whichever was the case, at the moment when he bound himself to his tempter, he had a vision that had no connection with the goal to be attained: he saw a wretch slumped against a wall, and a thin little blonde girl, and angel, holding out her hand to the vagabond and saying, with a sweet smile, the simple word: "Come!"

With an effort of will, he chased away the tenderizing image, unworthy of him, and stood up resolutely.

"Let's go to the Refuge," said Michael Gregor, getting to his feet in his turn. "Mohr ought to be there."

THE PRESENTIMENT

That evening, the field-hospital's ambulances never ceased shuttling back and forth to the battlefield, which was getting ever closer to the Polish capital, and to the refuge.

Dr. Mohr, in a white smock and a velvet cap, was presiding over the transshipment carried out by the young scout and the orderlies. Marie Sergines was attending to urgent care.

An artillery lieutenant had been deposited on a bed. Attentive to the examination carried out by the doctor, who had just recognized a dangerous wound above the lung, Ivan was waiting for his orders when he shivered abruptly."

"Ammunition, ammunition!" croaked the soldier, prey to delirium. "Why don't they send ammunition? We'll have to retreat. No, no! Rather die! Come on, artillerymen. Sabers! Sabers! Long live Russia, and *Vive la France!*" The words had been pronounced in French.

Distressed and emotional, Ivan leaned over the bed. In the face contracted by suffering he recognized features that had been familiar and dear to him.

"Monsieur Chantepie!" he said. "It's me, Ivan Damidoff. Don't you recognize me?"

The other looked at him with haggard eyes. A glimmer of intelligence was still alight in the soldier's brain, for he sniggered: "Oh yes, the nihilists! Oh, you worked well! Instead of thinking of the endangered fatherland, you...oh, the silent bomb! Ha ha ha! Well, it's time. Wre...wret...back! Ba...!"

He lost consciousness.

"Come on, calm down, calm down," Dr. Mohr had muttered, impassively, while he sounded the wound with a light hand. "A bayonet thrust," he murmured. "Dangerous."

Ivan was motionless, frozen.

Had the Frenchman recognized him? Was it really him at which he had hurled that series of bitter, cruel and bloody reproaches?

George Chantepie had witnessed the miracle at the sanitarium. He had sat by the bedside of the resuscitated man for several nights in succession, but in his relationship with the Damidoffs, save for Nadia, an irreducible constraint had been evident. He sometimes rediscovered the habitual surges of affection, but only to cut them off and stifle them immediately. One day, he stopped coming. They received a rather cold letter from him, announcing that he was in Odessa, enlisted in the artillery, and that he had received orders to go and do his duty to his friends without delay.

Ivan thought that the Frenchman as remembering a scene for which he, Ivan, had offered honest apologies.

I didn't think he was so vindictive, the young scout had said to himself, sincerely hurt. He replied to the letter without hiding his chagrin, but received no further news. How could he suspect that the poison poured by Dr. Mohr into the Frenchman's soul had gradually worn away the latter's sincere amity, as acid etches copper? How could he suspect that the former tutor was no longer unaware of Jude Iagow's past, and that, thanks to the cares of the old man, that past had been welded to the present and that a frightful crime had been attributed to the responsibility of the penitent and his son?

And now, after a year of hostile and icy silence, the Frenchman reappeared to hurl an insult in the face of his former pupil and friend, a reproach, phrases perfectly comprehensible to the latter.

Oh yes, the nihilists! Oh, you worked well! Instead of thinking of the endangered fatherland, you... Back! Back!

Had the officer, in his delirium, been addressing imaginary individuals, or had he really been addressing the young scout?

Does he know? The adolescent asked himself, as he went back to his lodgings, once the wounded had been installed and

156

bandaged. *And if he knows, how and by whom was my father's secret revealed to him?*

When he got up, he was pale and anxious.

"Nadia," he said, "I've seen Georges Chantepie, yesterday. He's gravely wounded. You know that he enlisted in the artillery at the beginning of the war."

"Yes. He went without saying goodbye to us. That hurt you a lot."

"A lot. He claimed that he had been upset by events, in haste to make himself useful to the country where he'd found subsistence and amity for many years. What do I know? Anyway, there must have been something else. What? You'll come to see him, won't you? When he's better. The good God will save him. Pray for him, won't you?"

"Yes," said Nadia. "I'll say an *Our Father*."

"This evening, dear Nadia?"

Ivan left, his head slightly bowed, this time.

Why did he evoke the nihilists? he thought. *He had recognized me, though, because he mentioned the silent bomb. Why was he shouting for ammunition? Why announce a retreat? Fever...unconsciousness. But why the nihilists? What were they doing in it? Does he know, then?*

He hoped to find the Frenchman in a better condition and to be able to obtain an explanation from him. Alas, the Lieutenant, after a long crisis of delirium, had lapsed into a coma. Dr. Mohr, on seeing him again that morning, did not hide the gravity of his condition.

"If he gets through it," he said, "He'll be lucky. I'd need another miracle for that, but this time, I confess that I'm impotent."

The adolescent felt large tears running down his cheeks. Georges Chantepie had been a charming and devoted friend; he had had a genuine affection for him. Was he going to lose him, and lose him without having washed away a terrible and odious accusation?

He went in search of the Catholic almoner and brought him to the dying man.

"Pray," the almoner said. "Dr. Mohr mentioned a miracle; God will doubtless contrive one."

When he had prayed hard, he thought: *My father will be glad to embrace him one last time. He'll be doubly dear to him, because he's a Frenchman who fell for Russia.*

Ivan Iagow went to the factory immediately. He was heading for the engineers' office when he bumped into a workman who was just going into a workshop.

"Pardon me," he said. "Oh! Nitchef!"

The other looked at him, impassively.

Ivan blushed at his mistake. The man had entirely white hair. Tattoos covered his face and arms. An enormous fold of flesh hung down from his left eyebrow. He was slightly hunchbacked and had a limp.

"Excuse me," said Ivan. "I thought you were someone else."

The man grunted and disappeared into the workshop.

"It's curious," said the adolescent, while he was on his way to the refuge with his father. "I thought I recognized Nitchef."

"At first sight," the engineer replied, "they have a sort of family resemblance. His name is Gorski. He's Polish. He had excellent qualifications, and he's already been singled out as very skillful and intelligent. Dr. Mohr brought him to me."

"Ah! Dr. Mohr!" murmured Ivan. And without being able to explain exactly why, he had the impression of a painful revelation.

THE ULTIMATUM

A fortnight had gone by since Dr. Mohr's protégé had started work at the Bargineff factories.

Gorski, in whom we have divined Nitchef, emerged from the canteen, where he had been for an hour with his head in his hands, thinking. A singular accident had occurred. The electricity supply had been abruptly cut off. The factory received its power supply from a generating plant situated three versts away, on the bank of a small tributary of the Vistula. Jude Iagow, appointed as chief engineer for days before, had told Gorski to look for the short circuit. Nothing had been found. It had been necessary to expose all the wiring. There had been a forced shut-down for a week. Exhausted by overwork and the slowness—excessive, in his view—of the realization of his ballistic endeavors, delayed by the incident, the engineer had flown into a violent for of wrath and, in front of all the workers, had told Gorski brutally to get out of the factory. He had almost immediately regretted his action and his bad temper, and had asked the electrician to come and see him in his office.

His pride wounded, the workman had refused. His hatred against these who arrogated the right to abuse other men under their authority—the hatred that he had almost diminished, perhaps extinguished, had flared up vividly at that moment. He had gone into the canteen to think, and to chew over the motives he had for hatred.

"If you want, Gorski, we can come out on strike immediately. The repairs to the cable won't be able to continue. They'll be obliged to take it back. We'll demand a public apology for you. Would you like that?"

Nitchef looked at the man who had spoken to him. "Where have I seen you before?" he asked. "Oh yes, I remember. You were with Michael Gregor the night...you're his intimate friend."

"Shh!" said the other, his gaze anxious. "Let's not talk about that. Do you want the strike?"

With one word, Nitchef could realize the dearest desires of Michael and his associates. A strike, for a justifiable reason, might spread, with incalculable consequences. The murmur of disapproval that ran through the ranks of the workers at the moment of his dismissal showed that his interlocutor was not speaking lightly. Why did he not reply immediately? His self-respect had been wounded, and cruelly.

"Do you want it?" the other asked, for a second time.

"Leave me alone," he said, in a surly tone. "I'll give you my answer this evening."

"We're at your orders, you know."

Michael Gregor's friend put out his hand; Nitchef affected not to see it.

An hour later, he went out in his turn, went into Warsaw and headed for the Vshi-Baja-Boiga.

He had to pass through the aristocratic district. In order to take the shortest route, he went through the side-streets of a square. Children were playing in the sunlight, uttering joyful cries, indifferent to the battle that was being fought for them, whose stakes ere equity and justice, on the brink of being eradicated among humans by an egotistical and brutal materialist philosophy. A balloon escaped from the hands of a golden-haired child had caught on the branches of a tree. The little girl was looking up in distress at the red globe bobbing in the air, retained by the string. She extended her hand toward it, but was too short to reach it, alas. Nitchef grabbed the branch, seized the balloon and handed it back to the child.

"Thank you, sir," said the girl.

Nitchef smiled. He felt strangely troubled. A mist rose to his eyes, because the little girl was looking up at him, gratefully.

He thought about Nadia.

Always her, always that pleasant image, in moments when his soul was prey to the blackest thoughts.

He went on slowly, and reached the Stork Hotel.

Michael Gregor was there.

"What's happened?" asked the student.

"There was a short-circuit," Vladimir replied. "You're smiling…you knew about it, then? Perhaps it was one of your friends who damaged the cable?"

Number Thirteen resumed his impassive expression, while his interlocutor moved his head like a wild beast harassed by a mosquito.

"So?" asked the spy.

"Damidoff has sacked me."

"Sacked you! That's a pity. Yes, because of the powder—but he's signed his death-warrant if he doesn't consent to take you back."

"He wants to."

"Well then, go back."

"What about my self-respect, my pride?"

"Bah! Who wants the end…you can avenge yourself later."

"I can avenge myself right away, by letting them come out on strike for me."

"That would cause a delay, and doubtless close the door to the special crew to you. On the other hand, I don't see the absolute inconvenience. A workers' revolt in the middle of a war might have capital consequences for Russia. In fact—go for the strike. Accept the proposal."

"I'll give my response when you've answered me one question."

"Speak."

"Who are you—you and Mohr? Who are you?"

"You know very well."

"I want a categorical reply."

"In sum, it's not your concern."

"I'll tell you who you are, then: you're Germans, German spies. I've always had my suspicions."

"So I've observed," replied Michael Gregor, calmly. "That's why, during our expedition out there, you refused to tell us where the formulae were hidden. You wanted to keep

161

them for yourself, and you made good use of them. I've no reproaches to make to you on that subject. You astonish me, though. Germans? But even if we were, what can that have to do with you, a citizen of the world, who claims to have no fatherland."

"I was mistaken, that's all. There are elements, deep down in a man, that he can't undo; there are instinctive affinities and repulsions. I've analyzed them and named them: race. I'm of a race different from yours, and I'm almost tempted to consider you as an enemy. Faithful to the principles of my entire life, I want to struggle against that sentiment, but I can't succeed in stifling it entirely. I sense that what I'm doing is wrong. For after all, which side are justice and right on? What is it that the Germans—our brothers, as you call them—have made of the most elementary rules, of natural law? The Belgians, women and children, slaughtered in a cowardly fashion..."

"You're remorseful?" said the student, finally, with biting sarcasm.

"Which is to say that I'm feeling sentiments of which I was unaware."

"What?"

"Pity, for example. A little girl taught me that."

"Ah!" said Michael Gregor. He stood up abruptly. "This is what they've made of you!" he growled. "Have you already forgotten the lessons of Nietzsche? Only egotism and pride make one strong, and you talk about pity! You want to be humble and loving—you, whom men have trampled, scorned and abused? Your debasement would sicken me, if it didn't alarm me. Your hesitation is a crime as great as your remorse; it puts humankind back two centuries. Come on, enough sophisms! You're a coward, and you merit the punishment that awaits you."

"Death doesn't frighten me," Nitchef replied, calmly. "But what I would have done a year ago, without scruple, now appears to me to be odious. I betrayed a country—my own—to whose profit?"

"To the profit of humankind."

"No—the scales have fallen from my eyes, and the light is dazzling. I betrayed Russia to the profit of Germany. Yes, someone telegraphs every day the number of shells manufactured and the route they're due to take. Four days ago, the train derailed. Yesterday, the munitions left by road: a bridge blew up as the first truck was passing over it. I've had enough. I don't want it any more. My duty orders me to denounce you—you and Mohr—and I'm going to do it."

The student laughed in a stinging fashion.

"Imbecile! You want to fight against Mohr! Who are you to dare to do that? We hold all the trump cards. One word, one gesture, and Jude Iagow and his son are arrested. It's the rope, you know. There's enough evidence against them, and Mohr's not stupid. No, my dear, believe me, don't attempt an impossible and ridiculous contest. Return to saner and more sagacious ideas. You were nothing; you've been plastered with mud; you've suffered. Enjoy life finally, in your turn. Bring us the formulae for the powder, such as you have them; we'll work on them. Bring them to us, and you'll be able to count a hundred thousand rubles in your hand. Tomorrow, at noon, you hear? Tomorrow, at noon. If not... Make your choice."

And Michael Gregor pointed to the door.

THE CONFESSION ON THE TIP
OF THE TONGUE

After visiting Michael Gregor, Nitchef waited impatiently for the following day. The link with the manipulators was broken henceforth, but the danger had suddenly become immense. Jude Iagow denounced was death and ignominy for Nadia's father. He knew that, and he knew the leader of the gang—which is to say, Mohr—well enough to divine that combat against him would be impossible. Only presumptions could be brought against the scientist, not proofs and certainties, while everything combined to doom the former convict and in consequence, himself—for he was the only guilty party, and he would not allow someone else to go to the scaffold in his place.

The spy's threat was not carried out. It was doubtless not in Mohr's plans to precipitate matters.

Then Nitchef went to find the engineer. Peace was made. A scientific conversation took place between the two men. The electrician emerged from it magnified.

When the wiring was repaired, Gorski became part of the secret crew. Thanks to his considerable skill—was he not entering into a known domain?—the powder was perfected.

The experiment that followed was conclusive.

The inventor, delighted with that success, congratulated the workman warmly.

He came to consider him more as a collaborator than a subordinate. He met with him at all hours of the day and night to discuss issues in need of clarification. He also gave him free access to his office.

One day, Jude Iagowski was having difficulty matching up the resistance of the steel with the expansive force of his powder. He was desperate.

"I'll never find a metal capable of resisting such a pressure," he cried, throwing down his pen. "It's enough to drive one mad!"

"You don't need a cannon, sir," said Gorski's voice behind him.

The engineer raised his head.

"What would you use, then?"

"An airplane."

"An airplane!" said Ivan's father, pulling a face. "An airplane is noisy, and we're searching for...we need...complete silence!"

"I'm not talking about an ordinary airplane but a reduction, an aircraft only capable of carrying a maximum load of twenty-five kilos. The force of your powder is such that a shell doesn't need to weigh any more than that to have an irresistible destructive power."

"But how would we steer it? How would we make the shell fall at the desired point?

"Our aircraft will have an electrical receiver, and we'll give our propeller and its rudders the necessary impulsion by the intermediary of Hertzian waves. The bomb will be suspended from the apparatus by means of an automatic release mechanism—the clockwork system of infernal machines."

The voice faltered slightly as it pronounced the last two words.

"Once the target is pinpointed," the workman went on, making his diction firmer, "and the distance measured, only has to do what one does with photographic apparatus suspended from a pigeon's neck, and our bombardment will be as precise as that of French 75s."

The engineer's face lit up. "Gorski," he said, "You're a credit to the fatherland, and that apparatus will bear both our names." He extended his hand, open for a cordial shake.

The workman took a step back. "No, no," he said, to hide the disturbance he felt. "My name is that of a simple manual worker. You've been the mind; you should have the honor— it's only just."

"Gorski," said the engineer, firmly, "It will be as I say, for what I say is in accordance with justice. The apparatus will bear your name. Within a month, we'll have constructed it and realized your plan. The minister, to whom Mohr has introduced me, is impatiently awaiting the results of our endeavor. To work, then! To work!"

After three weeks of hard work, a little airplane was flying around a tightly sealed hangar, and at the determined moment, dropped a bomb on a determined point.

"It's understood, then," said Jude Iagow, "The army commission will meet tomorrow on the experimental field. You'll be by my side. Yes, yes, in putting you at my height, I'm obeying the order of my conscience. With regard to the fatherland, you've become my equal. I ought not to hide anything from you any longer. Then again, it's necessary. Human beings are fragile. This period of excessive work, succeeding my accident, has worn me out. I might collapse and die at any moment. It's necessary that someone else should take my place and realize my—our—work and bring it into the domain of action. You alone can do that, Gorski. The definitive formulae are locked in the safe in my study. The secret combination is..."

"Shh!" said Nitchef, going pale.

"Why? You're worthy of it, and I owe it to you. The password that opens the safe is NADIA. If I die, you'll find everything necessary there. Furthermore, by a clause that I'm going to add immediately to my testament, I'll determine that you alone have the right to touch those papers, and you alone will supervise the manufacture of the silent powder."

Vladimir Obrenovitch was flabbergasted. Jude Iagow had just surrendered himself. Jude Iagow had just surrendered his fatherland.

He, Nitchef, had obtained something he could sell for an enormous price. He only had to go to Mohr and say to him: "Give me five million, ten million, and I'll give you the silent powder. Germany will be victorious! What does it matter to me? I'm a citizen of the world, and the quarrels of nations leave me indifferent. With your gold, I'll live and be happy. Give it to me!"

Why did the nihilist not budge? Why was his head bowed? Why was his fist clenched? What thought as upsetting him? What did he want to do? Was it so terrible, since he was making as if to flee?

He stopped. His gaze met that of his chief. "No," he said, "I don't want that."

"Why not?"

"Because..."

His hand had already seized the white wig that he wore when there was a knock on the door of the hanger, and Ivan's voice shouted: "Father, come quickly. Nadia's very ill, and Dr. Mohr is asking for you."

THE TAUBE

"Papa! Papa! Please don't leave me!"

"But my darling, I have to go to the factory. Gorski's waiting for me. I'll be back in an hour."

"No, no, I don't want you to."

Feverishly, Nadia clung on to her father's neck with her tiny clenched hands.

For two days Nadia had retained him, anxiously, by her bedside. If, when she fell into an agitated sleep, the engineer tried to slip out of the room, the invalid perceived it immediately and went into a crisis of despair. Calm only returned when the paternal hand closed gently on her own.

And Jude Iagow thought about his invention. The army commission had arranged to meet him the next day at one o'clock. It ought to be his own hands that would enclose the *Mortem Fulgurans* apparatus, as he called it, in the armored truck that would transport it to the experimental field. He could, of course, entrust it to Gorski, but he preferred to be present.

Besides which, he was experiencing a vague apprehension. He thought about this collaborator's refusal to appear beside him and the gesture he had sketched as he said "Because..." Ivan had intervened. Then he had left, in haste, his paternal heart turned upside-down by the doctor's summons. If Mohr was demanding his presence, it was because the matter was serious, The memory of the singular scene had come back to him later. What had Gorski meant?

He had, in consequence, a double reason for wanting to get back to the factory at any price.

Impossible! The fragile chain of that little arm extended toward him kept him riveted to the sick-bed.

For the tenth time, he had tried to escape; for the tenth time, Nadia had prevented him from doing so.

He made a gesture of fatigue and anger against fatality.

"You were wrong to excite the child, my dear Damidoff," said Mohr, who had just arrived and had witnessed the scene from the antechamber. I told you that she's going through a very serious phase, and I can't guarantee anything."

"However, doctor, it's necessary that I make a flying visit to the factory. My presence there is a capital necessity."

"Bah! The shells will be manufactured without you. Once the impetus is imparted, the machine runs."

"Oh, it's not so much that as my invention. It's ready. Ready, you hear?"

Mohr's eyes had a sharp gleam behind his spectacles.

"It's ready," Jude Iagow went on, becoming excited, "and time is pressing. Our forces are retreating at the rate of a verst per day. In three weeks, the others could be here."

"Bah!" said the scientist, laughing. "How you go on!"

"So be it—let's say half a verst a day; even so, they're advancing. It's necessary that when they get here, they find something to reckon with."

"La la, my dear boy—not so much excitement. Truly, you're alarming me. You work too hard. Your eyes are magnifying things."

"I see things as they are, alas! And I want to save my country, Mohr, do you hear? And I can save her!

The scientist's face contracted strangely.

"You don't believe it?" exclaimed the inventor, who perceived that. "You don't think my discovery is capable of rendering Russia an incalculable service? No, Then you, like the vulgar, are skeptical and blind to the truth. Why, then did you offer me a fortune in exchange for it?"

Jude Iagow had marched toward his savior, his arms folded.

"Come on, Damidoff, calm down," said the latter, in a tranquil tone. If I hadn't believed in you, would I have allowed Marie Sergines—my ward, so to speak—to furnish you with the capital? Who introduced you to the Minister of War?"

"That's true," the engineer replied, his anger dying away as if by magic. "Forgive me doctor; I'm in a state. Just think—

at the moment when I'm reaching my goal, a disaster is threatening me."

The unfortunate father pointed at his daughter, whose burning cheeks were like two bloody patches on the white sheet.

Mohr made an evasive gesture. "That's life..."

A violent detonation punctuated his sentence, shattering the windows into a thousand pieces.

Jude Iagow looked up.

An immense bird with crooked wings and a bifurcated tail, whose steel carapace was sparkling in the light of the setting sun as if it were made of crystal, had just appeared in the cloudless sky. The engineer immediately thought of the Apocalypse of St, John, in which the apostle announced the advent of legions of evil angels spitting fire and flaming sulfur over miserable humans forgetful of divine law.

"A Taube!" cried voices in the street.[29]

The armored aircraft, indifferent to the intersecting fire of machine guns, insolent and placid, was describing concentric circles around the city. It seemed to be searching for a precise point somewhere over the city. Having reached that point, it released a bomb and resumed its circling in order to come back to it.

"It's bombarding the field-hospital at the Refuge," someone said.

Mohr sniggered odiously. The engineer did not see it; he was leaning out of the window seeking information. He had

---

[29] The Taube [Dove], a monoplane designed by the Austro-Hungarian Igo Etrich, was the first aircraft mass-produced in Germany, by Edmund Rumpler, in 1910. It was also the first from which (very small) bombs were dropped, by Italian aircraft operating in Libya. Taubes were used to drop similar bombs over Paris, along with propaganda leaflets, late in 1914, presumably inspiring this episode, but the design had been superseded by the end of that year, and was replaced by various models of Albatros and Fokker.

just thought about Ivan, Marie Sergines and Georges Chantepie, three dear individuals, risking death at that moment. The bombs were falling with clockwork regularity. The aviator was making a sport of it.

"It's said that there's a signal," said a passer-by to the anxious inventor. "Yes, a signal installed on the roof of the hospital."

"Who is the wretch...?" wondered Jude Iagow, turning abruptly to the scientist.

The latter started involuntarily. "Oh, it's not...." He stopped, and went on, very coldly: "Oh, these people see espionage everywhere. A signal on the field-hospital! I ask you!"

At that moment, a banner dropped from the Taube unfurled in the wind, and, graciously offering to all gazes the colors of Germany, descended in a fluttering spiral, while the aircraft disappeared westwards, as read as a streak of fire.

The emblazoned strip came to land on the sill of the window where the engineer was standing. He grabbed it.

"Look!" he cried. "Read this! The insolent individual!"

"Greetings to the people of Warsaw from Lieutenant Hermann. We're coming. See you soon."

"Oh, you're coming!" sniggered Pierre Damidoff's heir, straightening up. "Well. we'll welcome you!"

He took a step toward the door.

"Father!" cried Nadia.

The engineer leaned over his daughter, and kissed her with a passionate tenderness.

"I have to," he murmured.

He replaced Nadia on her pillows, and released the hand clenched on his sleeve, with difficulty. The child went into a frightful fit. She turned violet. She was choking.

"You'll kill her," pronounced Dr. Mohr. "If you take another step, she might die. Who knows, Perhaps Ivan is..."

Jude Iagow hesitated, but he crumpled the banner in his hand.

"They're going to come," he said.

"You alone can watch over your child," the doctor insisted. "I'd gladly stay myself, but I'm receiving the officers of the sector over at the sanitarium tomorrow, and I ought to..."

"I have to," Jude Iagow repeated. "Let God's will be done." And at a firm pace, sacrificing his child to the fatherland, he went out, refusing to hear the agonized croak that escaped Nadia's contracted throat, and refusing the atrocious vision of his son's body torn apart by bombs.

In the antechamber, he took his hat off the peg. A piece of paper fell out of it. Astonished, he picked it up and read it.

"If the formulae and drawings of the invention are not deposited at the Muller Bank this evening, Jude Iagow, the author of the attempted regicide of 27 July, will be enounced to the police, and the Bargineff factories will be blown up."

He was momentarily stunned. Jude Iagow? The attempted regicide? What was this...? Oh yes! The reality was suddenly revealed to him, fulgurant. But he crumpled the note and threw it on the ground with a forceful gesture.

"No," he said.

And he went out.

THE FLYING BOMB

A little joy had returned to the abode of the little Countess. Nadia was getting better rapidly.

When Jude Iagow had come back from the factory he had thought he would find himself in the presence of his daughter's corpse; in the contrary, he had seen her sleeping peacefully. The bombs dropped on the field-hospital had only caused superficial damage, and that morning, Marie Sergines and Ivan being free, they had set up the dining table next to the bed in which the little girl was twittering like a bird. The gentle hostess, so pretty in her military nurse's uniform was smiling.

"I congratulate you on your courage," said Jude Iagow, marveling at her calm and freshness. "Truly, you have the heart of a soldier."

"Not entirely," Marie Sergines replied, softly. "I confess that I'm mortally afraid."

"That didn't prevent you," Ivan exclaimed, "from carefully supervising the evacuation of the wounded into the basements. Georges Chantepie was unable to hide his admiration."

"Is he better?" asked the engineer.

"He's saved," replied the young aristocrat, "thanks to the good Dr. Mohr, who has employed all his science in caring for him."

"A worthy man!" concluded Jude Iagow. "We owe him a great deal. We can never thank him enough. Beneath a sometimes troubling appearance..."

"An aged scientist has the right to be a trifle eccentric," Marie Sergines remarked.

"Certainly!" agreed the engineer. "He has an excellent heart; and if he's—how shall I put it?—a trifle…jealous, that's just human nature. I don't like him any the less for it—don't you agree Ivan?"

173

The adolescent had lowered his eyes to his plate a moment before. At his father's question, an icy chill ran through him.

"Yes," he said, evasively. "I'm impatient to get to this evening," he added, in order to change the subject.

"Oh!" exclaimed the radiant inventor. "You're in a hurry! Well, so am I. How much work, my God! What a struggle! What obstacles! In the end, I have no regrets: the victory is won."

"And what a victory!" said the little Countess, with a gleam of pride in her eyes. "You'll have saved Russia!"

"After the valiant men who are defending her and serving her, Marie Sergines," the inventor replied, gravely, "But obviously, that doesn't diminish the importance of the discovery. Fundamentally, it's a mere bagatelle: producing an effect in a field impenetrable to our senses. It's not impossible, but it was necessary to think of it. And think, Marie Sergines, think about that frightful thing: silent death; that unrevealed force, which passes by and smashes everything, people and things. You can see from fear the terror multiplying the prodigious force of these bombs tenfold; you can see from here the hordes fleeing the mystical assassins; for beneath their gross materialism, superstition persists, the belief in sorcerers and phantoms. They still see nature as their ancestors saw it, with the Totem protective of the tribe. They're the tree and the tree is them. By the nail embedded in the trunk they pin evil spirits therein, imprisoned forever, but no matter how many nails they hammer in, they'll never be able to pin down the silent death. Their fate is inevitable. In two hours, at the most, the army commission will have adopted the *Mortem Fulgurans* aircraft; within a month, the factory will be installed, the machines will be active; in two months, the first bombs will turn Teutonic fury into terror."

Listening to his father, Ivan shivered with joy and pride. He looked at him, as if he were looking at a genie; he admired him and venerated him. Oh, how proud he was to be that man's son!

The clock chimed one. Jude Iagow started.

"I'm talking, I'm talking," he said, laughing, and I'm forgetting the unforgettable!" He leapt to his feet. "They're waiting for me, aren't they?"

Impetuously, he kissed Ivan and Nadia, kissed Marie Sergines' hand, and ran to get dressed.

He was alert. He felt as if he went twenty years old.

The previous evening, on arriving at the factory, he had found Gorski standing sentinel before the chest in which he enclosed the silent bomb, whose key he had taken away with him. He had darted a final glance at his invention. Everything was intact, shining, delicate, finished like a precision instrument. Then he had seized his collaborator's hand and, in a transport of sincere joy and gratitude, had said: "Thank you!"

But the electrician had withdrawn his hand, as if the contact had burned him. An expression of unspeakable suffering and despair had passed over his face. He had opened his mouth, as if he wanted to speak, but he had immediately fallen back into a somber mutism.

What's biting him? Jude Iagow had wondered.

The care of loading the chest into an armored truck, which was to transport the apparatus to the test ground, chased away the cloud that had formed in his thoughts.

When the auto-taxi, taken when he emerged from the house, deposited him at the field, he had forgotten the incident. A truck sealed with a triple lock and surrounded by a picket of soldiers, armed with rifles, was waiting for him.

No indiscreet curiosity had been able to reach the aircraft.

The delegates from the Ministry of War appeared.

The engineer advanced toward them and greeted them.

"My collaborator will be here before long," he said. "I want him to be present."

A quarter of an hour went by, then half an hour. Gorski did not appear.

The general presiding over the commission gave the order to proceed. The apparatus was taken out of the vehicle.

Jude Iagow commenced the demonstration, but suddenly stopped. The apparatus seemed to be incomplete. One piece had been warped, a wing had been broken, and the bomb had disappeared. The aircraft could to longer fly. The experiment was aborted.

"This is an unfortunate setback," he said, containing his irritation. "Tomorrow, everything will be in order."

The officers withdrew, while the engineer, replacing the apparatus in the truck, noticed a large hole in the steel platform. Someone had used a blowtorch to melt the double metal wall.

Has the bomb been stolen? he wondered. *Or might Gorski be the author of this sabotage? Out of jealousy? But I acted honesty toward him. Oh, men!*

He sighed, and was giving orders to the soldier driving the truck to go back to the factory when he heard his name called. He turned around. He was confronted by a uniformed officer.

"Colonel Archinef?" he said "The chief of police?"

"The same," said the Colonel. "Tell me—it's been reported that a wireless telegraph apparatus is installed in the cellars of the Bargineff factory."

"Espionage mania," the engineer replied, coolly.

"My God, we receive anonymous denunciations every day—but the police have a duty not to let anything go uninvestigated, so I shall go back with you. It won't take long; I've been told exactly where I'll discover the wireless equipment. Let's go,"

"But Colonel," said the engineer, with a calm that would have seemed terrible to anyone who could look into his heart, "there's no need, I assure you. There isn't, and can't be a traitor in the factory. I can answer for all my workers and employees, as for myself."

"Hmm! Are you quite certain?"

"I..."

"It's also reported in the letter that the worker Gorski, who has become your intimate collaborator...as if by chance…is none other than a dangerous nihilist whom you hid and fed in your house for a year under the name of Nitchef?"

"You're saying…?"

"Not me, Damidoff, not me—the letter. The letter also says that you are affiliated to nihilism and that, in concert with the pretended deaf-mute Nitchef, you perpetrated the attempted regicide of last 27 July. I don't believe a…why, Damidoff, what's wrong?"

Jude Iagow had just beaten the air with his hands and collapsed, an inert mass, at Colonel Archinef's feet.

BROKEN TIES

The day before it was to be presented to the examination committee, the "terrestrial comet" had been carefully placed in the truck, and the truck parked in a garage.

The inventor and his collaborator had supervised the operation.

"I'll spend the night here," Nitchef had said.

The bell rang. The day shift had left the factory and had been replaced by the night shift, considerably less numerous. More than half of the immense workplace was plunged into complete darkness.

Lying down under the truck, Nitchef was asleep. He was woken up abruptly. Two knees were crushing his chest. Something was stuffed into his mouth. He was then gagged and tied up, in the blink of an eye.

Nitchef doubtless recognized the technique, for he thought: *Michael Gregor! I shouldn't have forgotten about him.*

A hooded lantern was unmasked. Two men were carefully circling the regimental vehicle.

"Armored," said one, pulling a face. "It's going to be difficult."

The two bandits tried to force the locks, but could not do it.

"We'll never get it out," said the second, in German. "There's only one thing we can do—make a hole with a blowtorch and try to take out the bomb."

"Let's try underneath," advised the first—who was, indeed, none other than Michael Gregor, number Thirteen.

The acetylene torch was dragged under the platform. After an hour, the result obtained was meager; they had discovered that the chest containing the aircraft was itself armored. It was necessary to be content with making a hole through which the bomb could be extracted and the apparatus damaged.

178

"That's Iagow stymied," sniggered number Thirteen.

"While awaiting tomorrow's dance with the Colonel."

The bandits' laughter was so sinister that Nitchef shivered. What dance were they talking about?

"Before then, let's see if the other wants to talk."

The men returned to their prisoner. Thirteen put a dagger to his throat.

"Do you want to reach an understanding with us?"

"Yes," groaned Nitchef.

"You'll give us the formulae, then?" asked Mohr's satellite, removing the gag.

"Yes, since you have the upper hand." The nihilist got to his feet. "Follow me, then—are you coming?"

"You go first," said the spy, replacing the gag. "At the first false move, you know that I'll kill you."

They went all the way through the part of the factory plunged in darkness. They arrived, without any inconvenience, at a stairway leading down to the basements.

After following a few short corridors they arrived at the workshop where the silent powder had been produced.

Number Thirteen closed the door and removed the prisoner's gag again.

"Where?" he asked.

"Untie my hands."

"Be careful!"

"You're stupid. Don't I hate Russia? I've done everything possible to forget, but I can't. Without those swine, would my mother have sold me?"

Those words had been pronounced in a tone of such sincerity that Mohr's two associates were convinced.

Once freed, Vladimir pulled away an immense oak dresser standing against the wall. Flasks and test-tubes were kept in it. Two seconds later, a panel in the wall opened and revealed a cellar some two sagenes deep. There was a chest there, with tools and aircraft components.

"Open the chest," Nitchef instructed Number Twenty-Four. "The formulae are inside."

Unsuspiciously, the other did as he was told. The cellar door closed on him like the door of a sepulcher, and while he shot the bolt with his left hand, Obrenovitch seized an enormous hammer that was lying on the ground, straightened up and smashed Michel Gregor's skull with a single blow.

The scene had only lasted a second.

Having done that, deaf to Twenty-Four's appeals, he pushed the dresser back against the wall and left.

He went to the sleazy hotel-room in which he lived. He had something to eat and drink, and went to bed. The next morning, he spent a long time pacing back and forth in his room, taking long drags on a cigarette, his mind elsewhere.

He went out at about eleven o'clock.

He went back to the factory, went down to the cellars, moved Gregor's corpse away with his foot and opened the cellar in which the spy he had imprisoned was moaning.

"Come," he said, harshly.

"Where?" demanded the other, whose face still bore the traces of the frightful anguish that he had endured.

"To the police, of course."

"Oh, no, no!" cried the other. "No, let me go. Listen, Vladimir—I'll tell you a great secret. You can still save your life, but let me go, I beg you. Listen, Number Forty-Eight—we only know one another by numbers—you know, Number Forty-Eight, who wanted to call a strike on your behalf?"

"Yes. Well?"

"Well, he's installed a Bickford fuse[30] that goes from an electric switch at the Mohr hospice—the same plant supplies us with electricity—to a powder bunker in this work-yard."

"So?" the nihilist interrogated, anxiously.

---

[30] William Bickford was the inventor of the slow-burning safety fuse, consisting of gunpowder surrounded by a varnished jute cord, which helped miners to avoid accidents while working with explosives. The term is obviously being used very loosely here to refer to an electrical wire used to trigger an explosion at a distance.

"So? The whole place is going to blow up, do you see? I'm astonished that it hasn't been done yet."

"You're lying."

"I swear to you. Now let me go."

The nihilist did not budge.

"If you don't want to save your life," said Number Twenty-Four, "I want to ransom mine. Let me go warn..."

"No! You might be lying. Go back into the cellar. Go! Hurry up!"

"But they're going to blow it up!"

"So much the worse for you. If you're crushed, that will only be one filthy beast less."

And with a blow of his fist, Nitchef knocked the man down and shoved him back into the hole.

In a few strides he was outside, and he ran to the director's office.

"The factory's going to blow up," he said, point-blank. "Order an evacuation."

"Blow up? The factory? Who's going to blow it up?" demanded the functionary, wiping his spectacles. "This is the tenth time I've been told that. I received an anonymous letter saying the same thing this morning. It's just like this story of the wireless apparatus! A wireless, I ask you! And installed by Damidoff, no less! Damidoff! Humph!"

The director shrugged his shoulders.

Nitchef became increasingly anxious. What he had just learned about the accusation made against his former master strengthened his conviction that Michael Gregor's associate had not been lying. The spy's threats were being realized.

"O assure, you, sir, that..."

"But who? Once again, who is going to blow up the factory?"

"Doctor Mohr," replied the nihilist, squarely.

The functionary was astonished. He looked at his worker as if considering a phenomenon.

"You're mad," he said. And he threw him out.

"Damn! said Nitchef, as he left, crushed by the weight of fatality. "Who will believe me? Who can believe Mohr capable of such a crime? It's written."

He headed toward the experimental field, and had reached the road leading to it when he recognized Colonel Archinef in an automobile arriving at top speed, and lying next to him, the inert body of Jude Iagow.

At that moment, an unknown, irresistible force lifted the vehicle up and slammed it against a wall, which collapsed, while he was blown away like a feather for a considerable distance.

A frightful cataclysm had just occurred.

THE ROC'S EGG

One man had provoked the frightful event that had just transformed an entire sector on the outskirts of Warsaw into a chaos of ruins. That man was Jude Iagow's persecutor, Dr. Mohr.

He had gathered the officers from the nearby fortress in a room at the hospice for a kind of party, and we find him, shortly after the catastrophe, in conversation with the general in command of the sector.

"It's agreed, my dear Doctor," the soldier is saying. "In accordance with your wishes, your sanitarium is requisitioned in order to be transformed into a field-hospital. We'll soon have need of it."

"I'm entirely at your orders, General, and staff too. All my patients will be transferred to Moscow, to my annex. I can put two thousand beds at your disposal."

"I accept. In addition, we might establish our general headquarters here. It's a strategic location of the first order. We're overlooking the city, the valley of the Vistula and twenty versts of the plain. If you'd installed yourself here with a military intention you couldn't have picked a better spot."

"Oh, General," Dr. Mohr replied, modestly, "in matters of strategy, I only know that which is known as therapeutic. It has one point of conformity with yours, though: it combats enemy legions, albeit infinitely small ones: microbes, not macrobes. It attacks them and disperses them with oxygen bullets instead of metal ones. But there are also important differences: mine loves nature and the rural sites she protects; your battalions of workers fell centenarian trees and dig up the virgin soil to excavate trenches and blockhouses, and create ruination where mine create life. Look at my park and those gutted pavilions."

With a despairing gesture, the old savant pointed through the open window at the hill and the valley, ravaged by an army of soldiers who were preparing defenses on the approach to Warsaw.

"What do you expect, my dear Mohr? Beauty is nothing when the life of a nation is at stake. A pretty woman is ready to sacrifice the vanities of her visage to escape death."

"Alas, yes," groaned the old man. "That is the rule!"

The reception was in full swing. Everyone was swilling champagne and smoking excellent cigars; everyone was chatting. No one would have thought, on seeing those calm faces and tranquil eyes that the majority of those men had escaped from recent carnage and were fully expecting to die in a struggle that could only end with the final crushing of one of the belligerents.

Not having sufficient munitions, the army sent to meet the Austro-Germans was being driven back step by step, opposing their moving walls to the invader, bristling with nothing but bayonets. It was retreating, and the officers present expected the anticipated fatal blow with perfect stoicism.

They were talking about anything except the invisible presence that everyone felt: that of death. The believers had long since consigned themselves to the will of God; of the rest, those who were lettered, were thinking about Plato's dialogues on the immortality of the soul and trying to model themselves on the noble figure of Socrates; others were still trying to stifle the mysterious voice of conscience evoking truths that they had never wanted to hear.

They talked about hunting, racing, social gatherings, while gazes continually strayed, in an intrigued fashion, toward two objects situated in the middle of the room. one placed on a kind of pedestal wrapped in green velvet, the other suspended above it from a crystal chandelier.

The former was a statuette of a nymph whose fingertips were holding a delicately-fashioned flower, the pistil of which offered the aspect of a little emerald bulb: the statuette that we have previously seen on the scientist's desk. Its artistic beauty had doubtless earned it the honor of a proud solitude in the middle of the reception-room.

The other was, or appeared to be, a nickel bomb. Probably with the idea of paying court to the soldiers, the eccentric host had thought such an ornament appropriate. Perhaps, too, it was simply a souvenir offered by a wounded man returned from the front-line trenches, and perhaps it had been hung up there without attaching any further importance to it.

Nevertheless, the question that was on the hovering on everyone's lips eventually came to those of General Damidieff, with whom Mohr was talking at that very moment.

"Would you like to explain to me, Doctor, what that bomb is? It is a bomb, isn't it? I've never seen one like it. One might think that it were some nihilist plaything."

"I'll tell you in a moment," the old man replied, having been summoned into the next room by the ringing of a telephone.

"Hello?" he said, when he had carefully closed the doors and picked up the receiver. Is that you, Thirteen?.... No, he didn't come back last night... Curious!.... At the factory?.... Yes, undoubtedly... Iagow?... In conversation with the Colonel?.... They'll be at the factory in ten minutes—perfect! Well, don't wait—get out. Warn you know who... Thirteen, Twenty-Four and Forty-Eight?... Well, too bad for them. Goodbye!"

As Mohr headed back to the reception room he muttered: "The lives of three men are nothing. There are many others who fall without knowing why. Too bad! As for Jude Iagow, he asked for it."

When Mohr returned to the General, his attitude had changed; there was something simultaneously solemn and sinister about it.

During his absence his servants had arranged tables in the form of a horse-shoe, in such a way that the statuette and the bomb were at the point where all gazes converged, half a sagene from the Doctor. With the General beside him, Mohr gave a singal. A hidden band struck up the national hymn. The audience listened to it standing up.

"Gentlemen," he old man said thereafter, raising his glass, "a solemn hour has just chimed over the world. Something great and immense is about to surge forth from a point in space and extend its wings over the world. That force is lodged in the shiny ball that you can see there. That ball in not a bomb; it's a roc's egg. The phoenix is reposing within it, waiting until it can escape and begin its irresistible flight. You won't hear that flight; it's muffled by silence. It will sow fear in the most intrepid heart and strike with death the power that I execrate will all the strength of my soul."

"Yes, death to Germany!" cried the officers, with a common voice, raising their foaming glasses. "Death to Germany and long live the Emperor!"

Death to Russia and long live Wilhelm, Emperor of the World! thought Mohr, as motionless and icy as a sphinx.

And with a violent gesture, as if he wanted to punctuate his guests' cry of enthusiasm, he struck the emerald ampoule of the statuette.

A mighty roar, hoarse and profound, originating from the confines of the valley, rose toward the soldiers, standing there petrified, while a great sound of breaking glass mingled with the impact of a multitude of little stones raining down from the sky.

The earth trembled. A kind of meteor passed overhead, whining.

Then there was silence: a deathly silence.

The Bargineff factories had just blown up.

PART FOUR

THE PAST

A splinter of wood that pierced his thigh at the moment when the automobile was hurled against the wall, provoking an abundant hemorrhage, saved Jude Iagow from madness or death. Pulled out of the wreckage along with Colonel Archinef and transported to the infirmary of the police station, he received immediate medical attention.

Two days later, he was strong enough to declare himself ready to fight.

Mute and calm, he watched the search made of the lodgings that Marie Sergines had accorded to him. He kissed Nadia and Ivan, lavishing recommendations to courage upon them. The little Countess had promised to consider Nadia as her sister, so he had no anxieties n that subject.

"You can see," he said to Colonel Archinef, "that there's nothing here. You wouldn't have found any more at the factory."

"I'm almost convinced," the officer replied, skeptical by nature as well as by profession. "We're going to go to X***, and I don't doubt that I'll be able to return you immediately thereafter to liberty."

"And to my duty," the engineer added, thinking about the silent bomb.

Having reached their destination, the Colonel sent for the Burgomaster. The giant with the reedy voice recounted in brief the anecdote that had concluded, to his great confusion, with the disappearance of an individual little esteemed in the neighborhood and not very respectable. No one could understand why an honorable man like Pierre Damidoff had taken in such a vagabond. The French tutor, Georges Chantepie, had claimed that he had found the fanatic tied up and stabbed when the house had been burgled. Ivan Damidoff's inconsequential action had cast doubt on the Frenchman's veracity, but tongues had wagged thereafter, and, putting two and two together, he had arrived at the conviction that the villa had been a nest of malefactors; in addition, mysterious things had been going on there when war was declared.

"I knew nothing about all this," said Jude Iagow, utterly astonished.

"Really?" said the chief of police, considering him from the corner of his eye.

"Truly."

The Colonel sat down at the engineer's desk while his agents searched the house. He opened the drawers and took stock of the papers.

Jude waited for the catastrophe; it occurred. A packet of yellowing letters was in the hands of the chief of police. With a dry click the latter tore the ribbon tying them together, and his eyebrows rose as he scanned the lines.

He looked at the engineer, and returned to the letters, which he studied one by one, reading aloud.

"*You promised me not to try to escape. Be brave, Jude Iagow. Your crime is great; you must expiate it. God will impart pity into the hearts of man. Your obedience, your repentance, will touch them; they will not be inexorable. Work and pray...*

"*Courage, courage! Why don't you have confidence in God? He has forgiven the most guilty...*

"*In a year, to the day, I shall come to see you; my saintly mother has promised. I want to save you I spite of yourself. Don't flee! Perhaps I shall bring you at least a distant hope of salvation. Be good, be just...pray...*"

Then there were letters in masculine handwriting.

"*I can't wait any longer. It's settled; I have to get out of the hell of the mine. I have to, or I'll go mad. Forgive me. Think about it: in perpetuity! To die here, far from every-*

one...in the frightful darkness. No, No! I can't. I have to escape!"

Another letter from the woman:

"*I don't have the courage to reject you, Jude, to send you back. It's wrong of me, but I'm a woman; I'm weak. I feel pity for you. And then, I can't destroy the work of a dying man, the work of a brave man. He's bequeathed you his name. Let it be that of an honest man, a Christian. Work, and when I've seen that you're entirely won over by verity, when I judge that you're the man I want for a husband, I'll grant you my hand. We'll bear the burden of the past together, until the day when you can demand to appear among men with your true name. Oh, that day of rehabilitation will be a glad one!*"

Alas, Anna Erloff had died without having seen that triumphant day. Would it ever come?

Those letters, poignant and touching by turns, did not have the ability to import any emotion into the stony heart of the Colonel. If they troubled his mind, it was by showing him that a redoubtable criminal had been living within arm's reach without him having the slightest suspicion of it.

What! A nihilist guilty of a frightful crime, a convict in violation of his banishment, had been able to hide with impunity beneath the features of correct, devoted functionary full of abnegation, and he had not had the perspicacity to sniff him out, to discover and unmask him? He had been able to speak him, shake his hand, eat by his side at official diners, grant him an honorable place in corteges formed to greet the Tsar, without experiencing the obscure anxiety that denounces danger? Jude Iagow! Jude Iagow! What policeman did not know the name of Jude Iagow? What anthropometric service did not permit his measurements? He had held the man's photograph in his hand many a time, and had not been struck by the resemblance? Imbecile!

"Ha ha ha!" he muttered, between his teeth. "He'll pay for that."

His fist came down on the desk.

At that moment, a policeman arrived, very alarmed.

"Colonel, we've just found this timer. The metal is exactly the same as that found on the track after the attempt against the Little Father—and to judge by what we've been taught about nihilist inventions, this timer had no other objective."

"Perhaps not," the police officer replied. "It rather represents a rough draft, groping toward the decisive confection. Where did you find it?"

"In the laboratory."

"Ah! There's a laboratory? Seize this man and bring him along."

In the blink of an eye, the policeman had put the engineer in handcuffs. He took him by the arm and dragged him toward the garden.

"Colonel," exclaimed Jude Iagow, when they reached the laboratory, "explain! What has this to do with the attempted assassination, about which I know nothing at all? When it occurred, I was plunged into a kind of torpor at Dr. Mohr's hospice."

"That's to be determined," replied the chief of police. "In the meantime, I'm charging you with the perpetration of a crime of regicide, and placing you under arrest. In any case, you're and escaped convict, and that's sufficient."

"But..."

"You can answer to a military court. Take him away!"

And Jude Iagow was obliged to leave the villa and go through the assembled crowd in handcuffs. The man who might have saved the fatherland was no more, in the eyes of the world, than a criminal and a villain.

How could the world think otherwise?

At that moment, all heads bowed, and, hearted constrained by dread, men and women alike recommended themselves to God. A 429 shell had just passed overhead, howling through the sky. Six versts west of X***, the victorious Germans had installed a heavy battery, and they were bombarding Warsaw.

UNDER THE SHELLING

Ivan Iagow was thinking about his father and waiting anxiously for an opportunity that would permit him to launch an investigation that he wanted to undertake by himself, and which he had sworn to carry through to the end.

While devoting himself to his duties at the refuge, he ruminated his thoughts.

The wretch who denounced my father, he said to himself, *has his days of rest numbered; he won't enjoy impunity much longer. With God's help—and he will help me—I'll unmask him. That's a piece of paper that couldn't have come from a humble paper shop or the lodgings of a factory-worker. It was on the desk of a rich man, and comes from the famous Leipzig factory.*

As he went past a window, the adolescent took out of his pocket the note that had fallen out of his father's hat, which he had picked up. For the hundredth time he examined its translucency. The wing of an eagle stood out clearly, along with the three letters ICK.

"Moreover," he said, "the handwriting is that of an educated man, of a hand used to manipulating a pen skillfully. I'll find out, and we'll see whether my suspicions are justified."

Why—reluctantly—did Ivan Iagow pronounce the name of Mohr?

He put the sheet of paper in his notebook, and ran to a wounded man who was asking for something to drink.

"Thank you!" said the soldier, when he had quenched his thirst—and, fixing his burning eyes on his, he said: "What news?"

"Good, good," he replied. "We'll have them!"

He fled, not wanting to allow the dolorous contraction of his features to be seen.

Added to his personal sufferings, in fact, were the sufferings of the fatherland. The danger was becoming urgent. The

191

evacuation of the official services was said to have commenced. Eventual success was not in doubt, but the ordeal would be terrible. Ivan could sense it coming, and he stiffened himself against the animal need to give way to discouragement.

No, no, he said to himself, *I won't weaken.*

A distant detonation punctuated his sentence.

He ran to the church and prostrated himself at the foot of the tabernacle. When he got up, he felt better.

As he emerged from the church, the first accurately targeted shell fell on the field-hospital; previous ones had so far only reached the outskirts of the city, but now the shells were falling with clockwork regularity.

When he reached the refuge, he found the governor general in conference with Dr. Mohr and Marie Sergines.

It was decided that the wounded would be evacuated to another city, transported by railway.

"I'll go with them, then," said the little Countess. "Afterwards, I'll come back."

"No, Marie Sergines," the good doctor interjected. "Your aid will be precious to me for my field-hospital. The battles are getting closer and closer, and I can foresee the moment when I'll be overflowing. I need you and all your staff. Although the Germans aren't respecting the city, perhaps they'll respect my sanitarium."

With a quiver of joy, Ivan heard the Countess accede to the doctor's proposal.

The adolescent went with the little Countess to the house where he had spent such cruel hours. She had taken Nadia with her and installed the child in a luxuriously-furnished basement. Mohr had arranged things well.

During the week that the preparation of the field-hospital lasted, the engineer's son did not have a moment to himself. However, he kept an eye on the wing of the building surmounted by the dome, which was reserved for the scientist.

Father's salvation is there, he said to himself. *I'll get in there.*

But there a strong guard was maintained on that part of the building; a Herculean orderly turned away all indiscreet individuals pitilessly.

And the Germans were getting closer every day.

One morning, the hill filled up with defenders. Then a furious cannonade began—but the sanitarium remained a kind of islet of calm and security in the midst of the cataclysm that was turning the region upside-down.

As the abyss attracts humans, the battle exercised a strange fascination on the adolescent's nerves. He experienced the irresistible fear that drives you into a corner where you stupidly seek shelter behind a clod of earth. He experienced the mental conflicts against stupidity and the prideful triumph of the soul. He experienced the irresistible surges that make you clench your fist around an imaginary weapon in order to run into the battle and take part in the carnage.

One day, he could stand it no longer. He set out with a party of stretcher-bearers and went with them to search for men wounded by bullets. He witnessed scenes splendid in their simplicity: military priests gliding between the combatants to bring back a wounded man or console a dying one. And he accomplished his duty, animated by that example, with a composure of which he would not have thought himself capable.

It was in the course of one of these excursions, in the heart of the action, that he brought the aid of his alert youth to a man: a brave combatant whom despair, in the face of inevitable disaster had finally seized by the throat...to Georges Chantepie.

COUPS DE THÉÂTRE

"Oof! To be shelled for sixty hours running, without being able to respond—what a fag! Finally, the food's here and the feast's beginning! Hold hard, lads! First gun, fire! Second gun, fire!"

And for the first time in three long days, the two guns commanded by Sub-Lieutenant Georges Chantepie spat out long jets of flame, followed by a wisp of smoke and a hoarse cough.

The battery was installed directly opposite the Damidoff villa, in a thicket of the park adjoining the manor house of the Polish woman. Two hundred sagenes away, in front of a double line of trenches, a barricade blocked the exit from the village of X***—or rather, what was left of it.

A few houses were still standing, opened up like houses of cards; others had melted into impalpable debris and were displaying, through their blasted walls, humble village interiors. The Damidoff villa had only lost its roof. As for the manor house, the upper story had been carried away by a blast as if sliced by a knife, but, in spite of reiterated orders, Madame Wandowska had refused to quit its ruins, and remained there, impassive, or rocking her dead daughter's dolls, with the old muzjik and his wife, under the rain of shells that swept the park and the forest.

Above the manor rose the gradual slope of the hill, laid bare like a field of wheat after the passage of the harvester. At its summit, Dr. Mohr's sanitarium loomed up, intact, doubtless protected by the banner of the Red Cross—which, it is true, had not been able to protect the field-hospital at the Refuge, transformed into a heap of ashes a fortnight earlier.

The complete annihilation of the Bargineff factories, which normally furnished the sector with its contingent of shells, had dealt a formidable blow to the defense. The Austro-Germans had been able to gain ground, advancing step by step, albeit at the price of terrible hecatombs. Their success had been halted by the Sacred Hill, the ultimate buttress of Warsaw.

For a week, an intense cannonade had been raging against it, but the order had been given to keep going to the death, and it was being obeyed.

Georges Chantepie, scarcely recovered, had replaced a fallen sub-lieutenant—the third—at a moment's notice beside the two guns under his command. He had been forbidden to fire a shot until it was absolutely essential—which is to say that he had had to endure fire without returning it, doing nothing until an enemy attack was launched.

That moment, long-awaited—with such impatience!—under a sixty-hour rain of fire, finally arrived, and the Frenchman, with an evident delight and a certain relief, gave the command so dearly desired.

The Germans were emerging from the village in ranks of four, to the sound of their shrill fifes.

"First gun, fire!"

The shell departed; two hundred meters away, it burst.

The first three ranks were scythed down.

"Close ranks!"

The orders given in a guttural voice were audible to the defenders during the complete calms the punctuated the howls of battle in such a strange fashion.

"Second gun, fire!"

The head of the advancing human serpent was crushed, like an egg hurled against a wall. The remainder of the body continued its advance.

"Close ranks! Close ranks!"

And the voids in the column were filled in automatically, while it gained terrain irresistibly.

In their trenches, weapons raised, the Russians waited for the assault.

Georges Chantepie's gunners were maneuvering with magnificent regularity. The shots struck home. The Germans fell, like lead soldiers knocked over by the hand of a child weary of his game.

At this rate, thought the Sub-Lieutenant, *they won't reach the trench.* "Hold hard, lads!" he shouted, suddenly. "We've got them!"

The men of the battery seemed invulnerable—but their leader had not perceived a certain ripple among the attackers and had hardly uttered his cry of triumph when one of the artillerymen stationed at the sun nearer to the hillside fell, and then a second and then a third. The men at the second gun began to fall in their turn. A machine-gunner, stationed who knew where, had targeted the battery from the side and as methodically accomplishing his deadly work.

The attackers, liberated from half the danger, advanced more resolutely. Georges Chantepie found himself alone, to load and to fire. He shivered with impotent rage.

"Aim and fire, Monsieur Chantepie," said a voice close at hand. "I'll load. I know how to how to operate the clearing mechanism."

"Ivan Iagow!" growled the Frenchman. "Get back. You aren't..."

He shut up. The adolescent had just looked at him with such an expression of astonishment, dolor and pride that the sentence was cut off cleanly.

"Well, so be it," he said, reluctantly vanquished. "But be careful—there's a traitor hidden in the wood."

"Am I afraid?" queried the convict's son, with a dignified arrogance.

While speaking, Ivan Iagow had picked up a shell and loaded it. The lieutenant fired. And the two of them, mute, with clenched teeth, indifferent to the bullets that continued to whistle past their ears, as well as to the wounds—fortunately slight—that blooded their faces and hands, did their duty heroically.

Already the Germans, numerous and well-armed, had set foot in the first trench. Already the Russians were retreating to the second, attacked from the rear and decimated by the invisible machine-gunner. Defeat was no longer in doubt. Once the Sacred Hill had been circled, the road to Warsaw was open. Ivan and Georges Chantepie took the movable breeches out of their guns, henceforth useless.

"Monsieur Chantepie," said Ivan, "As we're about to die, I swear to you that my father is an honest man. Now, good-bye—see you in the other world!"

"I believe you, Ivan," the Frenchman replied, shaking his hand. "Forgive me, and may God forgive me. Forward!"

The two of them had already launched themselves, side by side, toward the enemy, when a man—a soldier—whose face was half-hidden by a bandage, bounded out of the Damidoff villa. He had a bag slung over his shoulder, bulging with grenades and bombs. In a few strides, the man was within range of the attackers. His hand, armed with a globe of shining metal, whirled round. The object, abruptly released, described a curve and fell in the midst of the German horde.

No sound was heard but the screams of the wounded, but a kind of profound wave shook them. Another metal globe fooled the first. An enormous void opened in the compact howling mass, torn apart like a ripped piece of cloth.

Implacable, standing on a mound in defiance of the projectiles that surrounded him in a buzzing and whistling swarm, the soldier continued the series of his throws. When the bag was empty, he picked up a rifle with its bayonet fitted, and, uttering a savage roar, he launched himself forward.

The other Russians followed, and had only to plunge their weapons into backs. Fear had transformed the homogeneous troop of Wilhelm's soldiers into a herd of crazed beasts. The silent death had begun its work.

ARIADNE'S THREAD

"Now, Monsieur Chantepie, you know the plain truth in its entirety. My father was doubtless wrong to believe, in accordance with his philosophy, that the end justified the means, but he was young and his goal had grandeur. He has repaired his fault nobly. As for me, if I freed Nitchef, it was unconsciously, driven by the terror of seeing you discover my poor father's true identity. I should have trusted in your friendship. Much uncertainty and anguish would have been avoided."

"I understand the motive for your silence, my dear Ivan. In your place, perhaps I'd have done the same. Such confessions cost our pride too much. But if you have made mistakes in regard to me, I made one in regard to you, and just as great: that of relying exclusively on the tales of that wretched German, without obtaining a clear explanation from you."

"What German do you mean?" the engineer's son asked, frowning.

"Eh? Mohr! When I went to see him, anxious when you didn't emerge from the sanitarium, he told me that your father had been injured as a result of his own crime—that the gases or the shock of the blast—I'm not entirely sure—had plunged him into a profound lethargy; that you were nihilists..."

"Mohr is a German? Mohr, a German?"

Ivan had risen to his feet and was striding back and forth in the study of the villa, now open to the winds, its walls cracked or holed by bullets, its windows smashed and it shutters hanging down from their broken hinges. He stopped abruptly, and turned to face his friend, who was lighting a cigarette.

"I understand everything!" he exclaimed, with a triumphant gesture. "Come here."

The young Russian grasped the Frenchman's wrist and drew him toward an embrasure, from which the surrounding countryside was visible.

"What do you see?" he asked, feverishly. "Does nothing strike you? Well, look—here, there, there and there, houses in ruins; death and devastation everywhere. Up there, scarcely a roof chipped by a stray shell. That doesn't tell you anything? It tells me a great deal, and with good reason. The flag of the Red Cross? Was the Refuge spared? No, and that's all the more curious because there's a general headquarters up there. Now, what seems surprising, and makes the soldiers murmur, with good reason, is that our troop movements are almost always known to the enemy. I think there's a wireless telegraph installed up there. My father was accused of having set one up in the cellars of the factory. There was no proof of that, the explosion having destroyed everything, but there certainly was one, which must have corresponded with the one up there. Oh, I've thought about it, and mulled over a host of impressions and memories.

"Listen, Monsieur Chantepie. There's one thing that I haven't told you yet. One day, the day of your arrival at the field-hospital, I went to the factory to bring my father to see you. Mohr declared you doomed, barring a miracle, and I didn't want you to quit this world without having been embraced by one of the people who loved you sincerely."

The adolescent's voice trembled. Georges Chantepie squeezed his friend's hand affectionately. "Thank you," he murmured.

"As I was passing the door of a workshop," the young Russian continued, after collecting himself, "I bumped into a workman. 'Oh! Nitchef!' I exclaimed. The other remained impassive. He went on. Well, now I could swear that my instinct hadn't deceived me: that old hunchbacked and limping workman was none other than the deaf-mute taken in here by my father. The true author of the assassination attempt of 27 July is him. The manipulator of the hidden wireless at the factory is him. The probable author of the explosion of the factory is him again—for, admitted in the capacity of an electrician, he was introduced to my father by Mohr himself."

199

That's a veritable speech for the prosecution you're making there, my dear Ivan, "said Georges Chantepie, gravely.

"Yes, but the mastermind is probably Dr. Mohr, who is capable of planning the entire intrigue; he certainly holds its threads." Ivan moved so close to his companion that his lips were almost touching his ear. "And he's done even more, Monsieur Chantepie. The machine-gunner...the machine-gunner who took our troops treacherously from behind, for whom they searched and are still searching in vain..."

"Yes—go on."

"Might there not be a subterranean tunnel under the sanitarium? It's full of secret corridors. I was taken through one of them when I was transferred from the ward to the pavilion where I found Nadia and my father."

"It's possible," the Frenchman agreed, anxiously. "But where's the proof of all this? After all, you're accusing Mohr and Nitchef, but Nitchef gave evidence today of his patriotism. He saved us from a certain defeat."

"Oh, yes," said the young Russian, with an involuntary surge of pride. "The silent bomb! You've seen it at work. That's true, your observation casts doubt on my convictions on the subject of the mysterious V.O. So be it. Let's leave him. The culpability of Mohr, in my opinion, is entire."

"The proof! The proof! One doesn't attack a man like that without proof. Do you have any?"

"I have one; here it is."

The adolescent took the piece of paper bearing the watermark of the imperial eagle and the letters ICK out of his notebook, and showed them to the officer.

"If the formulae aren't deposited in an hour at the Hauptmann bank..."[31]

"A German bank," Georges Chantepie remarked.

---

[31] The author has forgotten that the note, as previously cited, referred to the Muller Bank, and gave a deadline of "this evening" rather than one hour.

"There you are—another clue," Ivan concluded, placing his finger on the name. "And I'll add that this attempt at blackmail was the last maneuver attempted for the acquisition of the silent bomb. If lightning hadn't struck the inventor, he'd have been killed and the formulae he was carrying stolen. Secondly, the false instruction I was given to send the papers via Nitchef. Thirdly, the abduction of Nadia and my own abduction. Fourthly, the tragic scene whose denouement as the resurrection of a living corpse. Promises, bargains, terror—everything was employed and everything failed, and they finally carried out the threat.

"The inventor of the silent bomb is lost to Russia because he didn't want to sell it to Germany. Do you understand, Monsieur Chantepie? The man who came to offer two or three million to my father in exchange for his discovery wasn't an eccentric, or an extreme pacifist, or a friend of humankind, or even a jealous colleague; he was a German. He would certainly have liked to have the inventor with the invention, for certain aspects of fabrication are only ever known to the former.

"Having not succeeded in buying him, circumventing him or binding him with gratitude, the German has killed the good that laid the golden eggs. Although he has the bomb, he doesn't have the formulae—but no one will have anything. He's made one error, however, for in his preoccupation, he forgot that he'd given himself away. Evil betrays itself. That piece of paper will take Mohr to the gallows. The other half of the sheet must be in his study, and I'll get it tonight."

"How will you do that?"

"Bah! In this time of war, the primitive human, with his faculties of a wild beast, has been reborn in me; I'll slip into that man's lair, and I'll find it."

"You'll have to," Georges Chantepie said, after having reflected. "Duty keeps me here; I can't follow you. Be careful."

"God will help me."

The two friends continued their conversation for a long time, discussing the chances of salvation that Jude Iagow might have. Darkness descended quietly over nature. The moon rose slowly into the sky, its sad light reflecting from the faces of the corpses heaped up in front of the trenches.

A bell rang in the distance.

"The Angelus," Ivan murmured.

The two young men knelt down and prayed.

As the Russian got to his feet, something white flew through the air, coming from behind the garden wall, and a dart fletched with a piece of paper fell at his feet.

Ivan withdrew the note from the notch, unfolded it and read: *No, Ivan, I didn't operate the wireless and I didn't blow up the factory. My crime was already great enough. My God forgive me! The machine-gun is hidden in the gypsy caravan. Beware of Mohr; he's slippery. As for your father, if God wills it, I'll save him. Kiss Nadia for me; she opened the unknown country to me. For God and the fatherland.*

The note was signed: *Nitchef.*

SUSPICION

The following dialogue took place in one of the cells of Warsaw prison a few days later between Ivan Iagowski and Dr. Mohr.

"You refuse, then?"

"I refuse."

"No regrets?"

"I don't say that, Dr. Mohr, but I don't want to be saved by you. My father...in fact, he thinks you're an excellent man, and perhaps he's begged you to speak in my favor; perhaps you've come on his behalf? Personally, I refuse your intervention; I don't want it. After all, it won't be as easy as you wanted to get me to listen, Dr. Mohr. Your subtle—too much or not enough. You've imprisoned us an in inextricable intrigue; you'd have difficulty unraveling it yourself. After all, I'm guilty—not my father, me. I'm guilty of having introduced myself into your house by night in order to rob you. You caught me—so much the worse for me. One thing puzzles me, though, Dr. Mohr—where did you spring from when you grabbed me by the collar? You certainly weren't in your study. Where, then? Is there, in the enchanted walls of your abode—I say enchanted, Dr. Mohr, because the shells and bullets are directed away from it in a supernatural fashion—a secret passage?"

"Shut up," said the old scientist, visibly annoyed and casting a sidelong glance at the cell door. "Listen: I got carried away by a fit of anger that I regret. I want to make up for it. It will be difficult, as you said—very difficult, especially at the moment—but not impossible. I want to save you, but on one condition."

"What condition?"

"You won't say anything."

"Anything about what?"

"Anything that you know."

"Do I know something, then?" asked Ivan, naively.

Mohr made a gesture of annoyance. "You're doing it deliberately," he growled. "One might think that you don't want to understand."

"Perhaps I understand a great deal, Dr. Mohr. So much, in fact, that I dare you not to withdraw your complaint against me, whatever the cost. As regards my father, you know very well that he was your guest at the time of the attempt to kill the Tsar, and you alone know it, because you've been careful to replace your entire staff. Where are the witnesses? Will anyone even look for them? From the moment that you affirm something..."

"You know that it's scheduled for tomorrow morning?" snapped the old man.

Ivan paled in spite of himself, but overcame the emotion that as gripping him.

"Thank you for telling me, Doctor. I'll make my preparations in consequence. Since you're all-powerful, Dr. Mohr, get them to bring Nadia to see me. I'd like to kiss her, as I'd like to embrace my friend Georges Chantepie. If I have to die, I don't want to die without that consolation."

Ivan Iagow might not have been exaggerating in talking about his possible death. The security of the fatherland demands pitiless sanctions. Although Jude Iagow and his son were innocent, it was possible that their innocence would not be admitted. Far from being victims of circumstance, were they not, on the contrary, guilty men delivered by immanent justice to human justice? And people had been put up against a wall for much less than they might have done. Ivan's ears were still ringing with the noise of executions that had been erasing wretched spies from humankind every morning for a week.

Faithful to his promise to Georges Chantepie—he had given him the anonymous note just in case—Ivan Iagow had gone back to Dr. Mohr's house. He had gone to join Nadia in her basement and had waited, holding the little girl's hand, until she went to sleep. Then, equipped with a little electric torch, he had slipped into a subterranean corridor. After innumerable comings and goings, wrong turns and gropings, he had finally reached the goal of his expedition—which is to say, the scientist's study.

Quivering with joy, he had already picked up the sheets of paper lying on the blotter, whose grain was exactly similar to that of the note, when the doctor, emerging from who knew where, had put a hand on his collar and called for help. People had come, and the adolescent had been taken away to prison between two soldiers.

His fate was sealed. To that introduction by night into an inhabited place and attempt at theft—theft of paper—had been added the more serious charge of having set free a nihilist, and the even graver one of being an affiliate to the terrorist organization.

That was certain death. That was why Dr. Mohr was considering the young prisoner with a certain admiration.

"What obstinacy!" he muttered. "He deserves..." In a louder one, he said: "I'll come back tomorrow," and added, brusquely: "If there's still time."

And having rapped on the celled door for the jailer to open up, he left, still muttering.

Ivan Iagow was left alone with his thoughts.

Perhaps he was about to die—to die without seeing his father again, without a kiss from Nadia, without having witnessed the victory of his fatherland.

He remained standing, motionless, plunged in thought. From time to time, violent explosions announced that the bombardment of the city was beginning again; the Germans were avenging themselves for the defeat at the Sacred Hill. All of his beautiful stoicism evaporated, and, collapsing on his bunk, he wept.

Time passed. No one came—no priest, no friend.

"I would have liked to see Georges Chantepie, though," he murmured.

He did not persist with such a futile cruelty. He awaited the hour of judgment impatiently.

All night long, he heard comings and goings in the corridor. He shivered at the slightest contact with the door.

Finally, at dawn, the sound of a key entering the lock brought him out of his bed. He commended himself to God.

A jailer came in.

"Follow me," he said.

Ivan obeyed. Through somber and glacial corridors, alternately going up and down flights of steps, he followed the man's lantern, mechanically, his mind empty, less tremulous than he had feared, more resolute than he had thought. He was content with himself.

Like a soldier! he said to himself.

Finally, a rectangle of light appeared at the end of a corridor, and he was soon in a courtyard.

A dozen policemen were stationed there, arms at their feet.

Were they about to proceed with his execution?

He was taken across the courtyard, and led into a cell, where he was left alone.

After a quarter of an hour as long as a century, a person came in at whom the adolescent could not help gazing obliquely, mistrustfully. It was Dr. Mohr.

"One final word," he said, advancing and directing his flashing pupils at the prisoner. "I'm an officially-accredited physician. I've been instructed to draw up a medical report on you and your father. I can save you or doom you, according to whether or not you say anything that shouldn't be said. Understand me: if a single disquieting syllable emerges from your lips, Nadia will die. She's in a location known to me alone, from which no human power but mine can remove her. It's your decision: choose."

In spite of the fear with which the threat against his little sister had pierced his heart, Ivan did not flinch.

He's scared, he thought. *But of what? Does he know that I have the paper? No, he's afraid of something else that I might have discovered. I didn't see him. In fact, he grabbed me from behind. Now, I can remember the configuration of the*

study quite well: he couldn't have been in the room itself.
Where did he come from, then? From the wall?

Ivan shivered. In the many days his thoughts had been uniquely preoccupied with the actions of the old man; the many days he had been studying mentally everything that he knew about him, everything that he had around him, people and things alike, everything that he had heard emerging from his lying lips; the many days he had watched him circling around the silent bomb, like a character is an imaginary world created by some novelist, he had ended up possessing the man in his entirely, as he possessed the environment through which he circled. His conviction was firm: Mohr was a German spy; Mohr possessed a secret wireless apparatus, and that apparatus was in a secret place, behind the wall of the study.

I'd swear to it! he thought.

He imagined and saw the thing so vividly that he almost pronounced an irreparable remark. He contained himself in time. The old scientist was watching him with visible anxiety, a threat apparent in the corners of his twisted lips.

"Dr. Mohr," said Ivan Iagow, "If you save me, can you save my father?"

"That, I can't promise you, and for good reason—but I'll do everything I can in that regard."

Good, the adolescent said to himself. *It's necessary, then, that I'm free this evening. My father won't be executed, even in the worst case, before tomorrow morning. Many things can happen in the space of one night.*

"Well then, Dr. Mohr," Ivan said aloud, "it's agreed. I won't say anything that might touch you too closely. With regard to the rest, you'll allow me to defend myself and my father."

"That's only fair."

As if by enchantment, Mohr had recovered his cheerful and benevolent expression.

EVERYTHING AT STAKE

"Father!"

"Ivan!"

The father and son embraced emotionally; then they turned to face the court, heads held high, with the calm and dignity of innocence.

One after another, they replied to the president's questions, disputed the facts straightforwardly, seeking to bring order and light into the chaos.

For Jude Iagow's part, he confessed the great fault of his youth, his escape from the mine, the inheritance received in dramatic circumstances. He admitted having pursued research into explosives for twelve years, but with the sole goal of the predominance of his Russian fatherland over the world. The liberation of Poland he had, many years ago, left to the will of Providence, which had recently manifested its will by giving rise to the liberator Tsar.

"Yes," cried Colonel Archinef, the President of the Tribunal. With generous indignation, "And that's the Tsar you tried to assassinate!"

"No, Colonel," Jude Iagow relied, calmly, "since the Tsar realized the hope of my entire youth, and my action, in such circumstances, would have been the action of a madman—and since, in any case, when the Emperor came to Warsaw, I was lying in a hospital bed, in complete catalepsy."

"The testimony on that subject is contradictory. Only the sworn evidence of Dr, Mohr, the medical examiner, is formal. You were brought to the sanitarium on the night of the assassination attempt."

"He's mistaken. Have his records been checked?"

"The steward having been mobilized," the substitute prosecutor said, "the evidence could not be acquired."

"The tribunal will take that into account. In any case, a wireless telegraph post was set up in the factory."

"That's possible—even probable," replied the accused, to the great surprise of his judges. "The misfortunes of the munitions trains are sufficient proof of that, but I was ignorant of its existence." Jude Iagow added, ironically: "It's impossible to deduce from that installation that I also blew up the factory."

"Accident or malevolence," the Colonel pronounced, "twelve hundred workers are buried under the rubble and five hundred people were killed in the streets. The tribunal salutes those dead and associates itself with the fatherland's mourning. You cannot be accused of a catastrophe whose causes still remain unknown. In sum, you admit your escape from the prison colony and you deny the rest?"

"I swore to Pierre Damidoff that his name would be respected and respectable; I've kept my word. I swore to my wife that I would always be a good Christian and a god Russian; I haven't failed my oath."

The voice of the accused had sounded very clearly in the silence.

"The court will decide," said the Colonel. "Sit down. Ivan Iagow, stand up. You're accused of having introduced yourself into an inhabited place in order to steal. The injured party, Dr. Mohr, has withdrawn his complaint. He had even demanded your release, but the council has deemed that it has a duty to proceed, considering that you have assisted the escape of an admitted and dangerous nihilist. What reply do you make to that?"

"I was wrong to set free a man at odds with the law," the adolescent replied, "but I was only listening to my heart. I did not want my father's past to become known before he was able to beg for the indulgence of the emperor and human justice, but I had nothing in common with the nihilists. The proof is that I have not hesitated for a moment in my duty. There had been a threat to kill my father if I talked, and my sister Nadia has been abducted. I sacrificed both of them for the emperor's life. Ask this man what he thinks of my conduct."

"You did well, Ivan," said the engineer.

"One fact remains certain," added the president of the court, "and that is that your intervention saved the Tsar's life.[32] Furthermore, as a medical aide, and in lending impromptu service to the artillery, your conduct has been above praise. You have been mentioned in dispatches, on the proposal of Lieutenant Georges Chantepie. But let's return to the matter in hand. You don't misestimate its gravity. You claim that our father knew nothing about the attempt itself and the circumstances that preceded it?"

"I swear it. I kept quiet out of filial respect and in order that Russia would profit sooner from an invention that ought to ensure her of victory."

"Let's not stray from the point," intervened the prosecutor, a man with a rigid expression. "Was Ivan Iagow an affiliate of nihilism, yes or no? Yes. One doesn't set free an enemy of the law if one is an educated person like the accused and a friend of the law. In my view, his complicity is flagrant. Let's not get away from the question at the very moment it's necessary to stick to it. How and from whom did Ivan Iagow learn about the assassination attempt?"

"Nitchef revealed the secret to me."

"I doubt that, and it's contrary to the mores of that species of criminal. A nihilist would not have revealed a secret of that kind to a child unless there was a link of occult fraternity between himself and the child. It really is time to stop youth on the brink of the abyss and make an example."

That speech, like a hatchet-blow, had put an abrupt stop to sympathy for the accused. The members of the court undoubtedly shared that way of seeing, and in the absence of an exceedingly clever speech for the defense, the fate of the two unfortunates would be sealed.

"The tribunal will decide," pronounced Colonel Archinef.

---

[32] It is difficult to imagine how Archinef could possibly think that, let alone that it is certain.

"Before proceeding to hear the witnesses, we shall hear Dr. Mohr, the medical examiner, whose expertise the defense has demanded. Usher, send Dr, Mohr in."

The old scientist appeared. He advanced to the witness-stand with a detached air, not without casting a glance at Ivan, which signified: *You've kept your word and I'll keep mine.*

And, indeed, the adolescent had avoided the question, perhaps suspect in his eyes, of what the doctor' role in the affair might have been.

"Monsieur President," said the official physician, "I would have recused myself from the invitation by the defense if I had not been driven to bring into this mater the humble light of science, and my love of justice. As I have already had the honor of explaining to you in my report, I conclude an exceedingly attenuated responsibility of both parts, if there is any responsibility at all on the part of the young man. The latter's sister, Nadia, is subject to fits of somnambulism. As for him, he is afflicted, as I have had occasion to observe on many occasions, with disturbances of sight and hearing. Those disturbances make him impulse, in the strict sense of the word. There is nothing astonishing in the fact that he has been hyp-notized by the hotheads that his father has doubtless made his intimate society."

If it's necessary to purchase liberty at that price…! Ivan thought, choking and on the brink of protesting, out of injured pride. *Oh, if I didn't need to be free this evening...*

He understood Mohr's strategy, which was to save them by presenting them as two puppets, obtaining from scorn an indulgence that would not be accorded to sane individuals.

The scientist's speech unfurled, alternately technical and sentimental, undermining the firmness of the judges with in-credible skill.

The accused listened, torn between two contradictory sentiments. It was salvation. Salvation was coming once again—but they were both revolted. Them, impulsive! Them, degenerates! Them, irresponsible!

211

"Pardon me!" cried the engineer, at the limit of indignation. "I claim, and we both claim, my son and I, full consciousness of our actions, and we take entire responsibility for them."

"The physician has spoken," the old scientist went on, phlegmatically. "The witness is at your orders, Colonel."

"On what date, exactly," asked the police officer, "was Jude Iagow brought to you?"

"On the night of 27 July, exactly. He was deprived of his clothing."

"A sage precaution of an accomplice, doubtless the undiscoverable Nitchef, to lead justice astray."

"I was taken to the sanitarium on the night of 7 July, shortly after being struck by lightning, which volatilized my clothes and paralyzed me."

"Did his body show any evidence of burning?" asked the President.

"Not the slightest."

"Such phenomena are exceptionally rare!" exclaimed the engineer. "Lightning is a fluid endowed with intelligence, and often humor. It transports people over long distances without doing them the slightest harm, snatches away knitting-needles and extracts nails from shoes without touching the individual."

"The defense is evidently very subtle," the Colonel put in. "Might it not have been the explosive violence of the infernal machine that undressed him?"

"That's quite possible," replied the old man, "and the gases produced by the explosion might have determined the nervous phenomena of which catalepsy was the consequence. The agents employed are doubtless new, and thus unknown in their effects—but I cannot affirm anything."

"Dr. Mohr," interrogated Jude Iagow, still self-possessed in spite of his increasing irritation, "what interest do you have in dooming me? Is it because I refused the two million that you freely offered me?"

"I could not offer two million for an invention of which I was ignorant."

"You did offer them, sir," said Ivan. "I was there."

"You're lying, child," said Mohr, mildly.

"It's because you're jealous of the glory that I would have earned!" exclaimed the engineer, with a slight nervousness

"Isn't that, Colonel, one of the symptoms of persecution mania?"

"The religion of the tribunal is enlightened," said Colonel Archinef, approving the scientist's declarations. "Thank you, Doctor, you can withdraw, Send in...who is it?...Georges Chantepie. A committee of enquiry has been held. What is its opinion?"

Jude Iagow is innocent," the Frenchman pronounced, in a vibrant voice. "I've brought the proof of that."

And Georges Chantepie, in the uniform of a lieutenant in the infantry, with the Cross of Merit shining on his breast, advanced to the witness-stand, with the little Countess on his arm.

He looked Dr. Mohr in the eyes.

REPENTANCE

At the moment when the spark had sprung forth, under the finger of the chief of the German espionage, that had annihilated the Bargineff factory, an unknown terror had penetrated the marrow of Vladimir Obrenovitch, the nihilist.

"I'm his accomplice," he had murmured.

He had got to his feet, had assisted in the freeing of Colonel Archinef and the engineer, and then had gone away, walking straight ahead at random.

A church happened to be in his path, the doors wrenched way by the blast of air that had shot through the city like a meteor. He went in, as ill-tempered and mean-spirited as a wolf, his head down.

I need solitude in order to think, he told himself, by way of explanation.

At nightfall, a man slipped through the rubble of the factory. He reached a fissure opened in the foundations and penetrated into the cellar reserved for the fabrication of the silent powder.

O joy! The cement-lined walls of the laboratory had resisted the formidable shock. There was enough powder to fill twenty shells already.

In another part of the factory Nitchef discovered empty bombs and grenades. He set to work.

The enemy had tightened its grip around Warsaw. Its forces had finally reached the Sacred Hill and had run into furious resistance there. But the losses of men were only of secondary importance, and the enemy was on the brink of overrunning the position when the nihilist, dressed in a soldier's uniform, had surged forth and put the marvelous invention to use.

The man who had spent forty years of his life ruminating his hatred against Russia gave victory—temporarily, at least— to Russia. The Russian soul got the upper hand over the soul forged by the Schopenhauers, Büchners and Nietzsches, the philosophers, odious corrupters of youth. The event proved that the will that presides over the formation of human beings and their societies is not as incoherent as that. After having forced the attackers back, after having fought like a lion, he had gone back to the villa, to the ventilation shaft through which, for a year, he had kept watch on the birth of the terrestrial comet. It was from there that, the following day, he had witnessed the conversation between Ivan and his former tutor.

The adolescent's accusations had upset him, and he had thrown the note that protested his innocence.

Come on, he had said to himself, *it's necessary that I go all the way to expiation. I'll go, then, but after having saved all three of them and putting down the infamous beast.*

He watched from a distance the sacking of the gypsy caravan, where the machine-gun was indeed discovered. Dr. Mohr displayed real despair at having protected such rogues. Nitchef watched their immediate execution with a patriotic joy, as calmly and coldly as a Cato.

Your turn will come, he thought. *But your hour hasn't sounded yet. It's necessary to be cleverer and stronger than you are.*

In fact, the nihilist was thinking about Nadia, whom Marie Sergines, entirely innocently, by taking her with her to the sanitarium, had delivered as a hostage to her cruelest enemy. Ivan Iagow's arrest had complicated matters singularly, but he did not despair, for his plan was well made and firmly established.

The day when the court martial was to meet arrived.

Georges Chantepie had elected to be domiciled in the ruins of the villa. His wound had opened again, and an intense fever had taken possession of him. Nitchef appeared before him.

"Monsieur Chantepie," he said, "You have to return to Warsaw immediately with Marie Sergines. It's necessary to save Jude Iagow and his son."

"Only you can do that, Nitchef," the Frenchman replied, having recognized him at the first glance.

"Undoubtedly, I could, Lieutenant," the inventor's collaborator replied, "but my presence is necessary here. Nadia disappeared two days ago, as you're not unaware. Marie Sergines must have told you."

"Yes," said the officer, dolorously. "She must have escaped during a new crisis of somnambulism, and got lost."

"That's not the case," Nitchef replied shaking his head. "Nadia's in Mohr's power, who is using that to ensure his victims' silence. The child must be imprisoned in the secret and mysterious redoubt that everyone talks about but whose location no one knows."

"It's necessary to find her."

"There's no need. Nadia is very suggestible. I've experienced that many times, for the magnetic sciences have always interested and attracted me. Nadia will respond to my appeal and free herself."

"Why didn't you take action immediately?"

"Because I wanted to act in the presence of Colonel Archinef. Nadia will take responsibility, on the same occasion, for unmasking the traitor, for the redoubt in which she's enclosed—where, according to legend, Mohr vivisects humans—is nothing but a wireless telegraph station. It's therefore necessary that you take my place out there at the court martial. These are the facts—the very truth—that you have to reveal."

And the nihilist, the repentant criminal, made Georges Chantepie a full confession of his crimes and those that the band of numbers had perpetrated under the orders of the professorial spy. After that, he handed him the half-sheet of paper of which the fraction of the watermark corresponded exactly to the piece the Frenchman possessed, given to him by Ivan.

"I discovered it in Michael Gregor's room," he added. "It's at least a commencement of proof. Here's Marie Sergines. May God guide you. You'll find me again up there, this evening. Don't fail to bring Colonel Archinef.

"You can count on it," replied the Lieutenant.

The little Countess arrived by automobile. Georges Chantepie obtained authorization from his Captain to absent himself for an hour, and, his heart beating rapidly, sure of finding the eloquence that would snatch his friends from ignominious and unjust death, he leapt in beside the pretty aristocrat, and the engine, roaring like a shell, started to turn over in fourth gear, carrying the vehicle away in a cloud of dust, toward the triumph of innocence and the defeat of treason.

THE ACCUSER

"Permit me first Colonel," said the tutor, turning toward the accused, "to offer Jude Iagow, since that is his name, and his son, the apologies of a friend who was wrong not to trust the impulse of his heart; he had been led into error by perfidious insinuations. And I say this: a man who abuses his high position in order to blackmail an unfortunate—I will say more, to steal from him the most beautiful invention of modern times—is an infamous villain. It's you I'm talking about, Mohr—do you understand?"

"This soldier is excusable, Colonel," said the old man, pityingly. "The fever..."

"No, Colonel," retorted Georges Chantepie, forcefully, "I'm not feverish. I'm fully in possession of my faculties. I repeat, this man is infamous: doubly infamous."

"I can't allow myself to be insulted here. I'm a witness, and the law protects me."

"It won't protect you much longer, Mohr, I warn you. When you claim that Jude Iagow and his son are dangerous nihilists, you're lying. When you affirm that Jude Iagow was brought to your house on the night of 27 July, the day of the attempted regicide, you're lying. When you insinuate that he might be the author of the attempt and that the deflagration might have stripped away his clothing and the intoxication produced by the bomb's gases provoked his catalepsy, you're lying."

"And the proof?" interrogated the old physician, striving to remain calm in the face of the catastrophe he sensed approaching.

"The proof will come, and the witnesses will see it, Mohr, have no doubt about it. In the meantime, Marie Sergines, who is here, and I have received the confidences—I dare not say the confession—of one of those unfortunates blinded by poverty and suffering who are more your victims,

Mohr, and the victims of your subordinates, than guilty parties. They have rehabilitated themselves, formally, by standing up to the invader. In the meantime, I have come to proclaim here—and Marie Sergines will proclaim it with me—the innocence of Jude Iagow, the inventor of the silent powder, the great Russian, the great patriot, enveloped in the threads of an intrigue subtle woven around him."

The Lieutenant paused, and then continued: "Colonel, if at this moment you can hear cannon fire thundering over the city, it is to that man that you owe it. I could, if I were a novelist, entitle this affair *A Drama of Espionage* or *A Pre-War Episode*."

Mohr had shivered and gone frightfully pale, but his disturbance was of short duration. "Bah!" he said. "Where's the proof of all this."

"Mohr, the chief of German espionage in Warsaw, tried to obtain from Jude Iagow, under the pretext of pacifist principles, the secret formulae of the powder. Having been unable to buy them and having failed in the face of the latter's patriotic sentiments, he has condemned him. The nihilists had, indeed, recognized Jude Iagow as one of their former associates. Faithful to the motto of his nation, *divide and rule*, Mohr had insinuated himself among those unfortunates, into the milieu in which he was fomenting hatred and revolution with great skill, and had thus discovered Iagow's youthful crime. He made use of it at the last moment since, two hours before presenting his apparatus to the army commission, Jude Iagow discovered a note in his had thus conceived: *If in one hour, the formulae are not deposited at the Hauptmann Bank*—a German bank, Colonel—*and Jude Iagow has not sworn not to deliver his invention to Russia, Jude Iagow will be denounced and the Bargineff factory blown up*."

At that reading a ripped of amazement stirred the tribunal and the people present at the hearing. Only one remained calm: Dr, Mohr.

"Rubbish!" he said.

"This note," Georges Chantepie continued, implacably, "came from Dr. Mohr's study."

"That's a lie."

"Pardon me," said the Frenchman. "Here is the note, and here is the other piece of the sheet from which it was torn. Look at them, Colonel; the watermarks match up perfectly."

The sergeant-at-arms passed the two pieces of paper to the police officer, who, having examined them, ordered that they should be entered into evidence.

Mohr had moved forward as if to take them; he shrugged his shoulders and took a step back. "I'm not accused, so far as I know," he exclaimed, at a gesture from the lieutenant of artillery. "I'm a witness, and free in my movements. I don't have to listen to such stupidities."

"By virtue of my discretionary powers," put in Colonel Archinef, "I request that you stay."

It was necessary to obey.

"I shall go on," Georges Chantepie continued, sensing the interest of his listeners becoming excited to the highest degree and beginning to see the light. "Jude Iagow," he said, "was struck by lightning and electrocuted on the evening on 7 July, after leaving my house and asking me to watch over his children. He was followed by German spies, who intended to throw themselves upon him at a crossroads in the forest in order to steal his drawings and formulae. They were knocked down themselves by the violent repercussion of the shock, after which, on the insistence of Nitchef, at that time the engineer's valet, the latter was transported, unconscious and naked—the lightning had volatilized his clothing—to the door of the hospice owned by Dr. Mohr, the leader of the gang. After having knocked and summoned a warder, the bearers fled precipitately."

"French imagination!" growled the old scientist.

"I have the names of the men present," Georges Chantepie went on, taking another piece of paper out of his pocket. "Here they are. I warn you, Colonel, that Michael Gregor, alias Koffer, which is his real name, inscribed in the secret records of German espionage as number Thirteen, is probably dead now, as is number Twenty-Four. As for the exact date of the entry of the naked man to the hospice—the man who had swallowed the thunder, to use the expression developed by the inmates of the sanitarium—it will be furnished to you by the wife of the concierge of the hospice."

"She's lying," stammered the old man.

Georges Chantepie glanced at him sarcastically. Then he went on, in a vibrant voice: "The veritable author of the attempted assassination of 27 July 1914 is not Jude Iagow but the individual know in revolutionary circles under the name of Vladimir Obrenovitch and at X*** under that of Nitchef."

"This Nitchef is acquiring mythical status," the President of the Tribunal remarked. "He appears whenever necessary to confuse the thesis of the accusation. He remains nevertheless, undiscoverable."

"He will reveal himself, Colonel."

"When?"

"The evening. I have his word, and he will keep it. I'll go on. This Nitchef, concealed under the identity of Gorski, a deceased nurse at the Mohr hospice, was introduced to the factory by the intermediary of the same Mohr."

"How could I know?" protested the scientist. "A man is recommended to me. He is suffering. I hold out my hand to him. How should I know where he comes from? It's not my habit to investigate him. And after all, of what am I being accused now? Of having saved Jude Iagow's life? A fine accusation, in truth."

"You saved him in your own interest," replied the Frenchman, categorically. "You wanted to obtain possession of the silent powder, not for the sake of your own glory. But to ensure victory for your fatherland: Germany!"

"You're insulting me! Be careful. The law..."

The old scientist was pale. Anger and terror was disputing possession of his heart.

"The law," the tutor interjected, "forbids the possession of a wireless telegraphy apparatus. You have one in your home, and you make use of it—to the profit of whom?"

"That's a lie!" cried Mohr, in a voice that had nothing human about it. "Have you seen it?"

"I haven't seen it, but I have no doubt that the apparatus installed in the cellars of the Bargineff factory was in correspondence with yours..."

"Colonel," said the doctor, smiling. "He has seen nothing. He knows nothing, but he accuses me. You judge."

AND A LITTLE GIRL APPEARED

The hearing had lasted well into the evening. A multitude of witnesses had filed to the stand, without, in reality, being able to shed any light on the affair. Contradictions collided with one another continually, confusing the facts and denaturing them. The presence of the paralytic at the hospital on 27 July was affirmed by some and denied by others, according to the extent of their fear of the director. In sum, the Lieutenant was invoking the testimony of nihilists and workers, all unreliable individuals. He was brandishing a piece of paper and a letter that were being seen for the first time. The only evidence he put forward of what he was saying was the accusations of an undiscoverable individual. Where was this Nitchef? Why was he not at the witness-stand? Why had he not come to demand the sanction of the law for himself?

At any rate, there was doubt, and as doubt benefited the accused, and as, in reality, Ivan's intervention had saved the Tsar's life, as the adolescent had been mentioned in dispatches, as Jude Iagow's invention was confirmed and had had a demonstration *in anima vili*, the entire army talking about nothing but the unknown soldier who had thwarted the attack on the Sacred Hill, the two accused were acquitted of the charge of the assassination attempt. Ivan was released immediately, and Jude Iagow detained in prison until his fate could be determined.

As Dr. Mohr sought to make off, his mind oppressed by a great anxiety, a policeman appeared inconveniently on his right and another on his left, while Colonel Archinef, followed by Georges Chantepie, Ivan and Marie Sergines, shouted after him: "Pardon me, Doctor; permit me to accompany you home. Monsieur Chantepie has accused you. Gallant man that he is, he desires that his accusations should be put to the proof immediately; if disproven, he will offer you all the apologies you desire."

223

"You aren't going to search my house?" the old man queried, haughtily—but while producing the words in a firm tone, he sensed his gaze vacillating under the officer's piercing and questing gaze.

The latter kept his reflections to himself. "Time is pressing," he said. "You'll permit me, in such circumstances, to dispense in your regard with the juridical formality of a warrant."

It was necessary to obey. In any case, the master of the sanitarium knew that the secret of his walls was impenetrable to the most expert gaze. He still retained an almost complete confidence in his star. Had he not played his terrible game thus far, in the midst of these Russian dullards, without danger? He would come through the ordeal untouched and stronger than before. Then, what vengeance!

Three automobiles—the doctor's, Marie Sergines' and a third crammed with soldiers and policemen—took the road to X***.

A dull and prolonged racket resounded, punctuated with bangs and whistles.

"The battle," murmured Georges Chantepie.

"The battle," Ivan repeated, his nostrils flaring. "Quickly, quickly, driver!"

"Calm down, Ivan," said the Frenchman, in a grave tone. "We're going to fight one that will be no less important to the fatherland. One traitor unmasked is a hundred thousand men saved for her."

And the automobiles plunged on into the descending dusk.

Fulgurant gleams traversed the skies. Aircraft passed overhead, engines throbbing, some white and others black: Taubes and Blériots, pursuing one another and attacking one another furiously. The closer they came to the sanitarium, the more intense the noise became. The immense rumor of death at work rose from the flanks of the Sacred Hill.

The hospice appeared to the travelers as an oasis of calm in the midst of a tempest. The quietude of a monastery reigned there.

Stretcher-bearers carrying bloody and moaning burdens were going in, to emerge again thereafter, silent bees gathering a frightful pollen.

"Permit me to lead the way," said the Doctor, totally self-composed, as he got out of the car.

The Lieutenant and his young friend were watching him anxiously.

Are we mistaken on his account? they wondered. *He doesn't seem at all troubled.*

They went through the courtyard, and eventually arrived, via the corridors, in the study.

Mohr switched on the electric light. "Please come in, Colonel," he said, bowing courteously.

The officer obeyed.

"You'll see, Colonel," the scientist continued, following the chief of police, that that accursed Frenchman is an infamous li..."

"Accursed Frenchman!" said Colonel Archinef, astonished by the hatred that the master of the house had put into his remark, doubtless involuntarily.

But Mohr had interrupted himself. He was looking at a man standing in the middle of the room, next to the pedestal on which the statuette with the emerald flower reposed.

"They haven't killed him," he murmured. "The imbeciles!"

The man was none other than Nitchef.

"Colonel," pronounced the Nihilist, addressing the police officer, when everyone had come in. "I'm the man you're looking for. I'm Vladimir Obrenovitch, the nihilist, the sole author of the attempted assassination of 27 July 1914. I've come here to put myself in your hands and to summit to laws that I recognize as just, good and necessary, but I don't want to pay my debt to society without having rendered a service to that which I've denied, that which I'm reclaiming for my fatherland, great Russia. This man"—he pointed his finger at Mohr—had established a Bickford fuse that linked this statuette to the powder magazine at the Bargineff factory."

"Liar!" cried the old man.

"Colonel," Nitchef pronounced, coldly. "A sounding will permit you to verify the fact. In the second place, a wireless telegraph apparatus is installed here."

"Again!" said the scientist, hiding the terrible fear that was gripping him behind disdainful laughter. "Where is it? Search! I challenge you!"

"Nadia! Nadia!" shouted Nitchef, his arms folded, his muscles tensed by a powerful effort of will.

A surprised and anguished silence had fallen.

Something was about to happen.

What?

"Nadia!" murmured Ivan, his hand clutching Georges Chantepie's wrist.

The latter was following the scene with extreme attention. "Shh!" he said.

Nitchef's face was expressing the tension of a violent and imperious will. Drops of sweat were running over his forehead.

"Nadia!" repeated the nihilist, in a muffled voice.

"No, no!" groaned Mohr, he too stiffened, in a contrary effort of will. "I don't want it!"

"Nadia!"

"No!"

A mute struggle was taking place between the man who was willing the event and the man who was trying to prevent it. It lasted for half a minute—a century!

Then a slight click was heard in the wall, behind the Boucher tapestry.

There was a grating sound, and the tapestry lifted.

Utterly white, her eyes staring, Nadia had just appeared in the frame of the secret door.

"Go up that staircase, Colonel," said Nitchef, pointing at the steps visible in the shadow. "You'll find a wireless telegraph post." With a bloodthirsty irony dressed to the devastated Dr. Mohr, he added: "And you'll be able to telegraph this man's compliments to His Majesty Wilhelm, Emperor of the World, savior of oppressed peoples and protector of the weak."

TOWARD TRIUMPH

A few moments later, Nadia had recovered consciousness.

Sitting on Marie Sergines' knees, receiving the latter's lavish caresses, the dainty creature was considering Nitchef with her large candid eyes. Nitchef knelt down.

"Little angel of the good God," he said, in a tremulous voice, "you have taught me pity. You have shown me that human beings are better than the breakers of dreams pretend, those accursed corrupters of the human heart known as philosophers. You have shown me the true road that a man ought to follow. Why didn't I encounter you sooner in my path, alas? I've spoiled God's work by denying it; I've spoiled my life, I'm accursed, for I've done evil. The hour of expiation has sounded for me. I didn't want to die before having seen you again, little saint of the good God, before having thanked you and blessed you."

The nihilist took the blonde girl's hand and raised it to his lips. "Adieu," he said. "Adieu, Nadia! Adieu, Ivan!"

Having risen to his feet, Nitchef bowed to the Frenchman, who was more emotional than he wanted to appear. "I scorned you for your patriotism and your beliefs," he said. "Forgive me."

And, advancing toward Colonel Archinef, who was coming down from the wireless cabin, edified, he added, in a firm voice: "I'm at your orders, Colonel."

Outside, the battle was raging furiously. Shells were bursting even in the vicinity of the field-hospital. Undoubtedly, certain expected signals had not been sent, and the negligent individual was being reminded of his duty.

Months have gone by since that scene. Vladimir Obrenovitch, alias Nitchef, after having been reconciled with God, has bravely expiated his horrible crime. Mohr has fallen

228

to the bullets of a firing squad, with a smile of defiance and menace on his lips. His last word was: "Soon!"

That meant: *Soon, the Kaiser will rule in Petrograd. Soon, the culture of our philosophers will be imposed on the world, prostrate before the genius of the German people.*

Mohr rendered his last sigh with the certainty that victory belonged by right to his own side.

And events had appeared to prove him right. But the Tsar has set himself at the head of his troops, and a first bloody defeat has been inflicted on the conquerors.

Material force has collided with moral force and rebounded, overcome.

A few days later, the Iagows, Georges Chantepie and Marie Sergines are meeting up in the little cemetery where the mortal remains of Pierre Damidoff had just been deposited, finally reunited with the dust of his ancestors.

Jude Iagow, the inventor of silence, has obtained his rehabilitation from the bounty of the liberator Tsar. His first action had been to fulfill the last request of Pierre Damidoff, his second to lay the first stone of the factory from which the comet *Mortem fulgurans* would emerge.

After which, taking advantage of a leave granted to the Frenchman, he has come, escorted by all those who are dear to him, in pilgrimage to his savior's tomb.

The sky is clear, the sun is shining. The cannons are thundering in the distance. All of them, their gazes turned in the direction from which the muffled sound is coming of a woodcutter's ax undermining the base of an age-old colossus, certain of the inevitable result, which will be the giant's fall, have the word spoken by the spy Mohr on their lips: "Soon!"

And when they emerge from the cemetery, Nadia, who personifies the future, the generations who will reap the harvest of the bloody and heroic sowing, starts to sing a little ditty that is going through her head, like the little warbler that she is. Is it not the prerogative of a songbird to announce the approach of spring?

SF & FANTASY

Adolphe Alhaiza. *Cybele*
Alphonse Allais. *The Adventures of Captain Cap*
Henri Allorge. *The Great Cataclysm*
Guy d'Armen. *Doc Ardan: The City of Gold and Lepers*
G.-J. Arnaud. *The Ice Company*
Charles Asselineau. *The Double Life*
Henri Austruy. *The Eupantophone; The Olotelepan; The Petitpaon Era*
Cyprien Bérard. *The Vampire Lord Ruthwen*
S. Henry Berthoud. *Martyrs of Science*
Aloysius Bertrand. *Gaspard de la Nuit*
Richard Bessière. *The Gardens of the Apocalypse; The Masters of Silence*
Albert Bleunard. *Ever Smaller*
Félix Bodin. *The Novel of the Future*
Louis Boussenard. *Monsieur Synthesis*
Alphonse Brown. *City of Glass; The Conquest of the Air*
Emile Calvet. *In a Thousand Years*
André Caroff. *The Terror of Madame Atomos; Miss Atomos; The Return of Madame Atomos; The Mistake of Madame Atomos; The Monsters of Madame Atomos; The Revenge of Madame Atomos; The Resurrection of Madame Atomos; The Mark of Madame Atomos; The Spheres of Madame Atomos*
Félicien Champsaur. *The Human Arrow; Ouha, King of the Apes; Pharaoh's Wife*
Didier de Chousy. *Ignis*
Jules Clarétie. *Obsession*
Michel Corday. *The Eternal Flame*
André Couvreur. *The Necessary Evil*; *Caresco, Superman; The Exploits of Professor Tornada* (3 vols.)
Captain Danrit. *Undersea Odyssey*
C. I. Defontenay. *Star (Psi Cassiopeia)*
Charles Derennes. *The People of the Pole*
Georges Dodds (anthologist). *The Missing Link*
Harry Dickson. *The Heir of Dracula; Vs. The Spider*
Jules Dornay. *Lord Ruthven Begins*
Alfred Driou. *The Adventures of a Parisian Aeronaut*
Sâr Dubnotal *vs. Jack the Ripper*

Alexandre Dumas. *The Return of Lord Ruthven*
Renée Dunan. *Baal*
J.-C. Dunyach. *The Night Orchid; The Thieves of Silence*
Henri Duvernois. *The Man Who Found Himself*
Achille Eyraud. *Voyage to Venus*
Henri Falk. *The Age of Lead*
Paul Féval. *Anne of the Isles; Knightshade; Revenants; Vampire City; The Vampire Countess; The Wandering Jew's Daughter*
Paul Féval, *fils. Felifax, the Tiger-Man*
Charles de Fieux. *Lamékis*
Louis Forest. *Someone is Stealing Children in Paris*
Arnould Galopin. *Doctor Omega*; *Doctor Omega and the Shadowmen* (anthology)
Judith Gautier. *Isoline and the Serpent-Flower*
H. Gayar. *The Marvelous Adventures of Serge Myrandhal on Mars*
Léon Gozlan. *The Vampire of the Val-de-Grâce*
G.L. Gick. *Harry Dickson and the Werewolf of Rutherford Grange*
Edmond Haraucourt. *Illusions of Immortality*
Nathalie Henneberg. *The Green Gods*
V. Hugo, P. Foucher & P. Meurice. *The Hunchback of Notre-Dame*
Romain d'Huissier. *Hexagon: Dark Matter*
Jules Janin. *The Magnetized Corpse*
Michel Jeury. *Chronolysis*
Gustave Kahn. *The Tale of Gold and Silence*
Gérard Klein. *The Mote in Time's Eye*
Fernand Kolney. *Love in 5000 Years*
Paul Lacroix. *Danse Macabre*
Louis-Guillaume de La Follie. *The Unpretentious Philosopher*
Jean de La Hire. *Enter the Nyctalope; The Nyctalope on Mars; The Nyctalope vs. Lucifer; The Nyctalope Steps In; Night of the Nyctalope; Return of the Nyctalope; The Fiery Wheel*
Etienne-Léon de Lamothe-Langon. *The Virgin Vampire*
André Laurie. *Spiridon*
Gabriel de Lautrec. *The Vengeance of the Oval Portrait*
Alain le Drimeur. *The Future City*
Georges Le Faure & Henri de Graffigny. *The Extraordinary Adventures of a Russian Scientist Across the Solar System* (2 vols.)
Gustave Le Rouge. *The Mysterious Doctor Cornelius* (3 vols.); *The Vampires of Mars; The Dominion of the World* (w/Gustave Guitton) (4 vols.)

Jules Lermina. *Mysteryville; Panic in Paris; To-Ho and the Gold Destroyers; The Secret of Zippelius*

André Lichtenberger. *The Centaurs; The Children of the Crab*

Jean-Marc & Randy Lofficier. *Edgar Allan Poe on Mars; The Katrina Protocol; Pacifica; Robonocchio; Return of the Nyctalope;* (anthologists) *Tales of the Shadowmen 1-10*

Xavier Mauméjean. *The League of Heroes*

Joseph Méry. *The Tower of Destiny*

Hippolyte Mettais. *The Year 5865*

Louise Michel. *The Human Microbes; The New World*

Tony Moilin. *Paris in the Year 2000*

José Moselli. *Illa's End*

John-Antoine Nau. *Enemy Force*

Marie Nizet. *Captain Vampire*

C. Nodier, A. Beraud & Toussaint-Merle. *Frankenstein*

Henri de Parville. *An Inhabitant of the Planet Mars*

Gaston de Pawlowski. *Journey to the Land of the 4th Dimension*

Georges Pellerin. *The World in 2000 Years*

Ernest Pérochon. *The Frenetic People*

Pierre Pelot. *The Child Who Walked on the Sky*

J. Polidori, C. Nodier, E. Scribe. *Lord Ruthven the Vampire*

P.-A. Ponson du Terrail. *The Vampire and the Devil's Son; The Immortal Woman*

Edgar Quinet. *Ahasuerus; The Enchanter Merlin*

Henri de Régnier. *A Surfeit of Mirrors*

Maurice Renard. *The Blue Peril; Doctor Lerne; The Doctored Man; A Man Among the Microbes; The Master of Light*

Jean Richepin. *The Wing; The Crazy Corner*

Albert Robida. *The Adventures of Saturnin Farandoul; The Clock of the Centuries; Chalet in the Sky; The Electric Life*

J.-H. Rosny Aîné. *Helgvor of the Blue River; The Givreuse Enigma; The Mysterious Force; The Navigators of Space; Vamireh; The World of the Variants; The Young Vampire*

Marcel Rouff. *Journey to the Inverted World*

Han Ryner. *The Superhumans*

Pierre de Sélènes. *An Unknown World*

Angelo de Sorr. *The Vampires of London*

Brian Stableford. *The New Faust at the Tragicomique;The Empire of the Necromancers (The Shadow of Frankenstein; Frankenstein and the Vampire Countess; Frankenstein in London); Sherlock Holmes & The Vampires of Eternity; The Stones of Camelot; The Wayward*

Muse. (anthologist) *News from the Moon; The Germans on Venus; The Supreme Progress; The World Above the World; Nemoville; Investigations of the Future; The Conqueror of Death*
Jacques Spitz. *The Eye of Purgatory*
Kurt Steiner. *Ortog*
Eugène Thébault. *Radio-Terror*
C.-F. Tiphaigne de La Roche. *Amilec*
Louis Ulbach. *Prince Bonifacio*
Théo Varlet. *The Golden Rock. The Xenobiotic Invasion; The Castaways of Eros; Timeslip Troopers* (w/André Blandin); *The Martian Epic* (w/Octave Joncquel)
Paul Vibert. *The Mysterious Fluid*
Villiers de l'Isle-Adam. *The Scaffold; The Vampire Soul*
Philippe Ward. *Artahe*
Philippe Ward & Sylvie Miller. *The Song of Montségur*

MYSTERIES & THRILLERS

M. Allain & P. Souvestre. *The Daughter of Fantômas*
A. Anicet-Bourgeois, Lucien Dabril. *Rocambole*
A. Bernède. *Belphegor*; *Judex* (w/Louis Feuillade); *The Return of Judex* (w/Louis Feuillade); *The Shadow of Judex*
A. Bisson & G. Livet. *Nick Carter vs. Fantômas*
V. Darlay & H. de Gorsse. *Arsène Lupin vs. Sherlock Holmes: The Stage Play*
Séamas Duffy. *Sherlock Holmes in Paris*
Paul Féval. *Gentlemen of the Night; John Devil; The Black Coats ('Salem Street; The Invisible Weapon; The Parisian Jungle; The Companions of the Treasure; Heart of Steel; The Cadet Gang; The Sword-Swallower)*
Emile Gaboriau. *Monsieur Lecoq*
Goron & Emile Gautier. *Spawn of the Penitentiary*
Rick Lai. *Shadows of the Opera: Retribution in Blood; Sisters of the Shadows: The Curse of Cagliostro*
Steve Leadley. *Sherlock Holmes: The Circle of Blood*
Maurice Leblanc. *Arsène Lupin vs. Countess Cagliostro; Arsène Lupin vs. Sherlock Holmes (The Blonde Phantom; The Hollow Needle); The Many Faces of Arsène Lupin*
Gaston Leroux. *Chéri-Bibi; The Phantom of the Opera; Rouletabille & the Mystery of the Yellow Room; Rouletabille at Krupp's*
Richard Marsh. *The Complete Adventures of Judith Lee*

William Patrick Maynard. *The Terror of Fu Manchu; The Destiny of Fu Manchu*
Frank J. Morlock. *Sherlock Holmes: The Grand Horizontals; Sherlock Holmes vs Jack the Ripper*
Jean Petithuguenin. *The Adventures of Ethel King*
Antonin Reschal. *The Adventures of Miss Boston*
P. de Wattyne & Y. Walter. *Sherlock Holmes vs. Fantômas*
David White. *Fantômas in America*
Pierre Yrondy. *The Adventures of Thérèse Arnaud*

SCREENPLAYS

Mike Baron. *The Iron Triangle*
Emma Bull & Will Shetterly. *Nightspeeder; War for the Oaks*
Gerry Conway & Roy Thomas. *Doc Dynamo*
Steve Englehart. *Majorca*
James Hudnall. *The Devastator*
Jean-Marc & Randy Lofficier. *Royal Flush*
J.-M. & R. Lofficier & Marc Agapit. *Despair*
J.-M. & R. Lofficier & Joël Houssin. *City*
Andrew Paquette. *Peripheral Vision*
Robert L. Robinson, Jr. *Judex*
R. Thomas, J. Hendler & L. Sprague de Camp. *Rivers of Time*

NON-FICTION

Stephen R. Bissette. *Blur 1-5. Green Mountain Cinema 1; Teen Angels*
Win Scott Eckert. *Crossovers* (2 vols.)
Jean-Marc & Randy Lofficier. *Shadowmen* (2 vols.)
Randy Lofficier. *Over Here*

ART BOOKS

Jean-Pierre Normand. *Science Fiction Illustrations*
Raven Okeefe. *Raven's L'il Critters; Rave's Faves*
Randy Lofficier & Raven Okeefe. *If Your Possum Go Daylight...*
Daniele Serra. *Illusions*

HEXAGON COMICS

Franco Frescura & Luciano Bernasconi. *Wampus*
Franco Frescura & Giorgio Trevisan. *CLASH*
L. Bernasconi, J.-M. Lofficier & Juan Roncagliolo. *Phenix*
Claude Legrand, J.-M. Lofficier & L. Bernasconi. *Kabur*
Franco Oneta. *Zembla*
L. Buffolente, Lofficier & J.-J. Dzialowski. *Strangers: Homicron*
Danilo Grossi. *Strangers: Jaydee*
Claude Legrand & Luciano Bernasconi. *Strangers: Starlock*
Thierry Mornet & Juan Roncagliolo. *Guardian of the Republic*
J.-M. Lofficier, M. Garcia, F. Blanco & J. Pima. *Strangers in a Strange Land*